# About the Author

Zoe Jae was born in Sydney Australia, where she works as an office manager at an environmental consultancy working on projects and writing articles on the waste industry. Zoe grew up with an intense interest in ancient mythology that has inspired her book *The Realm*. Zoe also has a keen passion for all things horror, leading to naming her two family dogs, Spooky and Mischief. Follow Zoe on her social media at zoe__jae_w for updates on her current works.

# The Realm

Zoe Jae

———————————————————

The Realm

Vanguard Press

**VANGUARD PAPERBACK**

© Copyright 2023
**Zoe Jae**

The right of Zoe Jae to be identified as author of
this work has been asserted by her in accordance with the
Copyright, Designs and Patents Act 1988.

**All Rights Reserved**

No reproduction, copy or transmission of this publication
may be made without written permission.
No paragraph of this publication may be reproduced,
copied or transmitted save with the written permission of the
publisher, or in accordance with the provisions
of the Copyright Act 1956 (as amended).

Any person who commits any unauthorised act in relation to
this publication may be liable to criminal
prosecution and civil claims for damages.

A CIP catalogue record for this title is
available from the British Library.

ISBN 978 1 80016 995 1

*Vanguard Press is an imprint of
Pegasus Elliot Mackenzie Publishers Ltd.*
www.pegasuspublishers.com

This is a work of fiction. Names, characters, businesses, places, events and
incidents are either the product of the author's imagination or used in a
fictitious manner. Any resemblance to actual persons, living or dead, or actual
events is purely coincidental.

First Published in 2023

**Vanguard Press
Sheraton House  Castle Park
Cambridge  England**

Printed & Bound in Great Britain

Dear Grandpapi, I hope you enjoy this finished book from beyond.

# Acknowledgements

First and foremost, thank you to my family for always being super supportive and encouraging.

Thank you, Mum, who said in response to all my complaining about the books I was reading, *"If you can't find the story you want to read, write it."* And here we are. You were the igniting spark I needed.

Marli, you are the strongest person I know, never ever doubt the strength you have.

Dad and G, sorry I didn't let you read the drafts, but thank you for your constant excitement.

Thank you Grandpapi. He unfortunately passed away before I had a finished book, but thank you for your honest critiques of my first twelve chapters.

Thank you Jo for your support and wisdom, and for listening to my constant chatter about my book from the beginning.

A massive thank you to Rochelle for creating the book cover of my dreams.

Last but not least, thank you to the readers for choosing this book, and apologies in advance.

# CHAPTER 1

For someone who was inherently lazy, Faye was never quite still. Her body was constantly in some form of motion. Some part of her was always twitching, flicking, stretching, picking, clicking, or scratching.

Like now. Faye found herself sitting in her usual spot at the back of the classroom, Angus to her left and Tash on her right. While her friends were both quiet Faye was tap, tap, tapping her pen on the desk in time to the clock ticking on the wall.

She wasn't sure how long she had been doing it, before a hand the size of a basketball smashed down on the pen, silencing it forever.

Faye shot a look at Angus from under her mane of thick red hair.

"What the fuck dude," she mouthed silently to him.

He simply shook his head once, dramatically rolled his eyes in the direction of the wall clock, then raised his gigantic hand with his fingers outstretched.

"Five, four, three." He enunciated each word in an overexaggerated manner, dropping a finger with each count.

Angus didn't even bother with the two and one. The bell rang and that's when the cacophony erupted around her as students began standing and throwing back their chairs.

"Okay, okay, okay. Hang on a minute," Ms Hamilton shouted over the noise.

"You all have the holidays to get this assignment done. Do a workup of your family tree. I want to see it go back as far back as you can. I understand each family is different so the outcome will vary but I will make no exception for those of you who don't put in any effort. These assignments will go to your end grade for this Second World War topic, so include any and all family accounts from that time period," the teacher finished explaining.

The tribe was rushing out of the classroom now, full steam ahead towards the spring break.

"Faye, can I see you for a quick minute please?" Ms Hamilton asked as Faye tried to leave the room as inconspicuously as possible.

Faye dropped her head back and swallowed the groan of agony that threatened to erupt from her.

"You guys go on — I'll talk to you later," Faye said to Angus and Tash, literally shooing them out the door. Whatever Ms Hamilton wanted her for, she didn't want her friends around to hear.

Tash hesitated at the door and said, "Call me."

"Stalk you," Faye replied continuing their running gag taken a from movie they had watched together in their kindergarten years called *Stick It*. Probably not age appropriate but it certainly left a lasting impression on Faye — for reasons she was still trying to work out.

And just like that she found herself in the classroom with Ms Hamilton and a few stragglers.

"Nothing to worry about Faye — I just wanted to check in with you before you took off for the holidays," Ms Hamilton said with a reassuring smile.

Faye liked Ms Hamilton; in fact, she was her favourite teacher, but she couldn't fathom why being singled out by your teacher at the end of class wasn't something to worry about. Nor why a bloody teacher didn't get that!

Faye returned her smile and tried to relax the tension building in her shoulders.

"I'm all good Miss — just looking forward to getting out of here and starting the holidays."

"I know things have been rough for you the past couple of months, but I just wanted to let you know, I think you are doing remarkably well. You have the full support of the school. If you need any help with your schoolwork — for any subject — just let us know."

The kindness in Ms Hamilton's voice nearly broke through Faye's carefully erected walls. She dropped her head as she started blinking quickly to fight back the tears threatening to fall. With her chin almost touching her chest Faye felt things starting to unravel, like she was going to lose control of herself, the situation, and her life.

Faye gave her head an almost imperceptible shake, and just like that, in the blink of an eye, or snap of fingers,

Faye got her shit together. Back in her body, and back in control.

She offered Ms Hamilton a small smile and quietly said, "Thank you — really, I'm okay," knowing full well that how she must look to her teacher was in complete contradiction with what she just said. "But I would like to just focus on my Mum's side of the family for the assignment if that's okay?"

"That's fine Faye. I know whatever you hand in will be great. Go. Fly. Be Free," she said shooing her student towards the door.

"Just know we are here if you need anything," Ms Hamilton called out as Faye finally made her way out the classroom door.

\*\*\*

Faye had never been more grateful for living only three blocks away from her school. She enjoyed the walk home, even laden down with a backpack full of heavy textbooks. Faye unlocked the front door and made her way inside. Having only a staircase to go before reaching her room, Faye pushed through the heaviness of the bag weighing her down and took to the stairs.

She didn't really want to go straight from school into an assignment but if it meant having a relaxing holiday break with no thoughts of school or incomplete assignments, she could suck it up for the next few hours and try to it get it done.

***

Faye was lying on her bedroom floor procrastinating. Her first thought was to just google her last name, Adkins. But that came from her dad's side of the family and the last thing Faye wanted was to spend any time thinking about him.

She decided to call her mum's dad, aka Grandpa Josh. Her close relationship with her grandpa had grown stronger since her parents' divorce and she decided then and there she couldn't do the assignment without him. His underlying Irish lilt and his mysterious past were also major factors subconsciously convincing Faye to involve him in the project.

Running with the idea, Faye quickly jumped up from her position on the floor to look for her phone. Not realising it was by her feet, she half stepped on the phone and half tripped over herself before unceremoniously landing right back where she began.

Leaning back till she was lying flat on the floor, Faye checked her phone wasn't damaged by her clumsy feet and called up her grandparents' landline, wondering for the millionth time why old people persevered with the archaic form of communication, when both of her grandparents owned mobile phones, though they more often than not forgot about them.

Waiting for the phone to be answered, Faye quickly crawled over to her bed, reaching up for a pillow in hopes of getting more comfortable. After waiting while the phone rang ten times, Faye pulled the phone away from her ear ready to hit the decline button, when she finally heard her grandma.

"Hello, Sierra speaking. How…" Faye rolled her eyes at the predictable formality of her grandmother.

"Hi Grandma," Faye interrupted before she could complete her sentence.

"I'll go get him," Faye heard her say just as quickly, before launching into repeatedly calling out "Josh", each one sounding with an increasing level of frustration. Still no word from her grandpa. Faye could hear a shrill note enter her grandma's voice. Faye of course found it all extremely amusing.

At the precise moment she thought her grandma would either hurl the phone at a wall or her grandfather's head, Faye heard faint mumblings and assumed it was her grandfather apologising.

"I hear you wanted to speak with me, Sprite." Joshua greeted his granddaughter, surprised by the sudden call.

"Well, those words never left my mouth but hello to you too," Faye said while walking down the stairs to the living room and plonking onto the couch.

"I'm feeling loved by your sarcasm Faye." Joshua sassed his granddaughter. He immediately brightened when chatting with Faye, given she encouraged him to behave like a teenager again.

"What did you want to talk about?" he quickly added before Faye could make another smart-ass comment.

Faye smiled, listening to her grandpa talk like they were lifelong friends, and in every sense, she supposed they were, just with the same blood running through their veins.

Faye caught her reflection in the blank TV, and her smile faded as her memory flashed on the happy moments shared in the living room, something that seemed so foreign now. Faye felt as if she had lost her essence — the thing that lit up her face from within. She stared at herself, taking in her bright red hair and deep green eyes as if seeing these characteristics of herself for the first time. Faye couldn't help but think it was a peculiar combination, especially since neither trait came from her parents. In her eyes she just looked strange, otherworldly.

"Faye?" She heard her grandfather say her name as a question. Once again, she found herself shaking her head, trying to refocus.

"Sorry, Grandpapi. I've got a school assignment with your name all over it, well technically all our names. I have the holidays to create a family tree with accounts of the Second World War. Would you be up to helping?"

There was a long pause in the conversation as Faye waited for a reply, so long she was beginning to wonder if her grandfather had phased out like she did. Maybe that's where she gets it from?

Joshua stood in his kitchen, his back against the wall, tangling his fingers in the long phone cord. Tossing up whether he wanted to revisit the past and open the old wounds he had superglued shut so long ago. He was honestly surprised the conversation had never come up with his own daughter when she was younger, but he knew it was inevitable now with Faye.

With a deep sigh, Joshua prepared himself.

"Do you want to come over for dinner? We can see how far back I can remember," Josh asked, trying to give himself the time to mentally prepare.

"Sounds like a plan Grandpa. Is Mum invited?" Faye didn't know why she bothered asking considering she already knew the answer.

"Of course; you two are a package deal," Josh answered, loving the close relationship between his daughter and granddaughter.

"Mum should be home soon, then we'll head right over," Faye informed him, with the soundtrack of her stomach rumbling in the background.

"I'll let your grandmother know about our dinner plans and we will see you two later." With that comment Joshua quickly disconnected the call.

Faye stared at her phone, chuckling at the fact she was just hung up on. Scrolling through her phone, she hit her mother's number, but the call went straight to voicemail. Slightly peeved with the outcome, Faye decided she had better wear something more presentable than her current attire: a pair of worn-out track pants and an oversized T-shirt. She jogged up the flight of stairs back to her room and went looking for an outfit.

Midway up the stairs, she felt the vibration of her phone. Faye pulled it from her pants pocket and was impressed to see her mum's name on the screen. It usually took aeons for a call back.

"What's up Buttercup?" Elaine asked her daughter when she answered the phone.

That nonchalant question reminded Faye that her mum was treating her differently since her father had left, like she was a fine piece of china, which would shatter with the wrong line of questioning. Faye knew for a fact her mum was also acting that way primarily in the hope of avoiding any uncomfortable questioning about the divorce.

Shaking her head, Faye tried to concentrate on the conversation she was about to have with her mum.

"Hey Mum. How does you, me and the grandparentals having dinner tonight sound?" Faye pitched her plan.

"Sounds good but may I ask why the impromptu visit?" Elaine asked. Confused, but not surprised, by the random plans, Elaine always counted on Faye to keep things off centre.

"Weeeellllll, I had planned on an interrogation over the phone with Grandpa about an assignment I have, but he brought my food kryptonite into the equation and so I thought why not," Faye said.

"I'm in. Having dinner cooked for me sounds like a dream," Elaine replied.

Elaine started packing up her office while she was talking on the phone. Shutting down her computer and slinging her bag over her head, Elaine mouthed a goodbye to her colleagues, as she made her way to the elevator.

"I'm leaving now, so depending on the traffic I'll see you in twenty minutes. Love you. Bye," Elaine rattled off quickly before jumping in the elevator.

"Bye. Love you," Faye said just before she heard the click that said the call was disconnected.

Faye focused on the task at hand, finding decent clean clothes. She tended to leave dirty clothes wherever she took them off, which nine times out of ten meant they ended up on the floor of her bedroom or bathroom.

Faye found a sleeveless shirt shoved in the back of the built-in closet and pulled it on. Taking a sniff as the shirt came over her head, Faye checked for any hint of body odour smell. Not picking up on anything stinky, she grabbed a pair of black jeans to match.

Faye left her room and headed downstairs to wait for her mum. She was so lost in her thoughts as she took to the stairs, she literally collided with something solid.

Faye was stunned to see it was her mum blocking her path.

"How did you get home so fast?" Faye questioned her mother, truly baffled.

"You were off with the faeries Faye; time passes different there," Elaine informed her daughter, in that weird jesting way of hers. Smiling, she turned around and started walking back down the stairs.

"Well, I'm ready to go when you are," Faye said following her mum and trying to figure out how she had spaced out for so long.

"Let's get going then." Frustrated with Faye's dawdling, Elaine playfully shoved Faye out of the front door and turned around to lock it. Overexaggerating the push by her mum, Faye staggered her way to the car door.

Relying on her mum to have forgotten to lock the car when she came inside, Faye pulled on the handle, opening the door. She jumped into the car and made herself comfortable as she watched her mum walk to the driver's side and get in.

Faye leant forward and took her phone out of her back pocket to shoot her grandfather a quick text letting him know they were on their way.

"Just texted Grandpa," Faye told her mum as she dropped her phone in the cup holder of the centre consol.

"Okay. Who should we listen to?" Elaine asked, pulling out of their driveway.

# CHAPTER 2

Receiving Faye's text, Joshua stood and turned to find Sierra standing behind him. By the look in her eyes, Josh could see her brain flicking through a million different meal ideas. Taking a step forward, Joshua caressed his wife's cheek, trying to ground her.

"If you think that hard, your head might explode." Joshua attempted to lighten the mood before he added to her stress.

"They will be here in the next fifteen or so minutes."

Hearing that, Sierra frantically scurried to the kitchen to get things underway. She settled on making spaghetti Bolognaise, given all the ingredients were ready at hand, and everyone loved it. While she set about cooking the Bolognaise sauce Sierra ordered Josh to get the dining room ready.

"Make sure to use the nice plates," Sierra called after Josh as he powerwalked around her and out of the kitchen.

Opening the cabinet that held their fancy tableware, Joshua hesitated, staring at the plates. Josh was always confused by why Sierra insisted on going all out whenever they had visitors over, regardless of who they were. Laying on all the airs and graces when someone came for dinner did not make sense to him.

Startled by a loud bang from the kitchen, Josh quickly got to completing his task at hand. With a quick look over at his sloppy attempt at setting the table, Joshua followed the sound of very loud, but extremely mild, cursing coming from the kitchen.

The closer Joshua got to the kitchen, the heavier the tension in the air became. Standing in the entry way of the kitchen, Joshua watched his wife pace. He quietly engulfed her with his arms, embracing her, in hopes of calming her down.

"You need to remember this is dinner with Faye and El. They are the easiest people to please when it comes to food." Joshua smiled lovingly as he tried to comfort his wife.

"I know, I know. But we haven't really seen Elaine much since Mason upped and left, and I don't even want to imagine what that was like. So, we aren't going mention anything to do with Mason or the divorce." Sierra rattled off quickly and matter of fact while shooting Joshua a stressed and pinched look.

"I wouldn't dream of mentioning that ass," Joshua stated.

Joshua and Sierra stood in silence, staring at each other, absorbed in their own thoughts about their daughter and granddaughter's situation. They took a long moment to get their emotions in check before Elaine and Faye arrived. It took the pasta boiling over on the stove to snap Sierra back into reality.

"Holy Moses!" Sierra exclaimed, finally breaking through Joshua's deep train of thought. He quickly grabbed the handle of the pot, took it off the stove and placed it on the heatproof counter. Sierra walked over with a fork, attempting to fish out a piece of pasta. Deciding it was ready, Sierra focused on the sauce.

"Strain the pasta, please," Sierra kindly ordered Joshua, not looking away from the stove.

Placing the colander in the sink, Joshua carried the pot over to the sink and poured the pasta in. He shook the colander, getting rid of any traces of water, as the front door opened.

"We're here!" Faye announced in her best impression of a child's voice out of a horror movie, as she let herself into the house.

Following the smell of food, Faye found herself in the kitchen, greeting her grandparents with hugs.

"So, what's for dinner?" Faye directed the question to her grandma, after being released from her hug. The question was a courtesy and totally irrelevant considering she would be happy with any dish her grandma made.

"Spaghetti Bolognese my lovely faerie," Sierra replied, walking back over to the stove.

"Cool, I'll grab the drinks. What's the order?" Faye asked, turning to the cupboard behind her that held the glasses. Faye initially grabbed five glasses, then remembered she only to needed four. Zig-zagging her way around her family to the fridge. Not needing to wait for an actual response as they all drank the same thing every dinner, Faye poured wine for each of her grandparents and soft drinks for herself and her mum.

While Faye focused on the drinks, Sierra filled two large bowls with spaghetti Bolognaise to take out to the dining room. Handing one bowl to Josh, Sierra headed for the dining room table with the other.

Quickly finishing pouring the drinks, Faye followed her grandparents out of the kitchen, impressing herself with her ability to carry four drinks at once.

They sat down at the six-seater table, Faye, and Elaine on one side, and Josh and Sierra on the other. The empty chairs at the head of the table drew attention to the fact that a certain someone was missing.

Faye found it weird that she could block out thoughts of her dad most of the time, but an empty chair at dinner was now causing a downpour of emotions she was always trying to ignore.

Sensing Faye's inner turmoil, like it was a tangible thing in the room, everyone turned to her. They all couldn't help but see the disappointment and sadness flash across her eyes, making her look older than she was.

"The food is going to get cold," Sierra said, hoping for a distraction.

At the mention of food, Josh and Faye shared a look then dived into the serving bowls. Elaine and Sierra sat back, sharing a smile that said, "Look at these two animals at the feeding trough". After loading up their plates, Faye and Josh placed the serving bowls back on the table and waited to start.

Once everyone had food in front of them, Faye started shovelling spoonful after spoonful into her mouth. She ate like she had never eaten food before, like it was her last meal. Faye couldn't stop her mind wandering, thinking about the things she would soon discover about her grandpa. What was his childhood was like? Who were her great-grandparents? What were they like? What was Ireland like in the forties?

\*\*\*

In what seemed like a flash, dinner was finished.

Faye was starting to feel a strange kind of electricity in the air. She was aware of a few quick glances her grandpa and grandma shot each other once the dinner conversation had died down, but she wasn't sure what it all meant. As usual her mum was unaware of what was going on as she kept checking her phone.

Faye decided to grab it as her moment to interrogate her grandpa. She sat back in her chair, drumming her fingers on the table.

"I'm going to start asking my questions so, tough luck," Faye stated matter-of-factly… but with that cheeky smile she reserved only for her grandpa.

Turning his attention to Faye, Joshua braced himself. He found when it came to the topic of his past, everything was connected. A simple question that meant no harm, could end up unravelling the bigger picture and that's where Joshua now found himself with Faye.

"Why did you move to Australia, all the way from Ireland? Why not move somewhere closer to home?" Faye fired the questions rapidly at her grandpa. *Go hard or go home,* she thought as she kept smiling at her Pa. As the seconds slipped by without a response, she started to sense the seriousness of the questions she had just asked.

Before responding, Joshua took a moment to collect his thoughts. He brushed his hand over his chin, scratching at his grey bristly stubble. Unknowingly he mirrored his granddaughter's private sentiments, albeit in an old man kind of way.

*In for a penny, in for a pound,* he thought.

Taking a shaky breath, he started talking.

"It's not a simple answer, Sprite. So, you're going to have to bear with me while I explain. I grew up with my Mum and Dad in a small town, a half hour away from Dublin. We were your average happy family: Dad worked, and Mum looked after me. Fast forward fifteen years, my Mum started to withdraw and isolate herself from Dad and me. We worried but gave her time and space to deal with what she had to deal with, but it quickly took a turn for the worst. She started disappearing in the morning and not turning up till late at night. No more breakfasts or dinners together; the house was devoid of any laughter or joy, everything that made a house a home. We didn't know what was going on with her, but this type of behaviour shot up all sorts of red flags, so we set up an intervention of sorts."

Joshua paused and took a deep breath to settle himself. He couldn't look directly at Faye while he talked about the past, but he was fully aware of her watching him intently, transfixed almost. Closing his eyes, he started again, flying back through the years, straight back to the little house on the outskirts of Dublin.

"I remember sitting on the couch with Dad, waiting for my Mum that night. We sat there for hours, until she finally walked in. I will never forget that startled expression on her face when she saw we were still awake. We asked her to sit down so we could talk, and I swear, you could have cut the tension with a blunt knife. Dad calmly asked where she disappeared to all the time, and she just blew up. She was talking so fast, I only picked up her saying she was free to do what she wanted and being a Mum or wife wouldn't change that. Then she was at the door saying we wouldn't understand, and she walked out the front door.

"When she didn't appear the next day, we went to the Gardai and filed a missing person's report. The Gardai weren't that interested to be honest. People go missing all the time apparently." Josh shrugged, with his eyes downcast.

"Days turned into weeks, weeks become months, and before we knew it, a year came around and still no clue where she was." Joshua's voice finally cracked. Fearing he could start crying at any moment, he reached for the glass of water sitting in front of him. He quickly gulped down half of it, giving him time to collect himself before placing the glass back on the table.

As he started speaking again all Faye could think was how thick her Grandpa's Irish accent was right now — how easily he fell back into sounding like Father Ted from the old TV show they used to watch together.

"A few days after the one-year anniversary of Mum's disappearance, my da got a call from the Gardai. They informed us they were shutting down the case, discontinuing the search because the chance of finding me Ma alive, was slim to none. Da never kid himself into a happy ending but being told that, flat out, straight to his face, it tore him apart. He became a shell of a man and was hardly a da to me any more. We stayed in our house for another year, before moving here. I was sixteen, nearly seventeen when we arrived." Joshua finished his story, and the room was silent.

Faye turned away from the heartbroken look on her grandfather's face. She stared down at the pen in her hand and the empty notebook — she hadn't written a word as her grandpa spoke. She was too engrossed with what he was telling her.

She shot a quick glance at her grandpa and pondered what to say or ask. She had no idea that was what had happened to him, when he was pretty much the same age she was now. No wonder they had such a strong connection — both their teenage years sucked because of one rogue parent.

She decided to keep it simple and asked, "Have you been in contact with the police over the years, to enquire about the case?"

Josh was having an inner monologue, debating whether he wanted the conversation to continue or to shut it down. Pushing on, he decided to get it over and done with in one sitting. He looked up at Faye, ready to answer her question and saw her looking down at her notebook, avoiding any eye contact.

"From memory, the last time I called was five years ago. They still had nothing, not that I expected anything different, with years of no searching and all." Joshua added with dejection, "It's not like they would find anything, other than a body."

With that final comment, Joshua got up and collected the plates as he moved away from the table. The rest of the family sat still, stunned into silence.

Faye sat still for a minute trying to process everything she just heard. Pushing her chair back from the table she stood and followed her grandpa. Each step Faye took towards to kitchen, the more a feeling of guilt took hold of her. Walking through the kitchen door, Faye saw her grandpa leaning against the bench, staring off into space. She quickly noticed the sink filling up with water and bubbles, so Faye walked around the human who seemed to have turned into a statue and shut the water off. Plunging her hand into the warm water and grabbing the plug, Faye watched as the water circled the drain and disappeared.

Faye finally faced her grandpa and couldn't stop herself from breaking down.

"I'm so sorry you went through all that and I just made you revisit it," Faye sobbed, covering her face with her hands. Faye felt her grandpa's arm wrap around her, trying to give some comfort.

While Josh and Faye tried to soothe each other in the kitchen, Elaine still sat at the table staring at her mother, almost in a state of shock over what her father had just shared. How had she never been told about it? Elaine felt betrayed by her parents, but at the same time she was angry with herself for never even thinking to ask about her own grandmother.

Elaine stood up and moved away from the dining table, still trying to process what she was just told. Before she could leave the room, Sierra grabbed her hands.

"I know you're hurt right now because we didn't tell you, but your Dad didn't want to burden you with all the sadness he has in his heart." She tried to clarify to Elaine.

Elaine's rational brain could understand the reasoning her parents had for not telling her, but she couldn't work out why he would start talking about it now — just because Faye asked a random question. Elaine continued moving towards the kitchen, just ahead of her mother. Getting there first, Elaine saw the heart-warming sight of her dad and daughter comforting each other, and in that moment, she knew she had raised Faye right.

As if Joshua could sense his wife, he looked up as Sierra walked into the kitchen. Realising they had an audience, Josh discreetly swiped his hand under his eyes to get rid of any tears. It took Faye a little longer to realise they weren't alone any more, and she slowly retracted from the hug, looking up to see a smile on her grandfather's face. Faye moved out of the way to give her mum room to hug Joshua.

"Finding it hard to breathe, El," Josh joked with his daughter as she squeezed him tightly.

Realising she was uncharacteristically going overboard with the PDA, Elaine shyly looked up and muttered an apology.

Faye felt terrible about how upset she had made everyone, but she couldn't stop more questions popping into her head; the cycle of being curious and feeling bad kept spinning inside her. She was so completely zoned out lost in her own thoughts, she didn't hear her grandfather talking to her.

"Faye? Are you even listening?" Josh asked Faye.

"Yes. No. What? Sorry, you were saying?" Faye stammered, shaking her head, trying to snap out of it.

Joshua didn't blame Faye for not paying attention. He could see the gears working away in her head and thought it best to volunteer some information.

"I asked if you wanted to know more about my Mum," Josh repeated. Faye was still having her internal battle about wanting to know more but not wanting to see her grandpa upset. Realising her grandfather was willing to share, she decided to go with the flow. Faye smiled and nodded, indicating he should continue.

Deciding he wanted to get more comfortable, Joshua walked to the living room. Following him in, everyone assumed their positions. Sierra and Josh chose the double seater couch, sitting side by side, holding hands, while Elaine chose the other couch facing them. Faye sat on the floor directly in front of Josh, looking straight up at him.

"Before I start, I'm going to warn you Faye, certain things might be hard to hear. I know tonight has been a lot to take in, but I would rather have everything out in the open all at once. I'm going to start with my Mum's name and the date she went missing," Joshua explained, directing his focus on Faye.

Faye didn't quite understand why she was being singled out, as if the information had implications directly for her, rather than the family as a whole. Joshua's hesitation only caused Faye's agitation and impatience to grow.

Suddenly, as if struck by a bolt of lightning, Faye understood the reason her grandfather was being so cautious.

"Her name was Faye," she blurted out. The feeling of surprise in the room was palpable. Josh and Sierra were surprised that Faye caught onto the fact so quickly, and Elaine was overwhelmed that she had unknowingly named her daughter the same name as her missing grandmother. A grandmother she had never heard of, let alone knew had gone missing.

"Yes, my Mum's name was Faye; she went missing on the thirteenth of August, nineteen-fifty-two," Josh calmly added, directing the information at Faye.

Faye's mind went blank. Like being in a pitch-black room, completely deprived of anything. Faye didn't know what to think or feel. All she could acknowledge was the ringing in her ears like right after coming out of a concert. Then lightning bolt number two hit home and she realised not only did she share the same name as her missing great-grandma, but she was also born on the same day and month she actually disappeared. Sure, there were many decades in between the two events but it was a spine-tingling coincidence that Faye couldn't help thinking meant something.

The feeling of being watched snapped Faye out of her thoughts, only to refocus and see three pair of eyes trained solely on her. Only then, as she stared back at her mother and grandparents, did it become blatantly clear she was the only one with deep, green eyes. Every other pair of eyes looking back at her were different shades of brown. Honestly, why had she never realised it before?

"What did she look like?" Faye asked quietly, curious to know if she got her eye colour from her mysterious great-grandmother.

Joshua opened his mouth to answer but stumbled as if he couldn't quite process the sudden subject change. Elaine and Sierra looked at each other also puzzled by the question. About to ask her daughter if she was all right, Elaine quickly decided against it, knowing Faye would only retreat into herself if she thought she was the one being interrogated.

Joshua regained his composure and answered in a steady, calming voice, "She actually looked a lot like you Faye. The resemblance is unnerving if I'm being honest. I always wondered why her green eyes and red hair didn't get passed down to me or your mother but when you were born and you were named Faye, well…" Joshua let out a long breath and finished his sentence. "It was just meant to be."

# CHAPTER 3

The living room was so quiet and still as the four of them sat mulling over the things that had been said. Only when the clock chimed ten times, did they realise it had got so late. Elaine darted a glance at Faye trying to grab her attention. Making eye contact, Elaine flicked her eyes towards the door, giving the signal it was time to leave.

"We're going to head home now," Elaine announced.

Seeming to agree with his daughter, Joshua got up from the couch and moved quickly out of the lounge. He made a beeline to the bedroom he shared with Sierra and headed straight to his bedside table. Rummaging through the top drawer, Joshua finally found the thing he wanted. He hadn't looked at the photo he held in his hand in a long, long time.

With the memories of his mother again raw and fragile in his mind he couldn't stop the tears building behind his eyes again. The resemblance between his granddaughter and his mother was staggering and he couldn't help thinking, *There's family resemblance and then there's family resemblance! Jesus, Mary, and Joseph! These two could be the same person!* Shaking his head to snap himself out of it, Joshua turned to head off back to the living room where Elaine and Faye were standing getting ready to leave.

Faye watched her grandpa reappear and walk directly into the coffee table. He grimaced as he bent to rub his knee.

"Do we need to baby proof the house Grandpapi, so you don't hurt yourself on any sharp edges?" Faye asked with a smile.

Curious about his disappearing and reappearing act, Faye made her way towards him, easily avoiding the same coffee table. Faye stood by her grandfather, noticing he held something in his hand.

Joshua decided against replying with another smart retort that would encourage their routine play fight banter. Considering the time, he settled on giving Faye a simple smile and a nod. Not wanting to waste any more time, Josh held his hand out to Faye, passing her the photo.

Faye saw the picture and instantly knew it was her great-grandmother. The photograph captured a moment in time as her relative sat in front of an ancient-looking tree, with beautiful red hair and startling green eyes that stood out against the black lace dress she was wearing. The closer Faye looked, the more details she picked up. She focused on the items hanging off the tree branches. She could make out old children's toys and a sock or two but couldn't make sense of it.

Faye was so absorbed by the photo that she didn't realise she was being puppeteered by her mother to the front door.

"You can take the photo with you," Joshua whispered to Faye, assuming she wasn't ready to give it back. Josh braced Faye in a bearhug as a form of saying goodbye.

Faye couldn't help the genuine smile that broke out on her face in appreciation. Glad she could take it home, Faye found the photo to be the perfect size to slip into the pocket of her jacket without folding it, yet another coincidence. Snatching another quick glance at the photo, she reluctantly put it away and returned her grandfather's hug.

Elaine got the sense of déjà vu arriving at the front door to see Faye and Joshua embraced in yet another hug. Elaine loved that Faye had such a close relationship with her parents, since Faye's relationship with Mason's side was non-existent.

Elaine and Sierra ducked around the hugging bundle that was Josh and Faye, heading out the front door.

"Hurry up you two!" Elaine shouted, rolling her eyes.

"Well, we were actually waiting for you two to catch up," Faye countered, making her way over to her grandmother and gave her a hug, while Joshua did the same to Elaine. When the goodbyes were over, Faye and Elaine jumped in the car.

With the keys in the ignition, Faye rolled down the window and blew air kisses to her grandparents, as her mum reversed down the driveway. Elaine gently pressed on the horn, tooting a final goodbye.

The trip home was filled with silence. Elaine focused on driving, while Faye stared at the photo her grandfather had given her. Faye felt like she was looking into a mirror: her face was staring back at her with the same hair and eyes. The significant difference was the Faye in the picture looked like she was in her mid-twenties. Faye couldn't help but wonder if it is what she would look like when she was twenty-two or twenty-three. She turned the photo over and saw:

*Faye Burke 10/8/1934*

The only thing the date helped with, was letting Faye know it was taken pre-Grandpa, considering he was born in nineteen-thirty-seven.

Flipping the photo back over, Faye stared at her great-grandmother and her surroundings. She swore she could feel the sun rays on her face, as if the photo was actually emitting sunshine. She felt swallowed by the image. Faye slowly reached out in front of her to touch the tree, as if it was right in front of her. She was brought back to reality with a thud when the car stopped moving.

Faye looked up to see the front of her house, illuminated by the porch light. Faye opened her door and hopped out, still holding the picture as she accidentally closed the car door with too much power, resulting in a loud slam.

Elaine shot Faye a look over her shoulder as she started to unlock the front door of the house, but Faye was oblivious, still looking at the photo as she made her way up the front steps. Her mother walked into the house and waited to hear the front door close, before making her way upstairs to get changed.

Taking the keys out of the door, Faye kicked it closed behind her. As she placed the keys in the ceramic bowl on the table by the door, she decided to change back into her comfortable clothes. Taking the stairs two at a time Faye was back in her room in a flash — the sudden burst of action took her by surprise. She surveyed her room from the doorway, looking over the piles of clothes on the floor, on her desk, hanging out of drawers, trying to find anything relatively clean. Finding a slightly stained grey singlet and shorts right at her feet she decided they would do. Walking across the hallway to her mum's room, Faye wanted to see if she was up for a movie but hearing the shower running and she decided to go down to the living room to wait.

Elaine needed to relax after the dinner with her parents and decided a shower would do the trick. So caught up in her thoughts, she didn't remember even getting into the shower let alone being in there long enough for her hands to get all wrinkled and pruney. Deciding it was time to get out, she reached for a towel and dried off. Pulling on her pyjamas, she made her way down to where she knew Faye would inevitably be: on the couch. Elaine was right; Faye sat there with the remote in one hand and her phone in the other, trying to find something the watch.

"Ladies and gentlemen, on your left you will be able to see Faye in her natural habitat," Elaine announced to her phantom audience.

Faye snickered at her mum and tossed her the remote to pick what she wanted to watch. Faye was thinking about what she had learnt tonight. One point in particular was bugging her: how did she end up with the name Faye if her mum had no knowledge of the family history? Faye looked over at her mum and decided to ask her straight up.

"Why did you name me Faye?"

It was a common question Elaine had been asked when Faye was little. People always found it an exotic sounding name for a young Caucasian girl, but Elaine never answered the question when strangers asked it. Now that Faye herself was asking Elaine knew she owed it to her daughter to tell her the truth. Elaine turned to face her daughter straight on.

"I had a dream the night before I went into labour with you. It was the most intense dream I've ever had — like it was real. A girl was dancing in this amazing forest, surrounded by what looked like small flying bugs but I quickly realised they were faeries. Hundreds of them. And they were all chanting, 'Faye, Faye, Faye!' Suddenly the girl was turning around in my direction and just as I was about to see her face, I woke up. I sat bolt upright in bed, desperate to go back into the dream. To get a glimpse of the girl, but sleep and dreams don't work like that. My only consolation was I knew I had found the perfect name for my baby," Elaine explained with a small smile.

When her mother finished speaking Faye didn't say a word but simply lay her head on her mum's lap. She was so content in their easy silence and as her mum gently played with her hair, Faye almost dozed off as she tried to process the story her Mum had just told her. But her brain refused to turn off or quieten down.

She was so, so tired. More tired than she had ever felt before. Everything she had learnt tonight from her granddad, and now from her mum was threatening to overwhelm her.

She detangled herself from her mum and slowly stood up.

"I'm going to head up to bed; it's too late to watch anything now anyway. See you in the morning. I love you," Faye said to her mum, leaning in to give her one last hug.

# CHAPTER 4

Faye stood staring into the mirror that hung on the back of her bedroom door, wondering why she couldn't see her reflection. She looked back over her shoulder and saw her bedroom. When her gaze returned to the mirror, replacing her missing bedroom were endless rows of trees, the branches interlocking as high as the eye could see. Her attention was drawn to a tree in the foreground, a tree that looked older than time itself. The mass of branches looked to outweigh the tree's trunk, calling into question just how the trees were staying upright. She furrowed her brow, concentrating on what she was looking at, when it dawned on her it was the tree in the photo given to her after dinner — the photo of her great-grandmother.

Faye walked towards the mirror and started to raise her hand. She expected to come in contact with the cold, hard surface of glass, but instead she felt nothing. When she took her next step, she was falling, endlessly falling, falling through the mirror, falling through time.

Landing, she waited for the pain, but felt only a soft, springy floor. Like she was bouncing on a trampoline. Realising it was grass that broke her fall, Faye pushed herself up off the ground. Turning around in circles, taking in her surroundings, she found herself in a scene straight out of a faerie tale. Every colour imaginable bombarded Faye, from the bright flowering plants twisted around the tree trunks, to the dappled rays of sunlight peeking through the leaves, giving everything a sparkling glow.

Faye could feel a breeze against her bare legs, and at that moment, looking down at herself, she realised she was dressed in unfamiliar clothes. Where did the beautiful white dress come from? It overly exaggerated her curves, hugged her waist, flaring out and reaching past her knees. Faye was so confused by the whole situation that she quickly turned around, hoping to find the doorway back to her room but all she saw was the dense forest of endless trees.

Having eliminated her options of getting out the same way she got in, she had a good look around.

Faye had never seen so many trees in one place before, living in a city does that, buildings replace the trees, creating a twenty first century forest. She would have found joy in the forest if there was just something else, anything at all. Faye was completely under stimulated.

A completely silent and motionless forest created a dangerous environment for Faye. Nothing to distract herself from dark thoughts or the situation at hand. She felt like she was drowning in the sea of trees.

Taking a seat on the grass, Faye took a few deep breaths before trying to anchor herself in the present. Choosing one of the many trees as an anchoring tool, she started to list visual aspects of the tree. The leaves a perfect mixture between summer and autumn, a yellow that showed death was near but hadn't yet taken the leaves away.

Making her way down the tree, she noticed a miniature door built into the trunk. She nearly missed it altogether, the brown tones camouflaging the door into the rest of the tree. Quickly looking at the other tree trucks, she could just see the outlines of other small doors.

This just solidified the faerie-tale vibe Faye was feeling. Strangely she didn't feel afraid, per se, just unsure of what to do. Her rational brain thought the best course of action was to ask for help, so she knelt and knocked gently and tentatively on one of the many doors. The sound was so incredibly loud, like a thunderclap in the dead of night. The noise ricocheted off the trees, causing an echo throughout the forest.

Startled, Faye fell back on her haunches, landing unceremoniously on her backside, where she sat and waited for any sign of life.

With the expected outcome of continued silence, Faye stood up, picking a random direction and started walking, hoping to find someone or something that would explain what was happening. She couldn't help looking over her shoulder, for one more view of the doors, waiting for someone, or something, to appear.

When nothing happened, Faye picked up her pace and focused ahead, dodging trees and roots.

\*\*\*

Faye had been making her way through the trees for what felt like years. There were no real paths to follow so she just continued, trying to walk in a general straight direction while winding in between trees. She stopped, watching a butterfly bouncing in the air, dazzling in the speckled sunlight when she heard a sharp sound, once again being reminded of just how silent it was. No birds singing, no leaves rustling in the breeze, nothing. When she strained her ears to try to catch any trace of sound, Faye was only aware of how loud her own breathing sounded. She cocked her head, and held her breath, straining to hear the sound again.

And there it was. The sound was faint, wafting through the forest from a direction to her left. Following the noise, Faye could make out a clearing, devoid of undergrowth, only a circle of stones filling the space. The sound was getting louder, like the humming of charged electricity running through the air. As Faye stepped through the last line of trees and made her way into the clearing the louder the sound became. By the time Faye was within touching distance of the stone circle, the humming was deafening.

Faye could barely stand the sheer volume and intensity of the sound. It literally reverberated in her skull. It was as if the wall of sound was a repellent, there to force anyone to back away from the curious forest enclosure. But Faye knew she had to continue, so undeterred, she took one last step, lifting her foot over the stones closest to her. When she stepped into the circle, in a blink of an eye, Faye was surrounded by a peculiar assortment of beings.

At first, she thought they were children. Children who had literally come out of nowhere. Within seconds she realised they were not children. Her gut was telling her she was looking at faeries, but that rational brain of hers, the part that had told her to knock on the door, was now telling her none of what she was seeing could actually be real.

The creatures in front of her were the height of a five- or six-year-old, reaching up to her hip level and dressed in earth-toned cloaks. Faye realised these beings looked more or less like her, with red hair and green eyes; with a random one or two with blonde hair. The thing that quickly stood out to Faye was the lack of dark hair or eyes. The battle between what she was seeing in front of her, and her sense of reality was swirling in her brain, making all other functions, like standing, halt working. As she crumbled to the ground, Faye sat looking up at these creatures.

Faye realised she could simply pick herself up from the ground and her height would allow her to tower over them, but she was compelled to stay where she was. These beings may be small in stature, but they radiated intimidating power and Faye started to feel the first real flickers of fear in her belly.

"We are descendants of the Tuatha De Danann. State your business crossing into our realm," said the being closest to Faye.

Faye assumed she was in charge as the others stood behind her, all looking in her direction, hanging on her every word waiting for a command.

"I honestly have no idea what is happening right now. I don't know where I am or if this is even real, so if you could point me in the direction away from here, I will be forever grateful," Faye replied in her polite yet panicky voice.

As the leader moved closer, Faye quickly scrambled backwards and started to stand, glancing over her shoulder first to make sure she wouldn't step on anyone or anything. With each step backwards, away from the faeries, they seemed to multiply in front of her.

"My name is Cahira. I am the Commander of this region, and it is under my protection. No one can just wander into this forest from an outside realm. You need to leave immediately, or I have no other choice but to apprehend you and take you to our Queen." The leader Cahira stated this with so much conviction that it left Faye speechless.

The silence didn't last long as Faye burst out laughing. Not just a simple nervous giggle: she was bent over, hysterically laughing, clutching her stomach trying to catch her breath. Wiping the tears off her cheeks, she shook her head, trying to collect herself before talking.

"Sorry, that was incredibly rude, but I must be dreaming. This can't be real," Faye stated, finally looking down at Cahira.

Taking in the murderous look on Cahira's face, Faye quickly staggered backwards, not realising an army of faeries had moved in behind her. Faye bumped into the swarm of creatures caging her in and she spun around. She started to scramble now, in a panic to get some distance between herself and these intimidating beings. Tripping over her own clumsy feet, she was falling again, this time landing headfirst onto a rock-hard tree root. She thought she knew pain but this was next level. Pain was bombarding all her senses, until it was all she could see or hear. It paralysed her, cementing her to the spot where she lay on the forest floor. All she could do was surrender to it and pass out.

# CHAPTER 5

Faye bolted upright, frantically looking around, trying to figure out where she was. When she realised she was in her bed at home, she started to calm down. Faye couldn't shake the feeling that her dream wasn't a dream at all as she reached over to her bedside table and started feeling around for her phone. Faye disconnected it from where it sat charging and quickly googled 'Tuatha De Danann' while she could still remember it clearly. With no clue how to spell it, Faye thought her best bet was to phonetically spell it out. Typing 'toouhhuh dey dahnuhn' into the search bar, Faye didn't expect any results to turn up but when what she assumed to be the correct spelling popped up in bold underneath her pathetic attempt, goosebumps erupted along her arms.

Clicking on the proper spelling 'Tuatha De Danann', Faye found a quick reference guide to Irish myths and legends, hoping it would give her some answers. When the website had finished loading, Faye found exactly what she was looking for: short sentences in bullet point form, making it easier to read and hopefully understand.

*Tuatha De Danann*

*\*Means the people/children of the Goddess Danu, in Gaelic.*

*\*In Celtic mythology, they were said to be skilled in magic.*

*\*Tuatha De Danann are said to have inhabited Ireland before the Milesians, the ancestors of the modern Irish.*

Faye shivered when she read that it related to Ireland. Was it a simple coincidence she had learnt of her secret family history and then had an intense dream featuring Irish mythology she had never heard of all in one night? She thought not. Eager to learn more, Faye continued reading.

*\*The Milesians defeated the Tuatha De Danann, banishing them underground, while the Milesians remained above ground.*

*\*Tuatha De Danann being underground starved them of affection, causing them to shrivel and wither until they became Little People also known as the Faerie Folk.*

*\*Tuatha De Danann were described as short and slim, with red or blonde hair, blue or green eyes, and pale skin.*

Faye stopped reading and instantly started to freak out. Why did the stuff she was reading exactly describe the 'little people' in her dream? And why did they just so happen to look exactly like her?

Shutting off her phone, Faye got out of bed deciding it was time for breakfast. As Faye was about to open her bedroom door, the sight of her mirror froze her mid stride. With her hand outstretched, inches from the door handle but inadvertently close to touching the mirror, she took a moment to look at her reflection. She was thinking back to her dream, trying to shake the unsettled feeling that was starting to creep into her stomach.

Faye pushed it down and opened the door, quickly heading across the hall to see if her mum was up yet. The door was open to her mum's room, meaning she was already up, not that it was a surprise.

As Faye reached the bottom of the stairs, she could hear a loud clattering in the kitchen, which signalled her mum was attempting to cook.

"Morning Mama, how did you sleep?" Faye asked as she came up behind Elaine, giving her a hug.

Elaine glanced down at her watch when she felt Faye's arm around her, realising Faye was up earlier than usual. Elaine turned and faced Faye, capturing her in a bear hug.

"I slept like a baby. Not the best phrase since babies wake up a lot through the night but I actually had a really good sleep." Elaine rambled on, only stopping to take a breath.

Elaine glanced at her daughter quickly before turning back around to finish cooking breakfast. Elaine noticed that Faye had dark bags under her eyes causing her to look deathly pale.

"Are you all right my love? You look a little pale," Elaine asked Faye as she dished up their eggs and bacon.

Both of them took their seats at the island bench and began to eat.

"I had a really odd dream that seemed so, so real. When I woke up, I googled some of the things I heard spoken in my dream, and to be honest Mum what I read really weirded me out," Faye told her mum in a rush with a mouth full of bacon. Elaine grimaced as she looked at her daughter, trying to think of something to say to calm Faye down.

"Last night's information took both of us by surprise, so it's not that much of a stretch to have a crazy dream the same night. How about we get loads of junk food and binge watch some crappy TV?" Elaine stated, hoping to help provide an explanation and a distraction.

Faye finished her last mouth full of food before looking at her mum with a smile and nodded, agreeing to the lazy day.

Realising both of their plates were empty, Faye piled the dishes as she walked around the bench to the sink. Running the water, Faye rinsed the plates and cutlery, before placing them in the dishwasher. Turning around, Faye simultaneously closed the dishwasher with her foot and opened the pantry door to check their snack supply.

Only finding two packets of lollies, Faye turned dramatically to face her mum, falling to her knees, clutching at her chest.

"I've been hit, Elaine. Supplies are low... we only have two packets... we need more if you expect me to get through a marathon of your TV choices," Faye dramatically said, resting on the floor.

Elaine got off her stool and walked over to Faye, nudging her with her foot before helping her up. Knowing Faye wouldn't stop nagging about food if something wasn't done about it, Elaine pulled Faye towards the front door.

"We'll have to go and get some more then, won't we." Elaine said laughing at her daughter as she pulled her shoes on. Grabbing the car keys, Elaine opened the front door and lightly shoved Faye out of the house, towards the car.

Faye recovered from her mother's push just in time to avoid slamming into the car. She flashed her mum a faux dirty look before getting in the car. Faye forcefully closed her door, reinforcing the fact she didn't like getting shoved and put her seatbelt on, while ignoring Elaine laughing.

"I didn't even use that much force, so stop sulking. I also want to point out that we are both still in our pyjamas," Elaine mentioned, as she put her seatbelt on.

Faye quickly looked down realising her mum was right but also not giving two shits. So what, she was going to the shops in a dirty T-shirt, tights with holes and just to top the look off, socks with thongs. Faye never took any real notice of what people thought of her. She gave Elaine a one-hundred-watt smile before turning back to gaze out the window, totally zoning out, consumed by thoughts of her dream.

Elaine looked over at Faye, seeing the blank look on her face she started the car, constantly amazed at how quickly her daughter could flick from one state of mind to the next.

***

"Do you really need all of that?" Elaine asked Faye, looking at the shopping cart full of lollies and chips.

Faye glanced at her mum as she grabbed a bottle of soda, smirking while placing it in the cart. Faye continued to walk down the aisle, knowing her mum would be right behind.

"It's not a case of need, Mother, it's a case of want… and yes I realllly want all of that," she said over her shoulder.

Not needing anything else, Faye walked to the end of the aisle intending to head to the checkout. In the split second Faye took to look over her shoulder to make sure her mum was following, she slammed into someone's chest. Faye quickly stepped back, dying a little of embarrassment.

"I'm so sorry. I wasn't looking, obviously." Faye apologised while staring at the floor and not looking up at the person she had bumped into.

Elaine was watching her daughter, amused at the site of Faye acting so timid. She was so distracted she didn't realise the stranger Faye bumped into was actually her ex-husband. As she glanced up and saw Mason's face, her happy mood evaporated immediately.

Faye felt the atmosphere around her change from delight to displeasure like the flick of a switch. Confused, she looked up at her mum only to notice her attention was focused solely on the person standing in front of her.

Faye understood why her mum's mood changed when she finally realised who the stranger was. Just like her mum, in that single instant, Faye's happiness disappeared.

"Why are you just standing there Mase?" Someone called out from behind Mason, causing Faye and Elaine to shift their focus to the new person. Faye couldn't think clearly as she saw an unfamiliar woman walk up to her dad and wrap her arms around his waist. When her dad mimicked the action, wrapping his arms around the woman, it triggered such a white-hot flash of anger in Faye that it took her by surprise. Immediately she thought, *So this is why he wanted a divorce. The cheating prick!*

There were no greetings between them all, no pleasant 'Hi, how are you?' The four of them just stood there and looked at each other.

"Who's this?" Faye broke the silence as she nodded her head in the direction of the mystery woman. Faye already knew that they were a couple but wanted to see if he had the balls to explain it straight to her face.

Mason stood staring at his daughter and ex-wife, blinking rapidly, trying to think of an answer that would soften the blow. In the end, he couldn't think of anything clever to defuse the situation, so he decided to simply state the facts.

"Faye, this is Candace. My girlfriend," Mason announced, looking directly at Faye waiting for her reaction... expecting her to blow up.

Faye knew her relationship with her father had always been rocky. Even before the divorce she wasn't as close to him as she was to her mum. But the feeling of disgust that hit her, made her stomach churn so badly that she almost dry heaved. Faye couldn't stand looking at her father any more, so she turned her attention to Candace.

She quickly appraised the woman and determined she was maybe fortyish. The only thing Faye based her decision on, was the fact she didn't have any major wrinkles. At least she didn't seem to fit the 'new girlfriend' stereotype that divorced middle-aged fathers seem to go for. No twenty-five-year-old blondes with big boobs and collagen lips. In fact, Candace looked pretty average, like anyone else with brown hair and brown eyes.

"Is this why you divorced Mum?" Faye couldn't stop herself from asking, the question flying out of her mouth before she could stop it.

It was obviously the first thought Elaine had when Mason came to her wanting a divorce, and it pained her now to know she never had the strength to ask him straight to his face. Elaine was so thankful for the courage and defiance she had instilled in her daughter, and a little ashamed that Faye had to ask the question she desperately wanted an answer to.

Once the question was asked and hanging in the air, both Elaine and Faye concentrated on Mason's face waiting for a reply. For a fleeting moment guilt appeared on Mason's face, but as quickly as it was there, in a flash it was gone, replaced with Mason's standard blank, vacant look.

Faye realised the nonverbal answer was all they were going to get, so she turned away from her father and towards her mum. Taking the shopping cart from Elaine, Faye headed straight for the checkout, trying to put some quick distance between them and the couple.

Elaine quietly followed Faye, not saying a word, knowing both of them needed to process what had just happened.

# CHAPTER 6

Silence had been a solid thing in the air since Faye had asked that question. There had been no talking as they went through the self-checkout or the car ride home. Now the silence continued as Faye and Elaine walked through the front door of their house.

Abandoning the bags of food in the kitchen, Faye walked into the lounge room and face planted into the couch.

Betrayal. That was the current emotion cocooning itself around Faye, trapping her. Replaying what happened at the grocery store with her father caused Faye's breathing to come out as short, sharp gasps and her heart rate increased. She knew a panic attack was starting but she didn't think she could stop it.

Dragging herself up to sit cross-legged on the couch, Faye worked on slowing her breathing. Inhaling through her nose for four counts, then holding her breath for seven seconds, before calmly exhaling for eight counts. After a few minutes, Faye's breathing began to steady again but her erratic heartbeat thumped on and on. Remembering cold water could do some good, she unwound her legs and made her way to the kitchen for a drink.

Faye found her mum unpacking the grocery bags alone, looking like she was trapped in her own deep thoughts. Faye felt a stinging jab of guilt for leaving her mum to do the chore on her own. She quickly swallowed a few mouthfuls of cold water before starting to load the bottles of soda into the fridge. Not bothered to put the junk food away only to get it out again when they started their TV marathon session, Faye piled the packets of crisps and lollies on the island bench. She was calmer now, the panic had abated as the routine task of unpacking groceries in the quiet, calming presence of her mum worked to keep her anxiety at bay.

With all the groceries unpacked Faye grabbed two cups from the cupboard beside the fridge and filled them with ice before pouring in the soda: Coca-Cola for her and lemonade for her mum.

Elaine picked up as much of the junk food as she could and walked into the living room, unceremoniously dumping it on the middle cushion on their three-seater couch. Elaine stood in front of the shelves full of rows and rows of DVDs. Of course they had a few streaming services, but they still did a lot of things old school in the house. Tangible things like DVDs, CDs, hardcover books, even LPs took up more space throughout the house than she really wanted to acknowledge. Elaine quickly scanned over the DVDs, knowing exactly what she was looking for and where they were. She made her selection. Elaine knew her daughter well enough to know watching people getting haunted and brutally murdered by paranormal beings would help her forget the drama of seeing her father — at least for a little while.

Faye placed their drinks on the coffee table then sat on her side of the couch, realising they still had not said one word between them. Elaine turned from the shelves and held her selection of movies up for Faye to approve. In that moment Faye was bursting with love for her mum when she realised, she had made the perfect choice: her favourite horror movies and Elaine's favourite go-to movie when she needed cheering up.

Elaine quietly slid the first disc into the DVD player and waited to make sure it loaded before sitting down.

Faye opened a packet of honey soy chips as she waited for her mum to make her way to the couch. She was so consumed by eating, Faye didn't even realise her mum was already sitting beside her with the remote in her hand.

"Are you ready?" Faye heard her mum ask; the first words spoken between them in over thirty minutes. Faye couldn't help a small smirk as she thought she should be the one asking that question considering her mum hated horror movies and was about to be scared shitless. Deciding against teasing, Faye removed her smirk and replied with a quick nod.

Elaine pressed play while trying to get comfortable and mentally prepared for the carnage she was about to watch. She really did hate horror movies. The silence between them continued as the movie rolled on and on. It actually wasn't scary at all just badly written and badly acted — in her opinion, anyway. *The Conjuring 2* just didn't carry the same clout as the first instalment. After an hour or so Elaine shot a sideways glance at Faye and wasn't too surprised to see her not paying any attention to the movie — she was looking in the general direction of the TV but definitely not watching it.

Elaine knew the last 24 hours would have taken a toll on Faye. The revelations dropped by Joshua last night about his mother, then running into Mason at the grocery store, so close to home, were almost too much for her to handle, so she couldn't imagine how Faye was processing all of it.

Elaine lent over and gave Faye a gentle poke on the shoulder, testing to see just how zoned out she was. Getting no reaction, Elaine took advantage of the situation and quickly swapped out the movies. Watching *The Devil Wears Prada* for the seventeenth time was better than watching that sad excuse for a horror movie.

Faye would usually be thrilled to spend a day watching movies and eating junk food with her mum, but today was different. She almost couldn't bear sitting back on the couch when the people she loved were hurting. With her mind whirling Faye started to devise a plan, hoping she can bring about some closure for her family.

Remembering her grandfather saying he had never been back to Ireland, not once since the day he left as a teenager, Faye started thinking that maybe they could go over and talk to the Irish police in person. As that idea formulated in her mind, Faye turned to face her mum, grabbing the remote off the table and pausing the movie.

It was only when she glanced at the screen that she realised her mum's favourite movie was on.

"Hey when did you change it?" Faye asked, flicking her eyes from the TV to her mum's face. Realising she was not really interested in an answer, Faye quickly continued.

"Never mind, that movie sucked. That's not what I want to talk to you about. I was wondering what you think about a holiday to Ireland?"

Elaine was stunned at the "how about going to Ireland" bombshell landing firmly in her lap. She knew her daughter was a somewhat impulsive and extremely empathetic person, very in tune with other people's emotions but in that moment, Elaine wondered if Faye was losing the plot. As that tangent of a thought was starting to ruminate in her mind, she shook her head, trying to clear it. Taking a deep breath in she answered Faye's question.

"I would say I'd love too, but I'm getting the feeling this is a more loaded question," Elaine replied.

Faye gave her mum a coy smile as she tried to gather her thoughts and formulate an explanation. Faye knew that since she was under eighteen, she couldn't go anywhere, least of all out of the country, without things getting complicated. Money was also a major factor even if she had some saved.

Faye decided to dive headfirst and started rambling in a rapid manic pace.

"I have been given a school assignment about our family tree that I need to do over the holidays. That's why I organised for us to go over to Grandpa and Grandma's for dinner — so I could quiz them about their branch of the tree so to speak. What Grandpa told us last night has totally freaked me out and I can see it has upset you as well. I have been sitting here while that crappy movie was on, thinking about Pa and how he had deal with all of that when he was so young. He was the same age I am now Mum!"

Faye took a breath and continued before Elaine could interrupt.

"I thought we could kill two birds with one stone, I could complete an assignment and hopefully bring closure or a bit of peace to Grandpapi. And why not travel somewhere we haven't been before. Plus, I'm sure the grandparentals would love a holiday." Faye finished in a flourish. She knew it was an out of the box idea and more than likely the answer would be no, but Faye was giving it a red-hot go.

"Not meaning to rain on your parade sweetheart, but your grandfather might not want to go back there," Elaine stated.

Faye was so caught up trying to fix old wounds that she didn't consider the fact going to Ireland might do more harm than good. Taking on board what her mum had said, she also noted that her mum hadn't said no.

Before overthinking it any more, Faye grabbed her phone from the armrest and called her grandfather. The phone rang and rang, as Faye pictured the old landline phone ringing right off the wall and contemplated not for the first time, why they didn't at least have a bloody cordless phone. Finally, her grandfather had picked up the phone and answered with a quick "Hello."

"Hi, Grandpapi," Faye said summoning up all the cheeriness she could.

"Wow. Two calls in less than a week! I'm feeling blessed, Sprite. How can I help you on this fine day?" Faye heard her grandpa say. Faye could see where she got her talent for being a smart arse from.

"Seeing as it took you so long to answer, I just might not tell you. But considering this call is about me being nice, I'll get straight to the point. What is your opinion on a family trip to Ireland and before you say no, can you please hear me out but if your answer is a quick yes, you need to have a full bill of health from your doctors? Since you're getting old and all." Faye rapidly pleaded while telepathically sending him puppy dog eyes. Before Faye could continue, she heard whispering on the other end of the line. Trying to make out what was being said she only ended up hearing gibberish.

Assuming her grandparents were having a discussion, Faye thought against interrupting and remained silent. As Faye waited with her phone against her ear, she grabbed the remote, and pressed play to continue the movie.

Faye would love to be a patient person, but the fact was, she simply wasn't. As the movie played on with the added murmuring of her grandparents, Faye had just about reached her waiting limits. All of three minutes had passed when, with a sigh, she brought her phone closer to her mouth and cleared her throat, extra loudly. Elaine and Faye burst out laughing and it seemed to have stopped Sierra and Joshua's conversation.

Not giving Faye a chance to talk, Joshua gave his answer, praying he was strong enough to go through with it.

# CHAPTER 7

Planning a trip to Ireland with her grandparents proved to be more difficult than Faye anticipated. After Joshua and Sierra both agreed to go and had been given the green light from a doctor who was impressed by their healthiness, Faye jumped right into planning the family holiday. She was enjoying it all until it came time to choose a date to fly. Thinking the problem would have been with her mum due to work, Faye was surprised that her Grandparents were the real trouble. It turned out Joshua and Sierra's social life was busier than both Elaine and Faye's combined. Between golf, lawn bowls and regular barbeques with the neighbours, Faye's grandparents were booked solid for the next few weeks, and they refused to cancel on anyone.

After taking everything into consideration, Faye thought the end of May would give everyone nearly a month to plan and organise what needed to be organised.

With a timeframe in mind, Faye started pitching the idea to everyone of flying out of Sydney around the twentieth of May and possibly staying in Ireland for a month. Not getting any clear objections to the plan, Faye moved on to looking at accommodation.

Faye didn't even know the name of the town her grandfather grew up in, so she thought the best course of action was to find a place to stay in Dublin. The one criterion Faye had when it came to their holiday accommodation was they had to stay at a family-run business. Throughout their travels Faye always found the best things were the least known, the hidden gems usually off the well-worn tourist tracks. After an hour or so of scrolling through lists of BnBs Faye finally landed on a link to a little Bed and Breakfast just outside the city called The Faerie House, and without a moment of hesitation she knew it was where they were meant to stay.

Faye had chosen the island bench in the kitchen as her trip planning space. Given it was a Monday morning and she had the house to herself, Faye decided to make the most of it, feeling it was time to get some thinking music playing. Connecting her phone to her Bluetooth speaker, she selected her 'Concentration' playlist from Spotify. Within a second the sounds of Amity Affliction were booming through the house. Her mum repeatedly told her how she was the best mother in the world for letting her play the "screamo" music out loud in the house or car. But it just made Faye laugh considering Elaine's playlist was full of nineties grunge rockers like Soundgarden and Stone Temple Pilots. Smiling to herself Faye spread her calendar sheets, notebook and pens around her laptop and got to work.

Still without confirmation from everyone about when they could go, Faye made sure to make notes on interesting places to visit and fun things to do — bookmarking any website that caught her eye. With her mind drifting back to her bizarre dream, and its link to Irish folklore, Faye typed some key words 'Irish', 'Faeries' and 'Trees' into the Google search bar before she realised what has happening. Within zero point six four seconds more than ninety-five million results materialised on her screen and Faye immediately started to scroll down the page, somehow knowing she would recognise what she wanted when she saw it.

She was right: clicking on the link called 'The myths and legends of a Faerie Tree', Faye literally gasped out loud when she saw the webpage. She knew she was looking at a website on her laptop, but the screen literally looked like a page torn from a medieval book. The design of the page was exquisite and reminded Faye of the old manuscripts she had seen in the history documentaries she watched with her mum — the massive old books historians lay on a table and open with white gloves and discuss in whispered voices as if the ghosts of past can hear what they are saying.

The page displayed ethereal cursive writing, with the first letter of each new sentence splendidly embossed, and a pattern of gold and green Celtic knots ran around the border — a smooth pattern with no beginning and no end.

Trying to stop herself being distracted by the splendour of the page Faye started to read.

*You may find a Faerie Tree standing alone in a field or along the side of the road. The Faerie Tree may be a Hawthorn, but it is not always so.*

*Do not harm a Faerie Tree in any way. Bad luck comes to all those who try.*

*Farmers know to plant their crops around a Faerie Tree. Removing the tree for the sake of the crop will only bring bad luck and bad health to them and their family.*

*Good health and good fortune to all who offer gifts and tokens to the Faerie Tree.*

*The blooming season of the Hawthorn tree coincides with the festival of Beltane. With the festival we mark the beginning of summer and offer praise to Bel, the life-giver.*

Faye scrolled down the page as she continued to read, with her attention immediately drawn to an illustration of a tree. Her eyes narrowed in on the bottom section of the drawing, depicting a circle of rocks around the base of the tree. Looking closer she found each rock was marked with a symbol. Realising they were letters; Faye jotted each one down in her notebook. Looking down at the letters C O S A I N T scrawled across the page she had no idea if it was an actual word or if they were even in the right order. Clearly not having a clue what any of it meant but engrossed all the same, Faye continued reading down the page, hoping to find some clarity.

*Cosaint is the Gaelic word for protection.*

*Placing a ring of rocks or boulders around the base of a Faerie Tree will protect the tree from humans. The ring will ensure no human unintentionally harms the tree, leading to bad luck befalling them from the Faerie Folk...*

Faye's intense concentration was interrupted by a deep rumbling in her stomach. Without realising it, more than two hours had passed with her sitting at the island bench doing her research. Sustenance was now required, and quickly. Her go-to snack was anything that included greasy food and caffeine — usually in the form of hot chips and gravy, and copious cans of Coke. Faye suddenly spun around on her chair, facing the kitchen, startled by a change to the sounds in the room. The music had been replaced by a shrill ringing and she realised she had an incoming call. Excited by the possibility of her grandpa ringing her back with a reply, Faye quickly leant over her computer, grabbing her phone.

Still slightly preoccupied with thoughts of her food options, Faye shot a quick glance at the screen. Seeing *'Grandpapi'* flash on her screen, she answered gruffly.

"Well, hello. I'm guessing you got my text and you finally decided to reply." Faye's impatience, hungriness and sarcasm mixed to form a greeting. An immediate pang of guilt coursed through her, leading to her offering a mumbled "Sorry" as a quiet apology.

"We're in. May it be. Send me the flight details, including price and I'll transfer the money into your account," Joshua stated, as if he hadn't even heard Faye's snippy greeting.

Faye decided to reply to her grandfather in the same controlled tone.

"I'm just waiting to hear back from Mum, about her leave from work, then I can buy tickets. Do you trust me enough to take care of the accommodation?" she asked. All of a sudden, pangs of doubt started to creep into her mind, daunted by such a responsibility.

"We're happy leaving everything in your very capable hands Sprite. Now get to it." Joshua added the last sentence with a smile in his voice before ending the call with a typical, "Bye for now, love."

'No pressure at all Faye. You only have to plan a holiday. To Ireland. With your grandparents. Nothing to worry about,' Faye muttered to herself, as her stomach rumbled loudly reminding her to feed the beast.

# CHAPTER 8

After three weeks of careful planning and eagerly anticipating the trip, departure day had finally arrived.

The first challenge of the day proved to be getting everyone to the airport on time. Who knew it would be such a stressful event for anyone. Faye and Elaine had set their alarms for five o'clock in the morning, guaranteeing they had enough time to triple check everything before picking up the grandparents.

The normal morning routine proved to be different for Faye, given the early hour of the morning. Managing to get shampoo in her eyes while showering and putting her shirt on inside out, did not instil in Faye a great sense of confidence for the day ahead.

With that in mind, she headed downstairs, going straight for the kitchen to make the biggest coffee possible. Flicking the kettle on, Faye took two mugs out of the shelf above, placing a spoon full of coffee in each, as well as a shit tonne of sugar. Musing that instant coffee was better than nothing that early in the morning, Faye could hear her mum making her way down the stairs.

Elaine's arrival in the kitchen was met with the whistling of the kettle. She mentally thanked the goddesses for Faye being one step ahead of her. Taking a seat at the kitchen bench, she watched Faye wordlessly pour the hot water into the mugs. Elaine remained silent, acknowledging that neither of them were morning people, and any attempt to start a conversation before the consumption of coffee was a death wish. Elaine lifted the mug to her lips, blowing the steam away before taking a sip the instant the mug was placed in front of her. The caffeine kick hit her, and she took a couple of quick gulps, looking over the rim of her mug to see Faye doing the exact same thing. Elaine watched as Faye finished her first cup of coffee in several swallows then turn to make another. Within sixty seconds Faye was disappearing out the kitchen door, second coffee in hand — and still not a single word had passed between them.

Faye sat on the arm of the couch, looking over their luggage, paranoid they were going to forget something. She always got anxious before they travelled. No matter how prepared she was. They had agreed a few days earlier that they would drive their car to airport and leave it in the long-term car park. Thus eliminating the stress and anxiety around waiting for taxis and Ubers and the logistics of someone else picking her grandparents up.

She went through her mental checklist, ticking things off: passports, her meds, wallet, phone, laptop, and on and on. Deciding they had everything, she started dragging their luggage towards the front door. Faye didn't realise how much stuff they had lying around the house until she had to navigate through it with two overly heavy bags.

Feeling puffed out before the real journey had even started, Faye opened the front door, enjoying the fresh morning breeze that hit her face. Waking up the final parts of her the coffee hadn't. After a quiet moment taking deep breaths, Faye started towards the car with one of the suitcases.

As she lifted the case into the boot Faye realised her mum was right behind her with the second one.

Faye wordlessly ducked around Elaine and headed back to the lounge room to get their carryon bags. Picking up her backpack and her mum's handbag, she walked back out to the car.

"If we stay any longer, I'm just going to overthink everything, and we won't make the flight." Faye said the first words of the morning.

Side stepping around her mum, Faye placed the carry-on bags in the back seat, before climbing into the front passenger seat. She watched her mum walk back to the house with the intention of locking it all up, as the nibbles of anxiety starting to creep up her spine. In a flare of impatience Faye leant over the center console and hit the car horn. The loud screech echoed in the driveway, giving Elaine the fright of her life.

"What the actual hell, Faye!" Elaine screamed over her shoulder as she turned the key in the lock with shaky hands. She took a long, deep breath, rattled the door handle to make sure it was secure and turned towards the car. Elaine purposely took her time reaching to the car as payback for her daughter's impatience.

"Just because I can't drive, doesn't mean I won't get in the front seat and leave you here," Faye threatened, letting her anxiety get the better of her. While Elaine settled in behind the wheel, Faye put her head back and took a moment to focus on her breathing, trying to keep the incoming panic attack at bay. She felt a soft pressure on her knee as her mum gently squeezed, then patted her.

"We're running right on schedule Faye," Elaine stated calmly trying to offer some comfort to her daughter, seeing the anxiety in her rigid body. Faye couldn't help herself when she opened on eyelid and shot a glance at the clock on the dash.

She nodded and said quietly, "Let's go get them."

\*\*\*

"How much luggage can two people pack? Like really!" Faye rolled her eyes as she looked at her grandparents standing in the driveway with their suitcases.

"Grandpa and I can load the bags if you two want to check the house and make sure you have everything," Faye ordered as she took charge. The look that passed between the three adults did not go unnoticed. Faye wasn't sure if it meant "we should have got a cab" or "just humour her until we get there" Either way she didn't care — she just wanted to get to the airport, check in and finally relax.

Faye stared at the crammed boot willing more space to magically appear and fighting down the urge to scream in frustration. Again, she felt a calming hand, this time on her shoulder, as Joshua said, "Let's drop it in the back seat hey, Sprite."

"It's going to be squishy, Grandpapi. I'll take one seat if you can suffer with me in the other?" Faye asked, as she swallowed down an urge to cry.

The creeping anxiety was battling hard to suppress the lightning bolt of realisation that her Pa knew her so well. He could always sense when she was on the edge and knew just what to say to bring her back.

"I guess I can sacrifice myself for the greater good," Joshua joked, giving her a smile as he shoved his wife's oversized suitcase in the back. Elaine and Sierra walked towards the car, sharing a bemused smile as they watched Joshua fold himself and two day packs into the back seat.

Faye found she had more space if she sat cross-legged, leaving room for her bag where her feet would have been. Noticing her grandfather was pressed for space, she reached around the luggage separating them and grabbed one of the day packs he was holding.

"You need to shrink," Faye told her grandfather, trying to focus on something other than the numb feeling taking over her feet and legs. She knew that when they arrived at the airport, she would have the worst pins and needles.

"Well, I think that comes with old age and I'm already there," Joshua acknowledged, trying to get comfortable in his cramped position. Relieved to watch the neighbouring houses blur past, Joshua was grateful for the fact that they lived so close to the airport.

Faye never knew ten minutes could feel like an eternity until she had to get out of the car with no feeling in her legs. Arriving at the departure zone she simply opened the door and toppled out. Since her side of the car was parallel to the kerb, she remained seated on the concrete while people hustled around her.

Luck wasn't on her side as Faye felt the prickly sensation that caused even the slightest of movements to hurt. It started at her toes and slowly crept up past her feet, settling in her calf. Faye struggled up to help her grandpa transfer their bags from the car to the airport trolleys.

"Are you okay while we go and park the car?" Elaine asked with a look that was halfway between a grimace and a smirk.

"Yep, no worries, Mum. We've got this, right Grandpapi?" Faye answered. She couldn't help but laugh at Joshua as he struggled to work out how to make the airport luggage trolley move.

"You need to hold the handle down Pa, then push."

"Lah-de-dah Miss World Traveller," Josh said in retort.

Elaine waved to them and called out, "See you at the check-in counter," as she drove with Sierra to the car park. She would relish the peace and quiet for the next fifteen minutes.

With their two trolleys piled to the max and threatening to collapse, Faye grabbed one of the trolleys and headed for the entrance doors. "Tally-ho, sir!" Faye cried out — almost a little too loud.

***

The third and final challenge of the day came as Faye sat in the plane and finally acknowledged she would be stuck there for the next twenty four hours. Sydney to Dubai, a two- hour layover then the final leg, Dubai to Dublin. Dubai to Dublin — that almost sounded poetic. Not for the first time in her life did Faye wonder why the hell Australia was so far away from the rest of the bloody world.

"Why don't you swap seats with me faerie? You can be on the aisle," Sierra asked her granddaughter, noticing the colour slowly draining from her face.

"It's okay. I just want to take off and this way, I can use either you or Grandpa as a pillow." Faye cheekily tried to steer the conversation away from any chats about her anxiety. "Maybe we can swap later." She watched her grandmother open her mouth to say something but was interrupted by the intercom.

"Good morning, ladies and gentlemen, this is your captain speaking. We are about to begin our flight to Dubai, where your connecting flights will take you onto Dublin, Ireland. Could all passengers please direct your attention to the closest air steward or monitors, we are going to start our emergency procedures and safety demonstrations. Safety exits will be pointed out and the closest one might be behind you. Please take the time to familiarise yourselves with the emergency pamphlets located in the seat pouches." As the captain continued rattling on, Faye took it as her internal signal to try to relax as much as possible.

# CHAPTER 9

The sense of relief Faye felt when she finally stepped through customs, and into the arrival hall at Dublin airport, was overpowering. After two long flights and the layover in Dubai, she was over sitting in one place. Her decision to stay sandwiched between her grandparents grew old after the first few hours. Considering they had all been awake since the ass crack of dawn, her grandparents were out cold, asleep almost as soon as they sat down. Faye on the other hand did not sleep so easily on planes, meaning she was trapped with no way out. No way to get to the bathroom or stretch her legs. Even her noise cancelling headphones couldn't block out the sound of her snoring grandparents.

After doing her research for the trip, Faye had warned the family that despite it being almost summer in Dublin the temperature rarely got any higher than twenty degrees Celsius. Of course, Joshua would have known that being Irish born, but he was old and had probably forgotten. It was still a shock to Faye when she finally stepped outside the doors and into crisp, cold Dublin air. Nothing like a six a.m. arrival time in a new city to keep you on your toes.

The scraping of the wheels against the concrete drew Faye's attention to the taxi driver loading the last of the bags into the cab. So lost in enjoying the cold, she had taken no notice of the rest of the family following her. For a second she realised her spacing out was becoming more frequent and all-consuming, leaving her with no memory of how she got from Point A to Point B.

She would have to work on staying in the moment, rather than drifting off — she wasn't even sure where she was drifting off to. Jesus — now she was sitting in the front seat of the cab, not standing on the sidewalk gulping in fresh Irish air… with no recollection of having moved at all. Faye continued her internal monologue, scolding herself for once again tuning out and moving through the real world without being consciously aware of it.

"Where am I dropping you?" The taxi driver's accent was so thick Faye assumed that was what he asked them. She had thought everyone would speak like her grandpa, but she quickly realised he had a hybrid accent — not quite Irish and a not quite Australian, but a weird mixture of the two. With the question hanging in the air Faye realised everyone's gaze had settled on her. Considering she had planned and booked the trip, everyone was expecting her to have all the necessary information at hand.

She was sure she saw a hint of a smile on her mother's face as she quickly blinked herself back into the here and now. Faye began flicking through the pile of papers she had in her hand and pulled out the printed confirmation of their Bed and Breakfast accommodation.

"It's near the entry into the Hill of Tara. Do you know where that is, or would you prefer the address?" Faye questioned, skimming over the page, looking for the address just in case.

"Don't worry, I know the place. I take many of you tourists out there. At lot of people want to see the Faerie Trees, but if I were you, stay away from em." Faye waited for her grandpa to correct the driver about not being a tourist, but he remained silent, though with all the bad memories he had, she didn't blame him for not admitting his connection. She suddenly realised he had barely said a word since they passed through immigration and collected their luggage.

"What's the name of the place you're staying at?" enquired the taxi driver, breaking the silence that encompassed the car.

"Faerie House," Faye answered without turning her attention away from the window, enjoying the irony of it all, considering what the driver had just said about Faerie Trees. She wondered how driving through the streets of Dublin could come with such an overwhelming sense of familiarity. She honestly couldn't remember ever feeling this excited — she couldn't wait to discover the city.

Faye was silently mapping out the week's activities during the thirty-minute cab ride. Although super keen to get in contact with the police department, she knew jet lag would be a bitch for at least the next day or two. And she wanted to be relatively coherent when she spoke to them. With that in mind she decided they should spend the first couple of days just settling in and getting their bearings, then tackle the police station at the end of the week.

\*\*\*

Pulling up outside a two-story building Faye smiled a satisfied smile — glad it would be her home for the next four weeks. She stared in wonder at the building that seemed to be made entirely of materials from the surrounding environment: wood and stone and wandering plant life. And it was old. Like really old. It seemed immense despite the fact that the building only had two levels. The thick forest of ancient-looking trees and the gardens that surrounded the property gave it an ethereal, mystical feel. Faye felt like she was entering into another world — one that was strange yet somewhat familiar.

Faye jumped out of the cab almost before it had come to a complete stop and bolted straight up the front stairs to the massive entrance door. She took a second to take in the grand entrance way before reaching up for the rusted, hand shaped door knocker, ready to knock. As if the door anticipated the coming knock, it flew open, and Faye found herself staggering forward and colliding with a small elderly woman. Faye struggled to regain her balance and composure as she made eye contact with the woman in front of her.

"Hi Faye, I'm Niamh. Welcome to the Faerie House and please do come in." Niamh greeted Faye calmly, waving her arm and gesturing for to her to enter. A flicker of fear must have flashed across Faye's face as Niamh set about reassuring her.

"Oh, don't be alarmed dear, by my familiarity. I'm not busy with visitors this time of year." Niamh chuckled. "That's how I knew who you were."

Faye couldn't help but return the smile Niamh was beaming at her. As that initial hint of panic disintegrated Faye stepped further into house and completely forgot her mum and grandparents were dealing with the taxi driver and all the luggage.

The transition from the outside of the building to the inside was barely noticeable. Faye looked around and noticed every possible surface was covered with some sort of vegetation. Every inch of floor space was filled with potted plants; flower baskets were hanging from the ceiling, and vines were climbing the walls. Faye had never seen anything like it. She expected to see hummingbirds and butterflies circling the flowers or faeries living in the plants but of course none were to be seen. A real sense of calm was quickly washing over Faye as she turned around taking it all in.

Niamh simply stood and watched as the wonder of her home took a hold of Faye. She was pleased her assumptions about the young lady all the way from Australia were correct.

"Oh, and this is Orla," Niamh said as her horse-sized scruffy grey dog came bounding towards Faye.

Faye eagerly greeted the dog. Not intimidated or scared by the sheer size of the dog, she didn't even need to kneel to pat Orla. The dog's head was almost at chest level.

"You're beautiful aren't you. Oh, yes you are," Faye babbled on in her baby voice. "What type of pup?" Faye broke out of her dog haze long enough to ask.

"She's an Irish Wolfhound."

Faye thought Orla definitely fit her breed. Niamh would never have to worry about break-ins with Orla guarding the house. Faye gave Orla one last scratch and smile, before she shot the older woman a quick glance, her version of asking permission to roam, then simply took off down the hall. With so many directions to choose from, she decided to explore the one thing that looked a little out of place: the staircase immediately in front of her. As Faye set off, she could hear the distinct sound of paws on the floorboards behind her.

Everything that Faye could see of the house was organic — made of wood or some form of plant life. But the staircase was metal — the old, spiralling forever upward, kind of staircase. It looked so old and rickety Faye almost hesitated about going up it. Almost.

Gently placing a foot on the bottom step, Faye tested to see if it would support her weight. With no groans or creaks of protest, she lightly made her way up the stairs. Winding around the spirals slowly, she took her time to take in the view of the room below her.

From that vantage point she could confirm there was a minimal amount of furniture and practically every inch of floor space was covered with some form of foliage. It literally looked like a jungle or forest with well-worn paths to follow between it all. In between the plants sat Orla, watching Faye's every move.

Faye was pleasantly surprised when she reached the top of the stairs, and they hadn't given way beneath her.

Faye refocused and approached the nearest open door. She managed to keep some semblance of being a guest in a BnB by making a conscious decision to steer clear of all closed doors. The lush plant life continued on the second level with the hallway full of creeping vines and potted plants. Faye found herself standing in the doorway to a bedroom which housed antique-looking furniture including a single bed, a side table, and a wardrobe. It had a magnificent bay window and of course several potted plants. Faye decided immediately that it would be her room for the duration of their stay.

Stepping backwards out the door, Faye caught a shimmer out of the corner of her eye. She turned towards the opened door that was resting against the bedroom wall, with her eyes landing on a shiny bronze plaque with 'Fionnula' carved into it. Faye guessed it was Niamh's way of keeping track of guests and allocating the rooms. She quickly looked over the other doors in the hallway and found a word on each. There were seven doors which she assumed led to seven bedrooms. Annoyed by her inability to understand Gaelic, Faye spun on her heels and took off back down the staircase — not quite as slowly as she had climbed up it.

"Niamh. What do the words on the doors mean?" Faye yelled out as she leaped off the bottom step, hoping Niamh would suddenly appear from amongst the plants. She stood for a fraction of a second waiting for an answer, until she heard the faint sound of chattering and clinking crockery coming from the other side of the house.

"They are names Faye, from an old Irish story." Niamh's voice seemed close yet far away at the same time.

Faye looked at Orla who had appeared besides her. "Okay, pup, take me to your Mamma."

Faye set off after Orla and wasn't surprised at all to find everyone crowded around an island bench drinking tea and chatting. She wordlessly squeezed into a gap between her mum and grandma and set her gaze on Niamh, waiting for further explanation.

"The names come from a story about a man remarrying after the death of his wife, this time to his late wife's sister. But it all turned ominous when the new wife turned his children into swans so she would have him all to herself. Well, her plan didn't work out completely, for he discovered what she did, and spent his remaining days by the lake with his kids. Who just happened to be swans." Faye watched Niamh intently as she told the story. Her main takeaway was the horrendous actions jealously could lead to, and how it more often than not resulted in the kids getting hurt.

"Well that's just peachy. Who comes up with these stories?"

Faye aimed her question out into the universe, too tired to converse with anyone specifically about it. Her defiance was quickly quelled as the jetlag started to overpower her. Faye crossed her arms on the benchtop in front of her, laying her head on the makeshift pillow. Just before exhaustion overpowered her, she felt a cool tap of metal against her wrist. Barely lifting her head Faye saw her mother giving her a look that said, "Sit up and pay attention".

"The keys I've given you have names on the keyring that match a door on the second floor. Head up and get some rest. Take your handbags with you but your luggage will be brought up for you a little later," Niamh said in a quiet yet matter-of-fact voice.

"Okey dokey. Thanks Niamh," Faye said, pleased to see 'Fionnula' on her keyring.

She turned to her family and added, "I'll see everyone after my hibernation. When we aren't dying from jet lag, could you and I go to the police station?" Faye directed her question towards her grandfather and hoped she wasn't bringing it up too early into the trip.

"We can go as soon as we are settled in, Sprite," Joshua said over his shoulder as he turned and made his way through the potted plant forest to the staircase.

# CHAPTER 10

As predicted, it took a few days for Faye and her family to acclimatise to the new time zone and get over their jet lag. Niamh was an amazing host and was so relaxed considering she had four random strangers in her home. She seemed to know exactly when they needed space and when they needed company. Faye could see that her grandma and grandpa were getting on particularly well with their elderly host. Maybe it was an old person thing.

The first two days were spent quietly at the BnB while they all struggled with disjointed sleep patterns and tested tempers. They tried to beat the dreaded lag by going to bed at their normal time, in their new time zone and setting an alarm for seven each morning. It failed miserably when nine thirty p.m. in Dublin was seven thirty a.m. in Sydney. It just didn't work — except to create a new level of tired tension between the four of them.

Faye now found herself awake at midnight, starving and left to her own devices in the strange, wonderful house. Case in point: she was standing in front of the fridge, wondering if she should help herself to whatever was inside. With a frustrated sigh Faye decided to swallow her hunger and stick it out for the rest of the night until everyone was awake. At least that way she could stuff her face with Niamh's delicious pancakes. She looked down at Orla who seemed to follow her everywhere and whispered, "Back to bed, Pup."

Faye was amazed at how comfortable she felt in the house after such a short period. She loved wandering around the succulent indoor forest on her own, even in the dark. She decided to head back to her room and try to get some more sleep. Faye took her time climbing the winding staircase and stood for a few minutes looking out the window before climbing back into bed. Trying to fall back to sleep with a growling, hungry stomach was not an easy task for Faye. She tossed and turned a few times before falling back into a restless, but dreamless sleep.

"Christ on a cracker!" she squawked into her pillow as her alarm went off at seven a.m. She lay still, face down under her covers as a sick squirmy feeling started to settle in her stomach. Faye wasn't sure if it was because she was still so bloody hungry, or a friendly reminder that she should be anxious about what lay ahead for her that morning.

The day to visit the police station with questions about her great-grandmother's disappearance had finally arrived, and the anticipation that had been building for over a month was reaching critical mass. Every second since Joshua dropped the bombshell about his family history that night at dinner had been leading to this day.

Faye dragged herself up to a sitting position on the edge of the bed and stared towards the window. Even though she had so many questions, the thought of speaking to real live police officers literally terrified her. She took a few deep breaths, giving herself a mental pep talk, and set about getting ready to head out with her grandpa.

\*\*\*

"I'll leave with or without you, Sprite!" Joshua yelled through the car window while watching Faye fumble down the front steps trying to put her shoes on. With the station in town, Niamh kindly offered her car and directions, guessing correctly that it was something Faye and Joshua needed to do alone.

Not dignifying him with a response, Faye got into the car and sat silently waiting for him to start the car. She knew her grandpa would be awash with emotions that morning — she figured sadness, frustration and anxiety would all be competing in his mind, and she didn't particularly want any of that aimed her way. She had enough going on in her own head.

Joshua gave her another sideways look, raised an eyebrow, and started the car.

"Right then. Let's get this over and done with."

Faye watched the countryside roll by out the passenger window, going over the little she knew about her great-grandmother and what she wanted to ask the police.

Before long Faye was completely spaced out, adrift in her mind, truly unaware of what was going on around her.

A loud bang snapped her back into the real world. She gave her head that little shake she did to clear the fog. Blinking rapidly Faye realised the sound was the car door shutting, and her grandpa was already out of their car. He was just standing there, stock still, with his back to her, looking up at the building in front of him.

Dunshaughlin Garda Station. It was a very innocent looking building, but Faye was frozen in place; the realisation of what they were about to do was finally hitting home. That place had played such a devastating role in her grandfather's early life and now she had dragged him right back to it. Faye threw her shoulder against the car door and got out before her terror got the better of her.

She stood next to Joshua and linked her arm through his. Only now realising they had not said anything to each other since he started the car twenty minutes ago, breaking the silence she simply said with a wan smile, "Let's do this."

Joshua and Faye knew all the police staff who worked on the disappearance of his mother would be long gone, and that in a way was a relief. Faye decided to take the lead as they walked in the front door of the building, constantly surprising herself at how quickly she put her anxiety aside when it came to protecting the ones she loved.

She stopped for a second once they were inside the door, getting her bearings. The building was like the bloody TARDIS: it appeared small from the outside, but it looked immense from the entrance door. In a flash the thought of her grandpa standing there, over and over again, when he was so young, trying to find his mum, threatened Faye's composure. Just before those dark thoughts sucked her into that blackhole of negative emotion she knew all too well, Faye saw an officer approaching them, walking briskly down the hall.

"Hi, excuse me, we are looking to speak to someone about an old missing persons case; could you point us in the right direction?" Faye asked politely as she intercepted the uniformed officer before he made it out the door. Not sparing a moment to stop and reply, he simply pointed back over his shoulder, in the direction of desks.

"Well thanks for that," Faye commented loudly enough to draw the attention of a few surrounding police officers. Embarrassed, she looked down at her shoes, as Joshua took her hand and gave it a tug.

They made their way over to the desks and Faye could see the tension on her grandpa's face, sure he was working hard to keep any feelings of hope locked away in the cage he created a very, very long time ago.

"Good morning, sir. Sorry to bother you." Faye addressed the officer who sat at a desk across from the unmanned 'Enquiries' counter. "I was hoping you would be able to talk to us about an old missing persons case."

Faye was trying to keep the shrill note of desperation out of her voice, but she knew she was failing miserably.

Joshua still simply stood quietly behind her.

"I'm Detective Inspector Quinn, but you can call me Seamus. If you could provide me with a name and date of the disappearance and your relationship to the victim, I'll have a look through our system." Detective Quinn attempted to ease the tension that radiated from the young woman and elderly gentleman standing in front of him.

"Faye Burke. Maiden name Davin. Thirteenth of August nineteen-fifty-two and she is — was, my mother." Joshua robotically recounted the information seared into his head. Flashbacks from his childhood mashed with his present of standing in the very station, talking about his mother.

"Considering the year of the case it wouldn't have been entered into our digital database, so give me a few minutes to look through the archives," the detective informed the pair, scribbling the necessary information on a Post-It note. As he simultaneously pushed himself out from beneath his desk and stood up, he peeled the note from the pad and made his way out the back.

"Huh, well that was easy," Faye said to her grandfather once the detective was out of earshot. She looked up at her grandpa and wondered if that was what her face looked like when she zoned out. He was obviously lost in his own mind — thinking about being there over sixty years ago. Faye couldn't control the sudden shiver that coursed through her body. Not sure if the tremor was a warning of an incoming panic attack, or a manifestation of the guilt she felt for putting her grandpa through the trauma again, Faye focused once again on her breathing.

"Righto then. I found the case file, covered in a thick layer of dust but nonetheless, here it is," Detective Quinn announced as he returned from the bowels of the building with a pile of files in his hands. He sat back down at his desk, laying them out in front of him and started to scan through the first folder.

Faye and Joshua stood, waiting on the other side of the counter, both nervously starting to drum their fingers.

"Soooo, quickly reading over this, I can tell you nothing was ever found. Area searches turned up nothing. No phone calls were made to or received at the residential premises indicating no contact was made nor were any bank accounts accessed. There was no information from any hospitals of a woman fitting the recorded description and the police interviews at the time with the extended family, neighbours and friends didn't raise any suspicions. It was as if she just disappeared off the face of the earth." Detective Quinn finished on a sombre note as he stood and made his way to the counter.

"I am happy for you two to have a look through these files yourself if you like — I can't see anything here that shouldn't be made available to the family. What's your connection, Miss?" the detective asked Faye.

"My name is Faye. This is my grandpa, Joshua Burke. And the missing woman is my great-grandma," she rattled out by way of introduction.

With a friendly smile, the officer handed the files across the counter.

Faye and Joshua accepted the paperwork and started to flick through the pages reading as they went, passing pages back and forth between them. The pages were only confirming exactly what the detective had just told them and what Joshua had said weeks ago that night at dinner. That feeling of guilt for dragging her grandfather across the world to listen to the same information he had been hearing his whole life started to creep back in, this time seriously threatening to overwhelm her.

Faye put down the sheets of paper she was holding and looked to Joshua for direction. She had based their whole trip on finding something new, some piece of information that would help to bring some sort of closure. She realised nothing new was going to miraculously appear on these pages and the trip to the police station had been a massive waste of time. Maybe the whole trip to Ireland was a waste of everyone's time and money.

She was waiting for her grandfather to take the lead, maybe ask the detective some questions, but he was still intently going through the pages, over and over again. She guessed he was waiting for that new piece of information to magically materialise and set him free. When nothing seemed to appear, her despair for control slipped away so she spun away from the desk and hightailed it out the door.

Joshua sighed and looked up from the file he was reading, first towards the front door Faye had just walked out of, then towards the young detective sitting at his desk.

"Thank you for all your help, Detective Quinn, and sorry for wasting your time." Joshua expressed his gratitude to the officer who had taken time out of his day to help a couple of strangers.

Detective Quinn looked at Joshua for a long moment and then simply nodded with a friendly smile. He rose from his desk and walked towards to the older man.

"All the best to you and your family."

Joshua shook the hand offered by the police officer then headed out the front door after Faye.

"I hope you find what you are looking for," the officer called after Joshua.

Joshua found Faye curled into herself, sitting on the pavement, resting against the car they had borrowed from Niamh. Noticing Faye's eyes had that familiar glazed look to them, he knew she was not yet aware of his presence. He knew a subtle approach was the best way to bring her attention back to the present, so Joshua purposely made his footsteps drag against the gravel.

"I know this wasn't the outcome you wanted, Sprite." Joshua tried to ease the disappointment and guilt oozing from his granddaughter.

"Come on. I want to take you somewhere. But fair warning — it's nothing cheery but it might help." Joshua offered out his hand to Faye, helping her back onto her feet.

The destination he had in mind was only a block or two away from the Garda Station, so he saw no reason to use the car.

"Come on. We're walking." Joshua started off, striding with determination away from the station.

\*\*\*

Within ten minutes, they were standing outside the gates of a cemetery and a new set of questions came hurtling into Faye's mind. Considering it was a place to the bury the dead, and Faye knew the body of her great-grandmother was never recovered, why was her grandfather bringing her there?

Turning her back to the cemetery, she faced her grandpa and waited for an explanation.

"This is the cemetery where members of my family have been buried for generations. Before we left for Australia my da and I wanted some sort of closure, so we got a headstone for my mother. Obviously, we didn't have a body to bury, so we buried some mementos of our life before you know…" Joshua stated very clinically. Leaving his explanation unfinished.

"You are more than welcome to have a look around, but I'll stay out here, by the gates," Joshua finished.

Faye stood for a few quiet seconds looking at her grandfather, the sadness that was radiating from him was palpable. But she also detected a note of anger in his last statement. She gave his hand a quick squeeze then walked into the cemetery.

The layout seemed typical of most cemeteries she had wandered in, rows of headstones fanning out from a church building. As with everything else in the town, the church and graves looked centuries old, with faded letters etching out the names and life spans of the folk buried beneath. Faye was trying to read each one she walked past, caught between the urgency she felt to find her great-grandmother's stone, and a yearning to know who everyone was, buried there in the graveyard.

Faye's attention was quickly drawn to loud squawking. She wandered a little quicker through the rows of headstones, trying to locate the source of the shrill sound, but still trying to read as many names as she could. She finally found the source of the disturbance: a large, black raven sitting on top of a head stone two rows across from her. She was entirely captivated by the bird, not afraid at all. The only conscious thought in her head was *Why is this bird making so much noise?*

Slowly and as quietly as she could Faye made her way through the maze of graves, coming to a standstill in front of the perched raven.

The majestic-looking bird was much larger than she anticipated, and she stared at it intently, sure in the knowledge that it knew exactly who she was and why she was there.

Breaking her gaze away from the raven, Faye looked down at the gravestone it was sitting on.

*Faye Burke*
*10th of September 1910 – 13th of August 1952*

Realising it was her great-grandmother's grave, Faye virtually collapsed onto the ground in front of it. In that same moment, the raven startled her as it flapped its wings and flew off. She got the distinct impression the bird had led her through the cemetery to that exact location. Now the avian guide was no longer needed, it was free to leave.

She didn't know what to think or feel as she stared at the headstone that she was so strongly connected to. Connected not only by the name, and family blood, but by something else that she didn't understand at all. She didn't understand it but the feeling of connectivity she sensed when she first stepped into the cemetery was growing stronger by the second.

She lifted her hand to trace the engraved letters and numbers, but as soon as her fingers touched the stone, her world collapsed in on itself. She felt like she was being sucked into a vacuum, devoid of any light, sound or air.

As quickly as the sensation engulfed her, it disappeared, leaving Faye with an intense feeling of vertigo taking hold of her as she struggled to stand, gasping, as her lungs filled back up with air.

Completely disorientated, Faye took in her surroundings. Looking to her left and right, she quickly realised she wasn't in the cemetery any more.

# CHAPTER 11

Faye forced herself to stop moving, waiting for the feeling of vertigo to pass. Rapidly blinking a few times, trying to make sense of her new surroundings. She wasn't in the cemetery any more but she had no recollection of leaving and going somewhere else with her grandpa. Maybe she had zoned out again. It wouldn't be the first time Faye had got so caught up in her thoughts she ended up somewhere with no recollection of how she got there. Or she could have passed out in front of the head stone and was dreaming. Faye knew enough about her crazy nightmares that pinching yourself in them didn't wake her up, but she tried it anyway.

"Yow — dang it! That hurt," Faye muttered to no one in particular after she gave her forearm a strong nip with her fingernails.

She looked around and every colour imaginable bombarded her eyes, creating a total sensory overload. A wave of vertigo was washing over her again, this time seriously threatening to immobilise her. She was surrounded on all sides by luminous plant life: flowers, trees, vines, and shrubs, glowing with the vibrant sunlight filtering through the leaves. She was struck by the incandescent beauty of it all.

"So, this is what it's like to be in a faerie tale," Faye couldn't help but say out loud.

As soon as the words left her mouth, she was hit by the sudden realisation that she knew this place — she had been here before.

Her dream all those weeks ago of the little faerie folk in the forest. Only this time she was still in her own clothes, and not in some old timey dress.

Faye felt no comfort with her observation, nor with the growing awareness she was not in fact dreaming. Her mind was starting to adapt to the notion that she was in fact awake, in her own body, in a different realm of some sort. Out of instinct she immediately put her hand on her jeans pocket to grab her phone. She knew she took it with her to the cemetery, she took the bloody thing with her everywhere, so she hoped it was still with her. Wherever she was.

She turned her jean and winter coat pockets inside out, quickly starting to dread what she already knew to be the truth — no phone.

"Fuck, fuck fuckety fuck!" Faye swore, as the familiar thread of panic lassoed her brain.

With no clear idea on what to do next, Faye did the one thing she was great at, ignoring her problems. In one swift motion she lay on the ground, shut her eyes and willed for it all to stop.

"I told you to leave, or I would make you my prisoner and take you to our Queen." An eerily familiar, disembodied voice brought Faye out of her stressful musings. In a most ungraceful manner Faye clambered to her feet, frantically looking around, trying to locate the person who had spoken that threat.

"I don't know what's happening here," Faye shouted into thin air. If she weren't so terrified, she would actually be amused at how squeaky her voice sounded. She steadied herself and stood remarkably still, for someone who always had a body part moving — not even a finger was twitching.

Faye took a deep breath in and focused her vision directly in front of her. Now she could see half a dozen small, cloaked figures emerging from within the brilliant shrubbery between trees.

"How did you get back here?" Cahira demanded, slowly approaching Faye, with the air and grace of a predator. And Faye, clearly her prey. Stopping within a metre in front of her, the smaller female figure waited for an answer.

"This can't be real. Is this real? No, this is obviously a dream," Faye rambled. But she was also terrified of the possibility it was, in fact, real. She had somehow been teleported, transported or Harry Pottered to another realm. Whatever you wanted to call it, she now found herself in a new, and very different world.

"You were warned," Cahira stated loudly, looking up at Faye with an almost bemused look on her face now. She seemed to be enjoying the mutterings of the confused young woman.

With a mere look in Faye's direction, a companion of Cahira's, seized control of Faye's body, locking her arms by her sides. It took Faye a moment to realise she literally could not move and that she was at their mercy. Her movements were completely constricted, with even the smallest effort to move causing severe pain to course through her body. She quickly decided pain was not her friend and gave into the weightless feeling, almost relieved when she saw Cahira flick her wrist, indicating to the other figures to be on the move and Faye started to move forward against her will.

With the troop of cloaked faeries marching behind their prisoner, Cahira and her patrol unit transported the trespasser to the realm's dungeon.

\*\*\*

Faye bolted upright. The first thing she noticed was her body was no longer being controlled by a small but extremely frightening 'person'. Person? Faerie? Whatever those creatures were Faye was not ready to acknowledge it.

The second thing she realised: she was no longer in a forest. Icy tendrils of cold began seeping into her bones as she took in her surroundings. Faye started to stretch her arms, back and legs trying to warm herself and relieve the cramps and the tension in her body. As she took in the cold, dank room, the only word that came to mind was 'dungeon'.

Faye had no clear memory of how she got there but she guessed she had passed out while she was being 'transported'.

"What in the actual hell is going on here?" Faye asked no one in particular, scanning around the room to see if any of the tiny people suddenly appeared.

Glad to have full control over her movements again she stood up and walked the length of the room — a whole four steps in each direction.

The dungeon looked like a converted cave with thick metal rods descending from the ceiling, dividing the space and creating individual cells. She couldn't help but compare the sight before her to something out of a horror movie. The feeling of dread that thought instilled in her was intensified by the waft of stale, rank air that filled her nostrils.

"Right so I've gone from a Cabin in the Woods scenario to Saw territory." Faye continued to talk to herself.

Truly embracing the sheer panic she was feeling now, Faye failed to notice the diminutive figure striding towards her until something clanged loudly against the metal bars.

"Fuuuuuuuuudge!" Faye screamed as she spun her attention towards the noise. The sheer darkness in the dungeon was transformed by a blazing light, beaming from the other side of the cell. Faye squinted and shielded her eyes, unable to look directly at it but unable to turn away.

She wanted to turn away, but she was transfixed by the sight before her. It was mesmerising.

Slowly Faye's eyes adjusted to the brilliance of the light in the dark dungeon, and she was startled by what she saw. Cahira was standing on the other side of the bars, radiating light like an angel. Faye took a short step back until she was pressed up against the cold cell wall, feeling hopeless, terrified and slightly in awe.

"You have been summoned." Cahira's voice floated from the light. The statement was delivered with a robotic tone. A matter-of-fact statement, almost like she was bored and annoyed with having to deliver it. Faye saw a flash of movement from within the glow and it took her a moment to realise the solid metal bars that contained her within the cell had vanished. Not opened but completely gone.

Conflicted between being amazed and terrified by the power on display, Faye froze, simply staring at the radiant being in front of her. Cahira seemed to sense Faye inability or unwillingness to move and with another flick of her hand two guards suddenly materialised in the cave on either side of Faye. Without actually touching her — at least she didn't think they were physically touching her — Faye was shoved toward the entrance of the cell and closer to Cahira.

"Hey! Okay, I can move on my own. Stop with the handsy, but not handsy stuff!" Faye said with as much bravado as she could muster. What she was hoping sounded like an indignant rebuke actually came out as a quiet muffled whisper.

She took a step closer to Cahira, so she was standing within the bubble of the light. She was stunned to realise her captor wasn't shorter than her any more. Cahira now stood at least a foot taller than her. In fact, Faye had to crane her neck up to look at her face.

Brilliant green eyes met hers as she looked up at a face that was exquisitely beautiful but devoid of any emotion.

Faye broke eye contact with a shiver and glanced past the being standing in front of her. She couldn't see any way out of the dungeon — no corridor or pathway. No sooner had that thought entered her mind, Faye felt an unnaturally icy hand clamp around her bicep, and the vertigo engulfed her again. In the vacuum with no air, no sound and no light, Faye fell to her knees. And in a fraction of a second the sensation was gone.

"That needs to stop happening or next time I'm going to puke," Faye moaned, doubled over wrapping her arms around her stomach.

Needing a distraction from the nausea threatening to physically manifest itself, Faye looked up to take in her new surroundings. Bright, shining light bombarded Faye's eyes, but this time there was a warmth too. Shielding her eyes, Faye slowly saw she was outside in golden sunshine.

*So not Cahira's brilliant radiance any more — just the sun* she thought, casting a quick side eye towards her captor to double-check she hadn't actually said that out loud.

Faye gasped in wonder at what she was seeing. An enormous tower, as high as any skyscraper she had ever seen, was in front of her. And it appeared to be built entirely of plants. The outside structure looked to be made of intertwined vines covered in moss and ferns, with circular spaces sporadically appearing, that she guessed were windows. These impressive towers paled in significance when Faye turned around and her gaze fell upon the immense cathedral behind her. It was like no building she had ever seen before. She had no point of reference to go by to even fathom its size. It was simply magnificently huge. The enormous sandstone blocks that made the foundation of the building reminded Faye of the pyramids of Giza. But they weren't in Egypt... right?

Faye looked at the structure and took in the impressive, gothic double entrance doors. Made of solid ancient wood, they looked too heavy for anyone to even move. Stained glass windows seemed to be ensconced in every wall. Faye's eyes couldn't really comprehend the enormity of the cathedral and the towers that surrounded it. It was a dazzling site almost too much to take in.

She was jolted out of her awestruck state by her body involuntarily stepping forward. She quickly noticed Cahira was walking away from her, in the direction of the cathedral. Knowing she had no choice but to follow, Faye put one tentative foot in front of the other and set off in her wake. As they climbed the stairs to the mammoth doors, Faye tried to work out if Cahira was actually walking or floating but gave up when the thought of Cahira floating threatened to trigger her brain into shutting down completely.

"Just go with it, Faye," she quietly muttered to herself, this time knowing she said it out loud.

The doors flew open as Cahira approached, and they entered the grand hallway. Faye was almost getting use to the sensory overload she encountered in this strange world. Almost but not quite. She gasped at the wonder of the colours that beamed in through the stained glass windows and the patterns those light beams were making on the floor. She stopped in her tracks and spun around in place trying to take it all in.

She also couldn't keep the smile from her face. She felt like she must be glowing as radiantly as the fractures of light coming from the windows.

Faye's spinning turn jerked to a stop when her focus landed on the throne at the end of the hall. Faye started to walk forward again, this time with a quiet purpose and of her own free will. She was closer to the throne now, almost hypnotised by the structure itself. It had a solid, dark oak frame decorated with carefully carved symbols and encrusted jewels, cushioned with a golden coloured velvet fabric. Faye was so engrossed by the throne itself she failed to notice the person sitting on it.

"You must be Faye," a woman's voice boomed down to her.

With that simple statement, Faye was brought out of her haze and back into whatever version of reality she was in. She shifted her focus squarely on the being who occupied the throne.

The immediate thing that Faye noticed was the woman before her looked exactly like her. An older version of her, dressed in weird clothes, but she was definitely her doppelganger. The woman wore a gown made of purple silk that reflected the light in the room, making it look like shards of light were emanating from her body. The gown included a magnificent embroidered golden corset connected to a flowing layered skirt, giving the dress the traditional ballgown look. Topping off the ensemble was a subtle crown made of twisted vines and thorns woven tightly together.

The familiarity of the woman's face emboldened Faye.

"Would someone like to explain what the hell is actually happening?" Faye said a little louder than she had intended. Faye was actually a little surprised and worried by how angry she sounded. She shot another sideways glance at Cahira for a reaction, but she was simply standing there, staring dead ahead, giving nothing away.

"That can happen later. First let's have a meal together," the woman on the throne commanded. And with click of her fingers they were no longer standing in the cathedral hall but transported into an elegant dining hall.

Just as she had warned earlier, Faye doubled over and emptied what little she had in her stomach all over the dining hall floor. Running out of energy Faye had enough wits about her to step away from the mess before she fell to the floor. The cool tiles were a nice contrast to the clamminess that had encompassed her.

She didn't take in the magnificent dining table with the ornate candelabras, crockery or cutlery. But on the edge of consciousness, she felt something press gently to her lips, but she was too far gone to do anything about it.

# CHAPTER 12

Floating in the flux of being not quite awake yet not really sleeping, Faye enjoyed the feeling of sinking into a cloud-like mattress. The further she floated in the in-between state, the further away her ambitions of fully waking up drifted. She was so lost in the familiar feeling of comfort, that she had completely forgotten where she was. That is until she decided to open her eyes to greet the morning. Rising up on her elbows it all came flooding back to her, the cemetery, the forest, Cahira and the little people, the cathedral, the weird older lady who looked just like her, a flash of a dining hall, and back to Cahira. Now she was in a bedroom, waking up in the world's softest, most comfortable bed. Alone.

From everything Faye had seen and experienced during her short time in the strange world, she was amazed to find a bedroom that resembled something straight out of an Ikea catalogue. Shit, maybe she was in Sweden?

Everywhere she turned was white on white. From the walls to the carpet and the bed frame buffered by bedside tables on either side. No personalised items decorated the room, creating another cage like vibe, only her current one was definitely more comfortable.

Faye found two doors on opposite sides of the room and hoped for a way out of her new dungeon. Sure, it was an upgrade from the cave cell she was in yesterday (was it yesterday — she couldn't tell how much time had passed). Deciding to check out the door on her right first, she was shocked to find a fully equipped walk-in wardrobe almost as big as her bedroom back home. The room was full of row after row of clothing. Faye looked around and saw elegant ballgowns, formal dining attire, tunics and cloaks, and if she was not mistaken, sleep ware. Below the hanging dresses stood a series of glass cabinets — on one side of the room the cabinets held hundreds of pairs of shoes, each pair as elegant as the gowns hanging above.

Faye stopped and looked down into one of the glass cabinets on the other side of the room and gasped. Faye felt like she was looking at a bright, sparkling, rainbow. She looked to her left and right and saw each of the cabinets was lined with exquisite pieces of jewellery: each piece unlike anything she had ever seen before. Necklaces, rings, brooches, earrings, and tiaras, all laid out on cushioned purple velvet.

Faye stood for a moment with her hand hovering over a glass cabinet containing an ornate bejewelled crown, almost spellbound by the beauty of it. She blinked, and in a flash, she was overwhelmed by the thought she really shouldn't be in the room. Faye quickly retraced her steps out of the walk-in wardrobe and across the bedroom to the other door. She grasped the cold door handle and threw open the door — fully expecting to see a hallway or corridor. The feeling of being a captive was reinforced when Faye found herself standing in a huge bathroom instead of a passageway out. As with the other two previous rooms, this one was white, white, and more white, but nothing was spared in terms of elegance and spaciousness.

It only took a quick glance at the toilet for Faye to realise she was still totally herself when the need to pee and shower surpassed any other feelings she was nurturing. She was so desperate to wash away the fear and stress of the past twenty-four hours she simply turned on the taps to the shower, adjusted the temperature and quickly undressed. Standing still under the showerhead, letting the water fall straight onto her face, Faye had never felt anything quite so heavenly. As the panic and confusion slowly washed away, a warm, comforting feeling of peace took its place. Faye stayed there, under the shower for what felt like an eternity.

Reluctantly coming out of her water induced hypnosis, she turned the water off and stepped out of the shower — stunned by the fact that a purple towel was neatly waiting for her on the rack. Faye looked around her and quickly realised three things: the towel wasn't there when she got in the shower, her clothes were gone, and she was stupid for having a shower in the first place.

"What the hell were you thinking Faye?" she asked her reflection in the steamy bathroom mirror.

Her anxiety started to rush at Faye with a vengeance. Questions were spinning through her mind at a rapid rate.

Where the hell was she? How were people coming in and out without her hearing or seeing them? Why did she feel like a goddam prisoner?

Struggling to keep some semblance of control Faye decided the best thing to do would be to get dressed and find Cahira — she seemed to be in charge. She stepped from the bathroom back into the bedroom with the intention of finding the least formal thing in the closet to wear. She stopped short when she found a gown already laid out on the bed. If Faye wasn't mistaken, the dress looked similar to the one worn by the Queen the day before, with the only difference being her dress had silver embroidered work on a sapphire blue corset.

"Of course you have chosen something for me to wear," Faye shouted out into the ether.

Faye grabbed the dress and walked back into the bathroom, kicking the door shut behind her. She was relieved to find she could secure herself in the dress with a zipper rather than laces of traditional corsets. Faye took a minute to look herself over in the mirror. She was amazed at how the dress fit her perfectly. The dress transformed her — she was still Faye but now, looking at herself in the mirror, she felt... regal. Regal. That was the word that popped loudly into her mind.

Turning away from the mirror and stepping back into the bedroom Faye was startled to find Cahira standing on the opposite side of the bedroom with her hood off. Even in the bright light of the room Faye found Cahira still seemed to glow. Now, standing there with nothing obstructing the view of her face, Faye understood why. Cahira had the most brilliant, hypnotic eyes Faye had ever seen. With a dark shade of green around the pupils that progressively turns into a lighter green, Cahira's eyes solidified the fact in Faye's mind that she was not human. The thought both terrified and intrigued her at the same time.

Not sure what to do next and trying to shake off the power Cahira's eyes seemed to have over her, Faye did one thing she knew how to do: nervously ramble.

"I guess standing here and staring at you won't get me any closer to an explanation as to where I am and what I'm doing here; will you answer my questions, or can you take me to someone who will?" Faye blurted out in rapid fire.

"Your presence has been requested," Cahira stated matter-of-factly, completely ignoring Faye's question. With no desire to keep the Queen waiting Cahira simply stepped toward Faye and enclosed her wrist with her own gloved hand, hoping to avoid any further delays.

***

Unlike the times before when Cahira had touched her and they teleported somewhere, Faye did not feel the need to decorate the floor with vomit when they reached their destination. This time she felt electrified, like she could feel each separate individual connection to every molecule inside her.

"You're looking well this morning."

Faye found herself in the grand hallway from the night before, with the Queen standing in front of her. Faye gave her a generic nod as her attention was distracted by the vast array of food laid out on the table in front of her.

With a complete disregard for the Queen, Faye walked around the monarch and quickly took a seat at the table. In front of her was an elaborate arrangement of breakfast foods, more than enough to feed a small army. Seated in front of a bowl of sliced fruits Faye did not stop to use cutlery, she just started eating with her hands — the need to eat eclipsing everything else.

"Your level of disrespect will not be tolerated," the Queen thundered as she turned and took her place at the head of the table.

Faye finished swallowing a piece of delicious melon and looked steadily at the Queen. Her level of fear had been dissipating with each mouthful of food she ate.

"The way I see it, respect goes both ways, and so far, I've been stuck in a cell in a dingey dungeon and then left in a bedroom with no way out. No matter how high class the room is, if it does not have a door that leads out, it's a jail cell," Faye finished, leaving the dining hall in silence.

Continuing to eat, she ignored the flabbergasted look on the Queen's face.

"If you had not taken ill last night, you would have received the answers to all your questions. But that was not to be, given your propensity for emptying your stomach's contents on the floor of my dining hall. I will spend this morning with you explaining the situation you now find yourself in."

The flash of a smirk crossed the Queen's face as she left that statement hanging in the air. She clicked her fingers and within the blink of an eye a faerie servant appeared beside the Queen and placed a white piece of silk across her lap, before disappearing again.

Playing witness to a new level of laziness Faye didn't know whether to be impressed or outraged. It literally took all her self-control not to scoff and laugh out loud. Faye was actually amazed when the Queen picked up her own cutlery and fed herself instead of having some poor servant do it for her.

"Okay, Your Majesty. Can I please have an explanation as to what is actually happening here?" Despite the reduced fear level Faye was feeling now, she still couldn't help but feel intimidated by the situation. And there was a definite hint of desperation creeping into her voice.

"I am your great-grandmother," the Queen stated, staring directly into Faye's eyes.

"That would explain why we look exactly alike, but my great-grandmother can't be alive today, and mostly definitely wouldn't be the age you are now."

"Maybe not in the Human Realm, but here…" The Queen raised her left eyebrow and left the statement hanging in the air, unfinished.

"While I was in the Human Realm I lived and breathed folklore. It was such an obsession of mine. I created a group in Dublin for other like-minded people who were dedicated to finding proof of the existence of faeries. Then one day he found us." The Queen took a moment to take a few mouthfuls of food.

Faye watched the Queen as she ate, waiting for her to continue and wondering who the hell "he" was.

"He showed us wonderful things, things you could never dream of, but it was all just a distraction from the real reason this faerie had made contact with us. He was sent as a scout to find a ruler for his realm. I was chosen and brought here, against my will. Before I knew what was happening, I was made to complete the Queen's Trial of Power." The Queen spoke without any indication of being traumatised by the events she was recounting. She simply shifted her gaze from Faye to the food in front of her and resumed eating her breakfast.

Red flags were starting to flap about in Faye's mind. So, this was her long lost great-grandmother! Her grandpa's mother — whom he thought was dead. And from his version of events Faye got the impression her great-grandmother chose to leave of her own free will. But now hearing her story, told with no ounce of emotion, Faye was wary.

For the moment Faye decided to stay clear of the questions she really wanted to ask in case she aggravated the Queen. She chose to start with something simple and off topic.

"Have I been shrunk to the size of the faeries, or have they grown, because when I first got here, they only reached up to my waist? But now everyone is the same size."

"Certain fae can manipulate perception," the Queen stated, watching with interest as a wave of terror swept across Faye's face.

"Right. Okay. I'd like to go home now." On instinct Faye needed to put as much distance between herself and the so-called Faerie Realm. Planting her feet firmly on the ground, she pushed her chair away from the table, creating an ear-grating screech.

Faye was pleased to see a flicker of annoyance cross her great-grandmother's face as she shifted her attention to finding an exit route.

Just like the bedroom she woke up in, there were no doors leading out of the dining room. Faye stood and pinched the bridge of her nose. Why would there be any doors if all the bloody faeries had the ability to magically appear and disappear?

Slowly feeling the walls closing in, Faye knew a panic attack was going to take a hold of her. And without being able to contact her mum, she had nothing to keep her grounded. The fear was swelling, and her heartbeat was pounding in her ears.

As if sensing Faye was going to break, the Queen's voice sounded clearly in her head: "I'll have Cahira return you to your room. We will talk again at lunch."

And with the end of that sentence, Cahira appeared right beside Faye. Feeling a firm hand take hold of her shoulder, Faye didn't have time to protest before she was once again whisked away.

# CHAPTER 13

This time it felt different for Faye when Cahira teleported her out of the dining hall. With Cahira's steady hand on her shoulder, she realised she could take a deep breath to steady her nerves. She couldn't quite explain how she knew when it was safe to open her eyes, but as soon as she did the coiled-up tension was released from her body.

Faye took a second to let her eyes adjust to not being scrunched tight in terror and she quickly realised she wasn't back in the bedroom. They were standing in the middle of yet another magnificent hall that was illuminated with an unnatural radiance., The hall was vacant of any furniture, bare except for a row of framed paintings running the length of each wall, as far as the eye could see.

"Where are we?" Faye asked, turning around expecting Cahira to be standing there, but instead she found herself alone.

Faye couldn't help but roll her eyes in a mixture of frustration and confusion. Not surprised at being left alone by the enigmatic Cahira but wondering why she would show her this place instead of taking her back to the bedroom — directly disobeying the Queen.

Faye didn't even bother looking for a door, avoiding the crushing disappointment she would no doubt feel, but instead walked closer to one of the hanging artworks, her eyes drawn to the gold metallic plaque shining underneath the frame. There, engraved in neat cursive script was:

*Queen Faye Burke 1952*

Faye drew in a shuddering breath, and she was now extremely reluctant to look up at the painting. She knew, clear in her mind, if she looked up at the painting, she would be looking at a portrait of herself. She shut her eyes again and tried her hand at teleporting herself out of the hall and out of the realm, as if saying "There's no place like home. There's no place like home," over and over again like Dorothy in *The Wizard of Oz*, was enough to get her out of there.

Opening her eyes just a fraction, Faye took a peek at the floor — knowing full well she was still standing in the bloody hall.

"Arghhhhh!" She growled in frustration.

"Right. Let's do this Faye," she said, giving herself a pep talk.

Biting the bullet, Faye looked up and immediately her suspicions were confirmed. Staring down at her was a painted image of herself — sure, the Faye in the portrait was a little older than she was but it was unmistakably her.

Faye was starting to grow a little weary of all the doppelgangers popping up everywhere she turned. Same face as hers, same name as hers. What she really needed now was an explanation. She suppressed the urge to growl again in frustration and resigned herself to the fact she would just have to wait until she met with the Queen again. Or maybe Cahira would actually speak to her, rather than just chaperone her through the crazy place.

Deciding to distract herself, Faye stepped to her left and looked up at the next painting. Any hope she was holding that it wouldn't look like her evaporated in an instant. Staring down at her — literally looking straight at her — was another portrait of herself. Same face, same long red hair, same green eyes. It was unnerving. The only difference between that portrait and the previous one was the shiny plaque sitting just below the frame had a different last name and year engraved.

The way Faye saw it she had two choices: give into the panic that was building inside her, curl up on the floor in the foetal position and wait for the next terrifying thing to happen. Or. She could embrace the crazy.

*"WwJLCd?"* Faye asked the woman in the painting staring down at her.

"She would kick your arse that's what," Faye answered herself, trying to channel Jamie Lee Curtis from every *Halloween* movie ever made.

Faye figured all the portraits hanging on the wall would look like her, but that knowledge didn't stop the rising surprise as she walked the length of the hall, quickly gazing up at each passing portrait and name plaque. She came to a stop at the end of hall. Standing in front of the first, and she assumed, oldest painting. Faye was slightly out of breath as she stood there, taking in the ancient-looking portrait.

She knew it was the oldest one in the hall. Not just because of the weathered, ancient frame and the raised cracks throughout the paint. In certain spots the paint had completely flacked off, revealing the faded yellow canvas beneath, and disfiguring the face of that particular version of Faye.

Faye dropped her eyes to the plaque below the painting and was surprised to see the words 'Goddess Danu' inscribed.

With a vortex of questions spinning around in her mind, Faye wished for Cahira to appear and make sense of the madness.

As if hearing her plea, Cahira materialised behind Faye, and before she could really register her presence, Cahira lay a hand on Faye's shoulder and once again they were miraculously moving through space.

***

Faye was almost getting used to it now. Still with her eyes closed she could sense when they had arrived at their destination, and it was safe to open her eyes. As with the time before, Faye was blinded by a light so bright she couldn't bear it.

Using both her hands to act as a visor, Faye slowly opened her eyes and blinked a few times — giving her eyes time to adjust to the light. The warm glow she felt on her skin made her realise she was outside. Faye couldn't help but gasp at the beauty before her. She lowered her hands and turned around to take it all in.

She was standing in a small clearing, surrounded on all sides by the largest trees she had even seen. They were so tall they could rival the tallest tower in any city, and the trunks were so thick, Faye thought it would take her an hour to walk around one. Faye looked around for Cahira and saw her on the opposite side of the clearing, just standing there as stoic as ever.

Between them lay a faerie ring similar to the one in her dream. Only this time the spaces between the rocks forming the circle were filled with large mushrooms in a beautiful arrangement of pastel colours. Faye was bewitched by the colours, and she felt herself being drawn down towards the circle, almost kneeling in front of it. Shaking her head suddenly Faye snapped out of her hypnotic state and turned her attention towards Cahira.

"A warning would be appreciated next time," Faye grumbled. She actually put her hands on her hips in a dramatic show of defiance.

"I'm getting really tired of being touched and teleported or whatever it is you do. All without my permission I might add. Are you going to stay and explain to me what's going on here, or zap me to another weird place and leave again?" Faye asked with a quiet calm she was starting to feel and embrace. She couldn't fight the feeling that she definitely liked being in Cahira's company.

"I have provided you with the tools you need to determine where to place your trust," Cahira stated, being frustratingly cryptic.

"What does that even mean, Cahira? You left me standing in a hall full to the brim with portraits of, well, me or people who look exactly like me. And I still can't wrap my head around the fact faeries are real — case in point." She gestured at the being who was now standing with in an arm's length of her. "And I'm actually standing in a Faerie Realm."

Cahira watched her patiently, knowing she wasn't finished with her rant.

"And don't get me started on the fact I am an exact replica of my great-grandmother, who is supposed to be dead, but is here, alive and well, and none other than the Queen of the goddam faerie kingdom!" Faye finished in a rush, quite pleased with herself.

"You have been told more lies than truths, Faye. You needed to be shown that." Cahira totally ignored Faye's questions and answered in riddles. Before Faye had the chance to open her mouth in reply, Cahira spoke again.

"I have been alive a long, long time and I know the signs of a power-hungry tyrant when I see one. The reign of this Queen is coming to an end, but she does not wish to relinquish her extraordinary power, and she will go against the natural order to keep it."

Before Faye had a chance to reply, she felt the cold grip of Cahira's hand on her arm, and she was transported back to the bedroom she had woken up in earlier that day.

\*\*\*

Faye sat opposite her great-grandmother, just as she had done that morning, literally staring at the woman across the table from her. She knew she was staring at the Queen, but she was too preoccupied with the information swirling around in her mind, specifically that of which Cahira had spoken to her in the forest. Faye was struggling to make any sense of it at all.

The magnificent dining hall was in darkness, save for the row of candles that ran down the centre of the table. The flickering flames cast a dim light over the plates filled with sumptuous looking food and threw shadows over both Faye and the Queen's faces.

"I want to go home," Faye stated clearly and as a matter of fact. "I've been gone too long; everyone will be panicking."

For the first time since being in the realm Faye allowed herself to wonder what her mum and grandparents were thinking and how worried they must be.

"You have no need to worry. Time moves differently here. A day in the Faerie realm is but an hour in the Human Realm," The Queen explained to Faye, not actually acknowledging her request to leave.

"How is that possible?" Faye asked, annoyed she was once again ignored, but also intrigued by what the Queen had told her.

"More things than you can comprehend are possible here," the Queen stated. She almost sounded wistful.

"Why not explore our realm some more, spend a few days here? I want to spend some time with you Faye, get to know you better. I lost my chance with my grandchild but you're here now."

It took Faye a second to realise she was referring to her mum, Elaine, with the last sentence. Faye stared at her great-grandmother, still slightly unnerved by her own image looking back at her. She clearly didn't have any choice in the matter. Leaving the Faerie realm was not an option for her. Not at the moment anyway.

"Enjoy the food you have been offered. Best to eat it while it's hot." And with that direction, the Queen shut down any further conversation.

Faye broke eye contact with her dining partner and took in the plates of food in front of her. There were plates piled high with meats that resembled chicken, beef and possibly ham, and bowls of steaming vegetables and lush looking salads. Faye gave into her hunger and piled her plate with a little of everything.

She sat quietly, shovelling food into her mouth, occasionally glancing at the Queen. She was unnerved to find the woman was just sitting there watching her, not eating, herself.

Faye swallowed a mouthful of chicken and put her knife and fork across her plate.

"I'm…" Before Faye could finish informing the Queen that she was finished eating, she was silenced by a loud click, echoing through the cavernous dining hall.

And just like that, Cahira appeared in the darkness behind Faye, and she was zapped back to her bedroom.

# CHAPTER 14

"Can't you take me home?" Faye asked Cahira as she sat on her bed the next morning, putting on her shoes. Doing the normal, mundane task reinforced her desperation to be back home with her family, pretending her time in the Faerie Realm had never happened.

"I don't hold the power to cross realms."

Faye struggled to believe it, considering all the teleporting Cahira had been doing while babysitting her. Surely if anyone could, it would be Cahira. Faye's thoughts wandered back to how she first got to the Faerie Realm and how she was sure Cahira had brought her. Now, with Cahira's statement, she had even more questions. It seemed every conversation she had with Cahira only led to more confusion and more unanswered questions.

"Well, someone has to," Faye tried to reason, more with herself than to Cahira.

"Only royalty can travel between realms. The Queen is the only one who can grant permission for others who wish to cross."

Faye was surprised she actually got a straight forward answer, no decoding needed and in her excitement she failed to comprehend the implications Cahira's answer had.

"Well look at us having a conversation," Faye said with a smile. And she was chuffed to see a flicker, just the faintest flicker, of a smile flash on Cahira's face.

Gaining more confidence Faye starting to pace the length of her bedroom.

"Okay then I want to get permission." Faye stated the obvious, coming to a stop directly in front of Cahira.

"Your request has been denied," Cahira stated flatly looking Faye dead in the eyes.

Faye almost stomped her foot in a temper tantrum "Who gives permission, because the only people I've spoken to is you and my great…" Faye's voice trailed off as the realisation settled in her brain: that her great-grandmother was the reason she was stuck and not on her way home.

"So, I just have to bide my time for the next few days as the Queen 'gets to know me' and then someone will take me back to the cemetery? Or will I just wake up from this nightmare back in my bed in the B&B?" Faye looked at Cahira for clarification but got nothing but another cold response.

"The denial is infinite."

Those four words weighed heavily on Faye as she contemplated what exactly her great-grandmother might consider 'getting to know her'. Whenever she had spoken to her great-grandmother, their conversations were short and awkward, and not to mention she found the woman extremely intimidating.

The optimism Faye was desperately holding onto about getting home was fading fast. She sat down on the end of the bed and ran through everything she knew so far. The Queen of the Faeries was her great-grandmother, who was also the mother of her grandpa, and she went missing decades ago and was long thought dead but was alive and well in the Faerie realm.

Her story of being kidnapped and taken to the Faerie Realm was a contradiction to her grandpa's notion that she left her family of her own free will. And while her story of being taken against her will was also how Faye found herself in the realm, the Queen's story left Faye with a bad feeling in the pit of her stomach when she first heard it.

And onto the hall of portraits where Cahira had taken her, without the Queen's knowledge, with painting after painting of different Fayes, including one that was apparently a Goddess.

Add in Cahira's comments from the day before about a power-hungry tyrant and she definitely had more questions than answers.

Trying to compartmentalise what she knew to keep an impending anxiety attack at bay, Faye decided her only course of action was to keep bombarding Cahira with questions, in the hope that her hard, faerie guard exterior would eventually crack.

"What is actually going on here?" Faye decided the direct route was the best route. Why beat around the bush?

"I have provided you with all the information you need, Faye," Cahira replied just as bluntly.

"You haven't told me anything! You dropped me in that hall, all by myself. How is that supposed to help? What information did that provide besides the fact that there has apparently been hundreds of people who look exactly like me?" Faye paused, running out of steam.

"What are you hiding?"

Cahira went to say something then hesitated before saying, "I have told you everything I can." And in that instant, Faye knew something terrible was going on.

"But you know more," Faye stated as a matter of fact. She hadn't missed that Cahira had said 'can' not 'know' and she knew someone was stopping her from telling Faye the truth — and she had a pretty good guess as to who that was.

Cahira stretched her open hand towards Faye, wordlessly giving her the option to trust her or not.

Faye looked at the hand and ran through all her options. Either she was being taken to breakfast, where she may be offered some answers or to some other random location within the strange place to meet her doom. With a shrug Faye decided to trust Cahira and reached out to take her hand.

\*\*\*

Faye was used to the teleporting business now, and she actually enjoyed it when she was a willing participant. She opened her eyes to find herself in another long, grand hall. And once again she was alone. No Cahira anywhere to be seen.

Just like the previous hall, the entire length of the walls was covered in art. Only this time it was immense tapestries that hung from the ceilings to the floor.

The tapestries were so large Faye struggled to comprehend what she was looking at. There were layers upon layers of woven cotton and fabrics creating depths to the tapestry Faye never knew possible with such a medium.

The tapestry Faye stood in front of was awash with competing colours, one half woven with dull, darkened tones that clashed diagonally across the middle with bright vibrant colours. When Faye stepped closer to the tapestry, she could make out the point where the two halves combined, and the area depicted a scene of two armies in battle. The fighters on the dark side held shields in one hand and weapons in the other. The weapons being held by the soldiers varied depending on their closeness to the centre of the battle. Those in the middle of fight held swords and axes; the second line of attack held spears, and the third line of soldiers, along the border of the tapestry, stood without shields but were each armed with a bow and a quiver of arrows strapped to their backs.

The army on the bright side of the tapestry did not hold shields or weapons of any sort. Each individual soldier was enclosed in a separate force field of light. From what Faye could make out, it appeared as if the light army was on the defensive against the opposing dark side.

Faye suddenly regretted not taking art as an elective at school as she stared up at the tapestry, trying to decipher its message. Faye looked around, trying to find anything that may explain what she was looking at. She was relieved to find a glimmer that indicated a plaque secured to the wall at the end of the tapestry. Faye counted out her strides as she walked to length of the tapestry to reach the plaque and was amazed when she finally stopped at 25.

The plaque was engraved with the following inscription:

*The battle between the Tuatha De Danann and the Milesians lasted three days, spanning over the land and sea. Overpowered by brute strength and weaponry, the bloodshed caused devastation throughout the Tuatha De Danann population. Goddess Danu took mercy on her people and sent them to live in tir na nog, to be free and safe.*

Faye stepped back and looked again at the tapestry, hoping it would all make sense. But she was still no closer to figuring out why Cahira had brought her there.

Moving onto the next tapestry, Faye found it portrayed an image of a man with his arms wrapped protectively around a woman holding a baby. Faye noticed the man wore a crown of gold encrusted in elaborate jewels and diamonds. As she stared at the crown it began to shimmer and glow, as if the sun was reflecting against a metallic object instead of woven textiles.

As Faye took a step towards the tapestry, she was hit with a devastating force — like being in a car that was travelling at a high speed before coming to screeching, sudden stop, causing the seatbelt to jerk tight against a chest. When Faye recovered from the shock of the physical jolt, she realised she was no longer in the hall looking at the tapestry.

Faye found herself standing in front of a man and woman laying side by side, in long, flowing grass, amongst the brightest flowers she had ever seen. A baby wrapped in an animal skin snuggled between them. In an instant, Faye recognised the family from the tapestry she had just been looking at.

*So now I am being teleported into tapestries — fan-bloody-tastic*, Faye thought to herself and vowed, then and there, to learn the depths of the powers available in the Faerie Realm.

Faye gazed upon the couple in front of her and saw the man open his mouth as if to speak. But in the blink of an eye he paused, frozen in time, and Faye felt like she was immersed in a 3D all sensory picture. The people were frozen; no wind was blowing, the flowers were still, and all was quiet. So, so quiet. Faye could hear her heart thumping in her chest, and the blood pulsing in her ears. But most frightening of all was when Faye tried to take a step forward, she couldn't move. She was frozen in the tapestry just like the family she was staring at.

"You have to take Faye and travel south. Stay on the inland roads and don't go towards the sea under any circumstances."

A man's voice boomed inside her head and Faye knew it was the man lying before her. His fingers were now outstretched towards the baby girl as if waiting for her to grab a hold.

"Why would I leave you, Lugh?"

Now a woman's voice, sounding almost frantic.

"I can't just pack up and travel with a newborn. This is our home. Where will we go? Haven't we found a balance between your commitments as the King and as a father?" the woman pleaded with man.

"It isn't safe for you or our daughter here. You know this to be true. Faye is the future of our people, and she needs to be protected." King Lugh tried to reason with the mother of his only child.

"Surely the safest place for us is with you."

"There is an army coming to claim this land and they will eradicate us all if they can. Both of you need to be as far away from me and our home as possible," King Lugh continued.

Faye wasn't aware of when the subtle changes were taking place within the tapestry, but the woman was now holding the man's hand, with a look on her face that was so defeated and worn it broke Faye's heart.

"When do we have to leave?" the woman asked quietly.

"This afternoon before nightfall. Everything is prepared. I have an escort waiting with all the supplies you will need for your journey. You and our daughter will be taken somewhere safe, where they can never find you. I will send word for you as soon as it is safe to return."

His voice grew stern, almost hard. "If the worst were to happen and you do not receive word from me, this land will eventually call for Tuath De Danann blood and you will know it is safe to return."

"Do not talk like that Lugh," the woman stated in a voice that now held a steely reserve. "I will take Faye and we will be safe. Just as you will."

As the woman finished her statement, Faye felt that strange jerking sensation again and she was jolted out of the tapestry and back into the hall.

She took a moment to steady herself back on solid ground, then looked for a plaque, hoping for some sort of explanation. To the side of the tapestry, she found the plaque on the wall that read:

*This marks the last time King Lugh, his wife Siobhan and their baby daughter Faye, were together before the death of the Royal couple.*

Faye felt such a heavy weight of grief fall over her, she nearly dropped to her knees. She wasn't sure how much more of the extreme emotional rollercoaster she could take.

Faye took a few deep, heavy breaths and looked to her left, wary of moving in front of the next tapestry.

Summoning up all of her inner strength she took several steps down the hall.

The next tapestry showed a silhouette of a person, standing in front of a large mound in the earth. There were bright beams of light shining from behind the figure, totally obscuring any facial details.

Faye's face felt flushed, and she swore it was from the heat of the light in the tapestry. As she raised her hand to touch her cheek, she once again felt a dramatic jolt, and in a flash, Faye found herself standing within the magnificent fabric artwork.

She immediately saw two striking differences between the image depicted in the tapestry Faye had been looking at from her spot in the hall, and the scenario she was now in the middle of. Firstly, the people in the 'tapestry' were moving and talking, interacting amongst themselves but seemed totally oblivious of Faye's presence. Secondly the bright beams of light were no longer shining behind the person in the centre and Faye could now clearly make out her features.

Once again, she was stunned to see her own face, just as she had back in the portrait hall. But this time it was more real: she could simply reach out and touch skin and bone. In the tapestry, Faye looked to be in her late twenties and Faye couldn't help but think if that was how she would look at that age, she would be happy.

Faye looked around and realised she was standing in a cemetery and the mound was a freshly covered grave. A fresh wave of grief washed over her as she pieced it all together: the Faye in the tapestry had lost someone close to her and she was standing there shattered and lost.

Faye was startled when a man's voice rang out.

"After all this time, we finally meet again."

A man suddenly appeared, standing on the other side of the grave, and Faye immediately knew him to be King Lugh from the previous tapestry. Despite him stating that time had passed, he looked as if he hadn't aged a day.

"Who are you?" the Faye from the tapestry asked in surprise. "Where did you come from?"

"I am King Lugh of the Tuatha De Danann, and I am your father. And you, my darling daughter, are the new Queen of our realm."

The Faye from the tapestry glared intensely at the man standing before her.

"My mother used to tell me stories about you and your land, and the magic you had. She died waiting for you to come back to her."

"I know, my dear, I know. It is one of the many things I regret in my long life. That, and not seeing you grow into the fine, beautiful woman I see standing before me. I fear I should not have come to you this soon as it is still not safe in our realm for you." The King hesitated, looking at his daughter with regret-filled eyes. "But I need you and so do your people."

Tapestry Faye screamed, "You know! What do you mean you know? How could you possibly know anything about my mother and me? You were never there!"

"Everything will be explained once we are back home." King Lugh said, in a reasonable tone. Tapestry Faye almost laughed at the preposterous statement.

"I already have a home. With my husband and my child. I will not abandon them," she said with clear authority.

"I wish that could be, but your duty is now to your people. Your husband and children will remain safe while you claim your title." King Lugh stated just as calmly. He was overjoyed to hear the command in his daughter's voice. She would make a magnificent Queen.

"Are you threatening me?" tapestry Faye asked, not hiding her distain in the question. She was clearly revolted by the man standing before her, claiming to be her father.

"Of course I am not threatening you Faye, or your family. They will be safer if you stay away from them. I had to make those extreme sacrifices with you and your mother. Siobhan understood that. Now it is time for you to do the same." King Lugh stated the last sentence as a command.

The real Faye was stunned when tapestry Faye practically shouted, "I will not leave them."

King Lugh looked both bemused and annoyed by the outburst, but he was growing tired of the defiance. Time was of the essence.

"Enough. We do not have time for this. Arrangements have been made."

"Make time!" Faye demanded "I am not going anywhere with you unless I have some sort of explanation."

King Lugh sighed and began. "I can guarantee the safety of your family and they will be totally unaware that you are gone. A mirror image of you, a changeling, will take your place in the Human Realm while you take your rightful place in the Faerie Realm. As time passes your children will grow and have children of their own."

King Lugh raised his hand to stop the older Faye from speaking. He continued with his explanation.

"Some time in the future a child will be born with the required markers of our original Queen. This child may be your grandchild or your great-grandchild, or so on. We do not know how many generations will pass before the next Queen will be born — but she will be your descendant and we will know she has been born the second she takes her first breath. Once this child comes of age, only then will you be able to return to the Human Realm. You will take her place in her life, and she will take your place as Queen in our realm."

Both Faye's stood in stunned silence. Real Faye was starting to make weird sense of what she had been experiencing in the past forty-eight hours, but tapestry Faye was clearly struggling with what her father was telling her. She had the advantage of knowing of the faerie world through the stories her mother had told her, but she was not prepared for the talk of being a Queen and having to rule her people.

"How is any of what you are saying supposed to comfort me? A stranger will be sent to my home, in my place, to live my life with my family. While I go off to some magical faerie land where I will rule as a Queen. Then when the "time comes" I will go and replace my great-granddaughter in her life. Do you hear how crazy that sounds?" The final question almost echoed the thought in real Faye's head.

Faye stood there, enthralled by the two people standing before her, the same two people who were totally unaware of her presence.

King Lugh took a step closer to his daughter.

"Faye, I have waited so long for this moment. You cannot begin to understand the sacrifices I have made. This is the only way for our bloodline to survive and for the rightful Queen to rule our realm. This is the only way for our people to be truly safe."

Faye could see the older woman contemplating what her father had said, and she could tell when the futility of her situation finally dawned on her. She didn't even have a choice. Her father was implying she could choose to go to the Faerie Realm or stay in the Human Realm, but she could see clearly now that was not the case.

"You promise my family will be safe and truly unaware I am gone?" she asked her father, more subdued now.

"Yes," he said by way of a simple reply, as he took another step closer. He was within touching distance now.

"I agree to your terms."

No sooner had those five words crossed her lips than a blinding explosion of light erupted and engulfed them all. As the sharpness of the light began to dim, they found King Lugh crumpled on the floor. Gone was the tall, stoic King and in his place lay a deathly ill old man. The King had aged decades in that flash of light. He looked like death itself — with sallow skin, barely breathing, and blank eyes.

"We have run out of time my child, we must leave," King Lugh whispered.

His frailty was staggering and when he held out his hand for his daughter to take, tapestry Faye reached out to take it.

Instantly Faye knew King Lugh was going to teleport back to the Faerie Realm, taking his version of Faye with him.

As soon as contact was made between the two hands Faye was ripped from the tapestry and she needed to take a few quick steps to steady herself when she landed back in the hall.

Faye knew the drill now. She quickly darted her eyes to either side of the tapestry to find the plaque displaying the title.

*The first of many Faye Queens to rule the Faerie Realm.*

Finally, she was starting to piece it all together. What had Cahira said to her earlier?

She had given her all the information she needed.

If what she had just witnessed in the last tapestry was true, and she combined it with the multitude of portraits and tapestry, she could come up with only one conclusion.

She, Faye Burke, formally Adkins, was a descendant of a Faerie Queen. But the one question that was sounding loudly in her mind was if what the King in the tapestry had said was true, why hadn't a changeling been sent to take over her great-grandmother's life while she was ruling in the Faerie Realm?

Faye decided to skip a few tapestries and stood before the last one in the hall, hoping it would show her great-grandmother. It depicted the side profile of two women, one standing tall and strong, the other kneeling before her, in a submissive manner. Faye looked closer at the women and realised she was once again looking at another, slightly older, version of herself. The two women in the tapestry were completely identical and wore the exact same dark-gold ballgown covered in a pale coloured lace trim. The only difference between the two was that the woman standing had a crown perched proudly on her head.

Faye felt the familiar jerking sensation and prepared herself to be thrown into the tapestry.

Faye found herself once again invisible, but this time she was able to move amongst a crowd of people milling about just inside the grand cathedral where she had first met her great-grandmother. The crowd's attention was drawn to the raised platform at the far end of the hall, upon which the throne sat. Sitting high upon the throne was an older version of Faye, dressed in the extravagant ballgown

Faye remembered seeing io the tapestry, and wearing the crown. Standing next to the throne was a younger Faye, dressed in the identical dress, but her head was crownless.

It wasn't until a woman's voice echoed through the hall that Faye realised it had been completely silent.

"Today we are gathered here to crown Faye the thirty-fifth, Queen of this Realm. I have spent the last century here and my rule has now come to an end. Faye the thirty-fifth has completed the Queen's Trial of Power, proving her right to the throne. She has mastered the required skills of teleportation, mind projection and manipulation, and creation and destruction. Thus she is ready." The Queen completed her speech and rose.

The Queen grasped the hand of the Faye standing next to her and guided her to kneel before her. Lifting the crown off her head, the Queen began to speak once again.

"Do you, Faye the thirty fifth, promise to rule justly?"

"I promise," the younger Faye answered.

"Will you protect the Faerie Realm with your life?"

"I will."

"When the time comes, will you guide the next Queen into power and return to the Human Realm?"

"I will."

"With this crown, I pronounce you, Faye the thirty fifth, Queen of the Tuath de Danann until the next presents herself."

Following that declaration the Queen placed the crown on the head of the young woman kneeling before her.

"You may rise and take your throne." With that, the previous Queen stepped to the side, allowing the newly crowned Queen to sit on the throne.

Suddenly the scene before Faye changed. No longer was she in the cathedral but standing in the now very familiar clearing in the forest. The two Queens, the new and the old, were standing barely two feet from her.

Faye noticed that the older woman no longer wore the ballgown, but instead wore a long, fitted navy skirt with matching blazer. The younger woman, standing tall and proud, still wore elegant attire of the crowning ceremony.

"I am feeling the call back to the Human Realm. It is getting stronger by the minute. I have been in this realm for so long I can barely imagine how much the Human Realm has changed. I cannot wait to take your place and meet Joshua. I haven't been a mother for so, so long." The previous Queen beamed with pure joy at the thought of returning to the human world — even if it wasn't the one she had left so long ago.

Faye was so fixated on the happiness that radiated from the older woman she failed to notice the dagger the younger Faye held in her hand before it was too late.

"I'm afraid I can't let you do that," the Queen stated coldly as she swiftly stabbed her predecessor in the heart.

Faye stared in horror as the terrifying murder unfolded before her. She was almost consumed by a searing pain in her chest, which left her gasping for air. Faye was so desperate to be out of the tapestry. She clutched at her chest and her head began to swim as voices started to chant her name over and over again and black spots appeared before her eyes. Just as Faye thought she would totally lose her mind it reached a crescendo then suddenly stopped.

And there she was, once again, standing in the quiet hall full of tapestries. No searing pain in her chest — just an all-consuming feeling of loss and betrayal. She had just witnessed a murder. Her thoughts were spiralling, circling like water around a drain, and she was trying desperately to hold onto something, anything, that could help her make sense of what she had just witnessed.

She closed her eyes and doubled over, trying to get her head down to her knees. The only tangible thought in her mind was she wished she never questioned why no one replaced her great-grandmother in the Human Realm. Because even if she had only asked that question in her head, it seems the Faerie Realm had a way of answering those types of questions. And Faye was not prepared for that answer.

# CHAPTER 15

The next thing Faye knew, she was back in the forest clearing with Cahira standing in front of her, wearing a perplexed frown on her face. Faye didn't remember Cahira coming to collect her from the tapestry hall, but that didn't really surprise her. The woman was incredibly stealthy, kind of like a faerie ninja. Then again Faye was also quite consumed by what she had just seen in the last tapestry.

Faye shook her head as if trying to clear the fog of the teleportation and the change of scenery.

"Why would... I mean how could she... How could anyone do that?" Faye rambled, trying to grasp onto a single question that could clearly convey her horror.

Overwhelmed by what she witnessed, Faye's body did what it always did when she felt unsafe, went into preservation mode. Her hands started to tremble, overstimulated by the adrenaline her body was producing in case she needed to run away. The classic fight-or-flight stimulus.

"Seeing is believing," was all Faye got as an answer.

"Stop being so fucking cryptic and answer me!" Faye literally yelled into Cahira's face. "You could have just told me about my great-grandmother. You didn't have to drop me in some magical bloody artwork so I could actually see and hear a cold-blooded murder play out before me. Why are you so cruel?" Faye was so pumped up and fuelled by the adrenaline coursing through her body she couldn't stop.

"Answer me. Or are you going to transport me be back to my room and disappear on me like you usually do?"

All the emotions Faye had been feeling over the past couple of days were rising to the surface, turning into anger. Angry at herself for feeling weak, angry at her great-grandmother for being so despicable, angry at being trapped in the Faerie Realm, and angry at Cahira for never answering her questions. Since Cahira was the only one in sight Faye aimed both barrels of her temper directly at her and unloaded.

"It must be great to be at the beck and call of a maniac like her. Every click of her fingers and poof, there you are, ready and willing. You're as bad as she is. Actually, scratch that, you more like her obedient little pet than anything," Faye finished, standing defiant with her hands on her hips.

"You can be as angry as you want with me, Faye, it won't change anything." Cahira stared back at Faye, ignoring her attempt to get a rise out of her. "You need to listen to me very clearly. You need to step into the faerie circle now. I know you do not trust me or believe me, but this is for your safety and mine."

"God!" Faye groaned in frustration.

"See, there you go again being all matter-of-factly without providing an explanation. I'm sick and tired of being scared and confused. All I've wanted to do since I've got here is get some clarity on what I was seeing and to be allowed to go home. But instead, I discover faeries exist, my missing great-grandmother is still alive, and a murderer to boot, and there's a long line of women who look exactly like me. So please, *please* tell me how getting in the circle will help."

Faye's anger was reaching critical mass. She knew Cahira didn't really deserve the verbal abuse she was spewing out, but she couldn't rein in all the hurt and anger that was churning inside her.

Cahira stood her ground, watching Faye closely as she yelled at her, getting more and more agitated. Taking a calculated risk, Cahira abandoned words and resorted to actions. Taking a quick step closer, within touching distance, Cahira made the bold move to shove Faye, just enough to make her take a stumbling step back into the faerie circle without falling over.

Relieved to see Faye was now standing wholly within the circle, Cahira stood back and watched, waiting to see if her gamble paid off.

Faye was momentarily stunned into silence by Cahira's actions. She literally could not fathom what had just happened. All the fear, anger and hurt she was feeling, whirled around inside her, all fighting for dominance of her soul. She was quickly unravelling and could feel the tangible tendrils of her anger embedding themselves and taking control.

Faye looked down at her trembling hands, suddenly realising she no longer felt the tight grip of her anxiety in her chest — that quickening of breath that seemed to be her constant companion. In its place was a seething anger that threatened to manifest itself in a physical form. Faye was oblivious to her surroundings as she tried to centre herself. She closed her eyes and inhaled deeply, trying to fill her lungs with as much oxygen as possible.

None of it worked as images kept flashing across her mind: finding the gravestone in the cemetery, arriving in the forest, having her body being controlled by others, being held captive, and witnessing a murder at the hands of her long lost relative. Like riding a merry-go-round, endlessly spinning around and around, Faye spun further and further out of control, her grip on reality loosening by the second.

No words could describe the emotional pain Faye was feeling, so she did the only thing left to express it. Faye threw out her arms from her sides, lifted her head to the sky and screamed. The sound she unleashed was a gut-wrenching wail that echoed throughout the forest.

Faye stood still for a minute once she was done, eyes closed, her face still pointing skyward. She felt amazingly calm now, as if all her anger had been released in that terrible howl. Her mind was clear, and she took a moment to bask in the quiet of the forest, with the sun on her face.

If anyone were to ask her how she felt right then, in that moment she would have answered serene.

Glad she now had a clear mind and was no longer racked with anger; Faye was determined to discuss the matters with Cahira in a rational manner. When she finally lowered her face and opened her eyes, Faye almost let out another scream. The beautiful, dense forest with its magnificent trees and luminous flowers was gone. All around her, Faye saw scorched earth and devastation, like a raging fire had swept through, killing everything in its path.

Only Faye remained untouched. She spun around hoping to see Cahira but saw no sign of her.

Faye looked down at her feet and realise she was still standing within the circle. There were thin bursts of blackened earth stretching out from the small gaps between the rocks where the mushrooms used to be. The scorch marks growing progressively thicker as they lead away from the circle. They had first swallowed the grass, flowers, shrubs and vines until they reached the trees, laying waste to the leaves and thick branches. All that remained was a smattering of skeletal tree trunks, making a mockery of the thriving forest that had stood there only minutes before.

"You are more powerful than she originally thought." Faye heard a familiar voice behind her.

She spun around and came face to face with a perfectly safe and non-burnt Cahira.

"Oh, thank the universe you're okay. You *are* okay right?" Faye asked with genuine concern. Not surprisingly Cahira did not answer her question, so she tried a different one.

"What happened here, Cahira?"

"You," The faerie guard stated. But that time it was almost a whisper, as if said in awe.

"What do you mean? Me? There is no way I am responsible for this. I am not like you — I don't have any powers." Faye stood staring directly at Cahira, then turned her head to take in the devastation before her.

"Why would you blame me for all this destruction?" The hurt she was feeling started to creep into her voice and Faye hated how whiny it made her sound.

"You have all the information you need, Faye," Cahira stated again. She was eternally patient, but it was taking too long.

"I am not an idiot Cahira. I get it — I look exactly like a long line of Queens who reign over a Faerie Realm. But I am not a faerie, nor do I have any magical powers. I'm not like you." Faye was pleased with the calm that had returned to her voice.

Despite herself Cahira smiled. A real smile, one that literally radiated light. It was breathtaking.

"If I'm honest with you I'm not sure this isn't all just a dream," Faye said with a sigh. She closed her eyes, forcing herself to stop staring at Cahira.

In a flash she heard King Lugh's voice booming in her mind.

*"You can return only when a descendant of yours present with the markers of the original. Then you will take their place in this realm, and they will take yours. This way our bloodline survives and there will always be someone to rule."*

Faye's eye snapped open, and she returned her stare to Cahira. The true meaning of her looks — her red hair, her green eyes, and why neither of her parents shared those characteristics — all fell into place.

When she finally spoke, Faye tried to convey all her thoughts into four precise statements.

"But I can't be Queen. My situation doesn't match the stories you have shown me. I am not married, and I do not have any children. It doesn't make any sense."

Cahira seemed pleased with the line of thought Faye was verbalising.

"Your time hasn't come yet," she provided by way of answer.

Faye felt frustration creeping back into the voice as she asked, "Then why am I here?"

Cahira actually looked troubled for a second, just a flash across her face as she tried to work out how she could answer the question. It was the simple question Faye should have been asking all along. Not the who, what, where, how… but why.

"It seems you must have been seeking answers in your realm — answers to questions about your family. As a result, you were summoned to the one place that can truly provide those answers."

"Why would my great-grandmother bring me here and risk me finding out she is a murderer?" Faye couldn't believe the Queen would make such a simple error in judgement.

"You are mistaken Faye. She did not bring you here."

Faye opened to her mouth to ask the question "Well who bloody well did?" but she knew it would be futile to ask. Cahira was blatantly deflecting her questions and answering her only in riddles.

Instead, she shifted her focus from Cahira's face and looked at the burnt forest around them. She looked down at her feet and realised the only patch of unscorched earth was contained within the faerie circle. She stood there for an eternity, surrendering herself to the realisation that she was responsible for the fire that destroyed the ancient forest.

"I caused the fire." It was a clear statement of acceptance made by a young woman ready to embrace all that came with it.

Cahira watched her carefully, wary now. The change in Faye was expected but the command with which Faye now spoke was impressive.

"It wasn't fire. It was a burst of energy. Pure energy that was born out of your anger."

Cahira took a step towards Faye with her hand outstretched, and the younger woman instinctively stepped back, out of the faerie circle.

Faye felt a ripple throughout her body, like a shiver. She sensed her familiar friend fear was coming back — reminding her she had just destroyed an entire forest with her mind. The sheer force of her anger caused the wanton destruction. What would happen when she finally got home and had an argument with her mum, would she accidentally do something terrible?

"It will be dinner soon Faye. We should return so you have time to process all you have learnt here today." Cahira's statement drew Faye away from her worries of the dangers she now presented to everyone she loved.

Faye knew Cahira meant to teleport her back to her room and she took several steps back, trying to put some distance between herself and the faerie guard.

"I don't want—" she started but Cahira was lightning fast and before she finished her sentence, she felt the familiar grip around her bicep.

# CHAPTER 16

As soon as Faye felt her feet back on solid ground, she jerked her arm out of Cahira's hold and tried to put as much space between them as she could. Her emotions were threatening to take control of her again and she was terrified of what might happen.

Faye backed herself into the furthest corner of the room and crumpled to the floor, with her head in her hands.

"You have two hours to prepare yourself for dinner with the Queen." Faye vaguely heard Cahira, muffled like her head was under water and Cahira was standing on the shore.

Faye made no move to respond or even acknowledge she had heard Cahira. She was so tired. More tired than she could ever remember feeling. The thing she needed now was time to process what was happening. She wished her mum was with her.

When she finally raised her head and opened her eyes, she saw she was alone: Cahira was gone.

"What a surprise," Faye said to the empty room.

She was struggling with the emotions whirling inside and the thought of having to sit at a dinner table with her great-grandmother and make conversation was next level terrifying. Faye had no way of processing the type of fear brought on by this woman, coupled with the knowledge she herself could be extremely dangerous if triggered. What if fear was a trigger as well? What if the Queen said something that pissed her off at dinner and she accidentally killed her? And what about Cahira? Faye wasn't quite sure how the faerie guard had managed to leave the forest unharmed, but she was glad she did.

The worst-case scenario in the forest, was she could have inadvertently killed Cahira, and ended up just like her great-grandmother: a murderer. That thought made Faye sick to her stomach and opened the door for another emotion she knew all too well: self-loathing.

Self-hate wasn't a new feeling to Faye. When her father first announced he wanted a divorce, she blamed herself. She always felt she wasn't good enough for her father, that he barely tolerated her as his daughter. She was constantly reading, getting lost in a world of fiction. It was the one thing that made her happy, but the one thing that seemed to annoy him more and more as each day passed.

It had taken her mother endless hours of patient explanation before she began to accept that she wasn't responsible. Her father was a grown man who made his own choices, and whether it was selfish, unkind or otherwise, he had to live with the consequences.

Faye knew that was her mum's way of saying her father was a selfish prick, without saying those specific words. Because even though he had definitely acted like one, her mum would never lower herself to his level and denigrate her father — not in her presence anyway.

But now she was alone, without her mum to talk her off the ledge and away from the self-loathing threatening to swallow her. Why on earth would someone who clearly did not have a very good grip on their emotions be given such a volatile power?

Maybe her mum not being there, her being alone and having to work it out, was for the best. That way she couldn't hurt anyone.

Faye dragged herself up from the floor and catapulted herself face first onto the bed. Within seconds she was tumbling down into a fitful sleep, with fear and self-hate battling for control of her dreams.

"The Queen does not like to be kept waiting." Cahira stood by the door to the walk-in closet. "You must change quickly so we can keep to schedule."

Faye did not move nor acknowledge Cahira's presence. She just continued to lie on the bed, face down, feigning sleep. She could feel the burning gaze of Cahira, watching her, knowing she was awake.

Hearing mention of her great-grandmother caused her body to convulse in an involuntary shiver. She had relived the moment of her great-grandmother killing the other Faye over and over in her dream and now she was left wondering what the Queen had planned for her. Her body jerked in response to that internal question and Faye curled up on the bed, still with her eyes tightly shut, trying to protect herself.

A few moments ticked by in silence before Cahira spoke in a quiet, almost gentle voice.

"I will see that your meal is brought to you Faye. But you must know, this is a one-time offer."

Faye remained as still as a statue; the only movement in the room was the rise and fall of her chest with each breath she took. She was almost dozing back to sleep when Cahira reappeared, this time with a tray of food.

Faye rolled over onto her back and stretched her limbs, enjoying the cracking of her joints.

"Honestly Cahira, you need to wear a bell. Or at least we need to introduce some form of system so you can let me know when you are about to appear. What if I had been naked?"

"What if you were?" Cahira asked in reply, as if the thought of walking in on someone naked was the most natural thing in the world.

If Faye was not mistaken, Cahira was actually joking with her. But that couldn't be, right... right?

"Dinner is served." Cahira made an elaborate display of revealing the tray of food and placing it down on one of the bedside tables. "Your nap has served you well. You seem in good spirits."

"I could say the same about you. Did you nap?" She knew very well Cahira did not have a nap in the time she was gone, however long that was. As a matter fact she didn't know if Cahira slept at all, ever.

"No Faye I did not nap. Now eat."

"I'm really not hungry." Faye was pleased with the relaxed banter between the two of them and she hoped Cahira would stay.

"You must be famished after today's events."

And just like that, it all came flooding back to her.

"Don't remind me," Faye growled at Cahira, with more venom than she intended. In a move that startled Faye, Cahira sat on the bed and put her hand on Faye's knee. It was the first time the faerie guard had touched her without teleporting her somewhere.

"Please eat something. You need your strength. Food will provide strength, while sleep will help to rest your mind and restore some balance," Cahira said quietly.

As Faye raised herself up on her elbows, Cahira twitched her head, ever so slightly, and she was gone.

"What the heck. I will not be getting used to that any time soon," Faye said to herself as she fell back onto the pillows.

She rolled onto her side and took in the tray of food before her. Just looking at the food was enough to make her stomach let out a rumble so loud she was sure it would summon Cahira back. She sat up straight, with her back nestled into the pillows against the wall and dragged the tray to her lap. Having not eaten since breakfast, the whole "I'm not hungry" act was a total lie.

Faye started to shovel food into her mouth and washed it down with a big glass of water, not her favourite drink by any stretch, but would have to do. She couldn't deny how delicious it was. In this instant she decided to embrace being there in the realm alone, and she found a new level of peace settle over her as her fears began to be assuaged.

# CHAPTER 17

Cahira appeared in Faye's room the next morning to find Faye still asleep, stretched diagonally across the bed.

"I assumed you would be up and ready to start the day."

Faye groaned loudly, startled awake by Cahira's commanding voice.

"Frack-a-doodle, woman! What did we say about warning bells? You obviously assumed wrong. Now leave me alone." Faye was never happy being woken up, no matter what the time or who was doing the waking.

Although Cahira was amused by Faye, she would not allow Faye to dally.

"That is not an option. The Queen did not appreciate your refusal to dine with her last night, and I might add, you have also missed breakfast this morning. She certainly will not tolerate you refusing to be by her side when she visits the village today."

A little niggle of fear crept into Faye's belly when she heard mention of her great-grandmother. She had done a good job of compartmentalizing her worries last night and her fear of the Queen was in the biggest box for sure.

As if knowing what Faye was thinking Cahira urged her, having no time to waste.

"Have a quick shower and freshen up. There will be fresh clothes ready for you when you are done."

Faye reluctantly dragged herself off the bed and walked into the bathroom. She stopped in front of the mirror and stared at the face reflected back at her. She hardly recognised herself any more. She saw her great-grandmother, the Fayes from the tapestries, and all the Fayes from the portraits. She didn't know where they stopped, and she began.

As she stared, she saw the face of the Queen totally morph into her own, even her red hair and green eyes seem to darken into the older woman's shade. Faye gasped at the power the Queen seemed to have over her but with one blink she was gone, and it was just Faye, seventeen-year-old Faye, looking at herself in the mirror.

With the steaming water finally running over her, Faye shuddered when she realised the smell of smoke still lingered on her skin. She scrubbed and scrubbed at her skin, until it was red and tingly, in the hopes of washing away the olfactory reminder of her power.

A flash of anger burned bright in Faye when she realised Cahira had entered the bathroom while she was showering to deliver a clean set of clothes for her.

"I made light of it before, Cahira, but you had no right coming into the bathroom while I was showering." Faye marched out of the bathroom after she was dressed.

"I did no such thing," Cahira replied. With a wave of her fingers, the tray of food disappeared from her bedside table and a bowl of fruits appeared in its place.

Faye let out a loud breath, calmed by the visual explanation Cahira provided. If the woman would just explain some of her powers, it would cut down on the stress building each day.

"I thought you said I missed breakfast," Faye stated as a way of deflection.

She sat back down on the bed and shoved a handful of fruit into her mouth, unable to stop herself until the bowl was empty.

As if sensing Faye's next move, Cahira stepped forward just as the younger woman started to fall back onto the bed.

"Oh come on," Faye muttered as Cahira placed a hand on her shoulder and they were out of the bedroom in a flash.

\*\*\*

It was as if Cahira thought Faye needed a brutal reminder of how powerful she was. Why else would she have taken her back to the forest and all its devastation. It truly was the last place Faye wanted to be right now.

"Why did you bring me here?" Faye couldn't help but ask as she dropped her head and closed her eyes. The thought that she was responsible for so much wanton destruction was almost enough to break her.

"Everything heals with time Faye," Cahira said in a whisper. She gently raised Faye's chin with the tips of her fingers and turned her face towards the forest.

Faye was caught off guard when she felt Cahira's soft touch. It was so out of character for her guard.

"Open your eyes."

Faye did as she was commanded but kept her gaze locked on the ground at her feet. Her breath hitched in her throat when she saw the sprinkles of green grass starting to appear in the ash and soot. She raised her head and looked first back at Cahira, then followed her gaze out across the clearing to the first line of trees. Where they were previously burnt out and blackened, the trees now displayed clear signs of regrowth and rejuvenation. Branches were beginning to grow, and bright green leaves were starting to sprout, literally growing as she watched. An intense feeling of ardour washed over her as she stood and watched the rebirth of the forest she had destroyed.

Faye realised she was crying when she turned to Cahira for an explanation.

"Young fae are brought here when they first show signs of their gift. Here they learn control and discipline. It is a safe place, to minimise the risk of harming others," Cahira informed Faye, pointing to the circle where Faye had stood yesterday.

"It didn't do much good yesterday," Faye replied. She found it difficult to believe the circle of rocks and mushrooms could protect anyone unless they were thrown at your head. Faye knew better than to voice her disbelief out loud, so she simply stared at Cahira waiting for a response.

"These trees have experienced it all before. They will continue to regrow and tomorrow you will not be able to see any of the damage."

Cahira stepped towards the nearest tree and peeled off a layer of dusty, charcoaled bark, to reveal a healthy brown trunk underneath. She turned and walked back to Faye, taking her hand and leading her to the rock circle.

"I don't want to do this Cahira. I'm not ready." Faye tried to extract her hand from Cahira's.

"That is why we are here, to learn control," Cahira stated calmly. She held out her other hand to Faye, showing her the burnt piece of bark. They watched as it started to disintegrate in her palm.

Faye's eyes followed the ash as it got caught in the wind, and floated away from her, quickly disappearing from view. She was silently wishing all her problems would disintegrate to dust and fly away.

"That's not what I mean. I don't want to learn control Cahira. I don't want this power!" Faye cried out vehemently as she flung her hands out towards Cahira, willing the faerie to take it from her.

Cahira took a step back from Faye, watching her intently as the young woman stood within the circle, arms outstretched. The irritation Faye was feeling was palpable, but it was the fear Cahira could sense that was holding Faye back.

"Fate is unavoidable. To be Queen, you must have control."

Faye dropped her arms to her side and almost pleaded with Cahira.

"You said it wasn't my time yet. And I will repeat myself just in case I wasn't clear before. I *do not want to be Queen*. I do not want any of this." Faye enunciated every word very slowly and clearly.

"You do not have a choice in this, Faye," Cahira stated just as slowly.

"You cannot deny who you and what you are. The energy running through your veins will react to all your emotions, manifesting in a physical form according to what you are feeling. The more negative the emotion, the more destructive the energy becomes. As we witnessed yesterday, your anger and fear levelled the forest."

Faye opened her mouth as if to argue with Cahira. In a moment of clarity Faye realised the only way she would get home, back to her mum, grandpa and grandma was to go along with her captor. If she wanted to be safe back in the Human Realm, and not a danger to her loved ones, she would need to learn control.

"Where do I start?" Faye asked with clear determination.

Cahira almost heaved a sigh of relief. The hard part was over. Now onto the training. "This energy is an integral part of you. We call it *Forsa Beatha* or life force. You need to embrace it, use it. If you do not, it will build up within you and become unstable. It will cause an irreparable imbalance between your mind and soul," Cahira continued, slowly putting a little more distance between herself and Faye.

"I want you to tap into your emotions, Faye. Concentrate on whatever you are feeling in this very moment. Feel the buzz of it just beneath your skin, coursing through your body. Can you sense it there, vibrating from the tips of your toes to the top of your head?"

Cahira spoke patiently, watching Faye with each word she spoke.

"Now harness the energy you are feeling and guide it into your fingers. I want you to channel it into a physical form," Cahira instructed.

Faye had her eyes closed tight, hypnotised by the soothing sound of Cahira's voice. It didn't escape her that she had never used this tone of voice with her before. She was almost amused when she heard the sound of Cahira's voice getting further and further away — she was obviously worried what might burst out of Faye.

She put those thoughts aside and concentrated, trying to focus sharply on the hum she felt within. The years of work with her therapist to curb her anxiety was paying off, with each deep breath she took, Faye felt the energy surrender to her control. An unbidden image of ET with his glowing outstretched finger popped into her head and she knew in that moment she could do it.

"Open your eyes," Cahira commanded.

Faye did as she was told and opened her eyes. To her delight a red-tinged orb of light was dancing on her open palms. Like a flame dancing on a wick of a candle, the manifestation of her internal power was a sight to behold. She felt a quick rush of excitement at what she had achieved and was enthralled as the orb flickered to an ardent violet colour. Then with a quick flash of light, it disappeared.

"It worked, it actually worked!" Faye exclaimed with sheer joy and wonder, and she looked to Cahira for encouragement.

Her faerie guard, now chief instructor, did well to hide how impressed she was at what she had just witnessed.

"Try again," Cahira demanded, in a voice devoid of emotion.

Faye was instantly disappointed that cold Cahira was back. She liked the quiet Cahira who touched her chin so softly only minutes before. Knowing there was no point in arguing, Faye sat cross-legged in the rock circle and closed her eyes again.

Clearing her head, Faye tried to summon the Forsa Beatha for the second time.

\*\*\*

"We must leave now Faye," Cahira suddenly announced, in what Faye knew as her 'Commander' voice.

A small orb with a light red hue had been dancing on her hand, and Faye was transfixed by it. At the sound of

Cahira's voice, the orb imploded, disappearing without a trace. She quickly looked from her now empty hands to Cahira's face and couldn't read her expression. Was she impressed, or maybe a little afraid? It was so hard to tell because her facial expression hardly seemed to change.

"What do you mean? I'm just getting the hang of this now," Faye said, deciding to ignore what she had just heard. She couldn't understand why Cahira would get her started on it, then make her stop before the day was over.

"As I mentioned to you earlier, your presence is required at the Queen's side today as she takes her regular walk through the village."

"Right, sure, I forgot." Then another thought popped into Faye's head, and she couldn't help asking it. "Cahira, what does the Queen think we are doing now?"

"I do not presume to know what the Queen thinks. She commanded me to watch over you so that is what I am doing."

The thought of spending any time with her great-grandmother was abhorrent to Faye, especially now she knew the lengths the woman would go to, to get what she wanted. At least now she knew she could quell her fear by focussing on the energy within her.

With those thoughts in her mind, Faye was the first to move, gathering up herself to stand in front of Cahira. She extended her hand towards the faerie, hoping her gesture would convey the trust she now held in her heart for her.

# CHAPTER 18

Faye didn't know what had woken her. At first, she thought it was Cahira arriving in her room in her usual stealthy fashion. But when she opened her eyes to take a peek, the room was empty.

It must have been her dreams, because she was certainly dreaming of the woman who was so pivotal to helping her navigate her way out of the realm.

Despite the fact that the room was windowless, with no source of natural light, Faye could tell it was early morning. She had noticed the change in the room's lighting the night before when she returned from dinner. Not only was the light dimmer, but she could also sense a calm vibration in the room she hadn't noticed before. Her last thought before she drifted off to sleep was that she must remember to ask Cahira about it.

Now she was lying awake, in the most comfortable bed she could have ever imagined, trying to wrap her head around yesterday's events. She was now so aware of the Forsa Beatha coursing through her veins, and she took comfort in it.

Faye realised now she had spent her whole life feeling something was not quite right with her, like something was inside her, clambering to get out. She had put it down to her anxiety because that's what the doctors had diagnosed her with. A nice label of Social Anxiety Disorder to go with her side order of depression. The knowledge that maybe her mental health issues were a result of unused energy and not a chemical imbalance, was almost a welcome relief.

The time she spent with her great-grandmother yesterday passed without incident. Faye almost enjoyed it. She welcomed the opportunity to walk through the village and watch how the other fae folk responded to the Queen. As Cahira walked a few steps ahead, constantly watching for danger, Faye felt the most relaxed she had since she had arrived in the Faerie Realm.

She wished she could spend the whole day there. Or in the forest with Cahira working on her powers. But she had agreed to spend the day with her great-grandmother, and she surprised herself by not actually dreading it. Faye couldn't deny she was actively terrified of the Queen, but that fear was quelled a little by her newly found, as yet untrained, power.

There were surprises all round that morning when Cahira teleported into the walk-in closet, knocked on the door and waited for Faye to grant her access to her bedroom. The look of surprise and appreciation on Faye's face even made Cahira smile. Her eyes quickly took in the fact Faye was actually dressed and ready for the day and it was her turn to be stunned.

"Who are you and what have you done with the real Faye?" Cahira asked in mock seriousness.

"Good God!" Faye exclaimed, matching her faux alarm. "Was that a joke, Commander Cahira? I could ask the same question: who are you really?"

The question seemed to still Cahira for a moment as she stared intently at Faye. Searching for something Faye wasn't quick enough to grasp. And in a flash, it was gone as Cahira stepped forward to take her to breakfast.

"Shall we?" Cahira asked.

"We shall," Faye answered with a smile and that time she placed her hand on Cahira's shoulder.

\*\*\*

"Good morning my dear. Are you excited about our day together?"

Faye watched her great-grandmother stand up from her throne and walk down the stairs towards her. The dress she wore was less formal than those she had worn on their previous encounters. It reached just above her ankles, showing off a modest pair of high heels. The dress and shoes the Queen wore amplified her essence of power through the golden fabric and bejewelled footwear that seemed to pulsate as she moved and spoke. The crown was still secured firmly on her head, not moving an inch as she moved or talked. Faye wondered for a moment if it was permanently attached to her skull.

Faye felt severely underdressed in the long silver tunic-style dress she had chosen to wear. The outfits she had worn the previous days had full-blown corsets that were torture to wear. There was method to her madness: she hoped she would get a chance at some stage to work on her magic with Cahira, and this attire would be much more suited to that activity.

"It is my understanding you have not been shown the moss towers. We will visit there now — they are the living quarters of the realm," the Queen said as she turned her back to Faye and started to walk outside.

Faye didn't move a muscle until she saw Cahira make an appearance out of the shadows and follow after her great-grandmother, pausing briefly at her side before continuing.

The small township was a delight. There was a constant murmuring of voices, that only got louder wherever the Queen went. Faye was instantly surprised by just how many fae folk there were, swarms congregating around the steps of the cathedral.

Faye had a clear view over the crowds, while standing next to her great-grandmother on the landing of the cathedral. There was a sea of red hair standing out against the earth tones of the towers and cobbled stone ground. The cathedral sat at the epicentre of the life in the Faerie Realm; the moss towers circled around the structure creating a barrier from the encroaching, dense forest.

The Queen wasted no time before descending the stairs and being swallowed up by the sea of green- and brown-toned cloaks. Faye would have lost sight of her great-grandmother if not for the shimmering crown acting as a guiding light.

"Is that where I'm staying?" Faye called after her great-grandmother, eager to learn as much information about her living arrangements as possible, quickly moving to catch up.

"Don't be silly. We live under the cathedral." Faye watched as her great-grandmother laughed at her question, like it was the funniest, or stupidest, thing she had ever heard.

Faye had to quicken her pace to keep up, amazed anyone could walk as fast as the Queen was, given how she was dressed. The heels she was wearing, and the cobblestone path did not seem to hamper her speed at all. Faye had been grateful that morning when she saw her own pair of white Converse shoes in her closet, and she was glad to have them on as they strode briskly down the path.

Faye stopped walking when they finally reached the bottom of the pathway. She turned and looked back, up at the cathedral towering above them, in awe of the magnificent structure. After a minute she rotated one hundred and eighty degrees to take in the towers in front of her. She remembered passing them when Cahira transported her from the forest that very first day.

God was that only three days ago, Faye wondered to herself. So much had happened it was hard to believe such a short period had passed.

It was mid-morning and as Faye gazed up at the towers, she wondered if that was the sun in the sky. Sitting behind the nearest tower, it cast a shadow over her and the Queen. If it was the sun, was it the same sun she saw back in the Human Realm? So many questions and never any answers.

These towers were impressive when viewed from afar, but they were spectacular up close. Faye was certain they were alive: a living, breathing creature, rather than a steel or metal structure. The green vines that snaked up all sides of the tower seemed to grow as she watched, while the darker green moss seemed to pulsate as if in rhythm to a heartbeat. It was so beautiful that Faye felt tears springing to her eyes.

"As you can see, this realm has no need for the standard form of housing that is utilised in the Human Realm," the Queen explained, breaking Faye out of her revelry. She turned and realised the Queen, with Cahira once again by her side, were waiting for her by the entrance to the tower closest to them.

Faye took a couple of quick steps to catch up to them, then followed as they passed what served as a doorway. She touched the plant material that covered the walls in the foyer and was surprised when her hand came away wet.

Inside the building Faye followed as she was led down a long, dark hallway that eventually opened onto a dimly lit room. The room was bare except for three candles burning on a stone slab that lay in the centre of the room. The only other thing Faye could see in the room was a stone basin filling from a small trickle of water that flowed out of an ornamental faucet in the wall.

"I have brought you here to show you where it all began. This was the first room to grow at the creation of this realm. It isn't much to see but back then comfort wasn't a priority, as basic survival was the goal. But as you saw outside, things have changed over time, and the towers have evolved to fit the needs of our people," the Queen explained as she headed back towards the door.

"Each family gets a floor, as it is a common practice for all generations of the same family to live together. Some separate when new families begin, but the young are required to take care of the old." Faye listened to every word as her great-grandmother spoke, thrilled to finally be getting some information on the strange realm.

Faye followed them both back down the hallway and into the bright foyer. She lingered in the interior open space, with both her hands against the walls, feeling her fingers almost sink in. She took a few deep breaths and felt a blast of sheer energy shoot through her fingertips right to the soles of her feet.

"Forsa Beatha," Faye said in a quiet whisper.

\*\*\*

"Unfortunately, I have been called away to attend to an urgent formal matter. Cahira will show you the next tower. This one is a particular favourite of mine as it houses the silk spinning rooms that provide the fabrics for our gowns.

Please take your time there; pick a gown from the many on display there. Cahira will see that it is promptly fitted for you."

And just like that, her great-grandmother was gone, disappearing before her eyes. She knew she shouldn't still be surprised by the sheer act of power, but she was. Faye thought that no matter how many times she saw someone dematerialise in front her, she would never get used to it.

"Do we have to do that?" Faye asked, turning to Cahira with a mopey look on her face. "The last thing I want to do is look at fabric and pick out another bloody dress. Can't we go to the forest so you can teach me more about my powers?"

Faye watched as Cahira gave her a hint of a smile and a small shake of her head before she felt the familiar touch of Cahira's hand and lack of solid ground beneath her feet.

When Faye opened her eyes, she wasn't greeted by the expected sight of the forest but of mounds of earth, covered in grass.

"This is my home."

Faye looked at Cahira, confused by what she was being told and seeing. She had just been shown where the fae folk lived, in the towers. In stark contrast to those amazing structures, there were no signs of habitation anywhere in the hilly field.

"I don't understand. What do you mean? Don't you live in the towers?"

"The people of the Faerie Realm are segregated depending on ability. The ones with a talent or ability that benefits the throne, are housed in the towers, the rest are left to fend for themselves here."

Faye remained silent as she tried to process what Cahira was telling her, combined with what her great-grandmother had said earlier. But once again only lies seemed to pass through the Queen's lips.

Faye couldn't believe the old woman would lie to her about something as simple as living arrangements, but by the look on Cahira's face she knew it was true. She really was related to a megalomaniac, and that thought was enough to trigger her anger. She truly hated the injustice of it all.

"I'm at a loss for words," Faye said as she turned her head to Cahira who was looking down at one of the mounds.

Her words broke through the dull silence of the open field and Faye wondered where everyone was. As if sensing Faye's internal questions Cahira stepped toward her, touching Faye on the shoulder.

Faye was so familiar with being teleported now she just closed her eyes and waited to feel firm ground beneath her feet again. She was startled when she felt the ground beneath her feet give way slightly. Looking down she realised they were standing on soggy earth in a dark underground cave, made purely of dirt. The first thought in Faye's mind at that moment was *I'm standing in a burrow*.

They were most certainly underground, and Faye guessed they were now inside the mound they had just been standing on top of. She turned her head from side to side, trying to take it in. The small burrow was dark and damp, the only source of light was a tiny candle glowing in the corner. As with most of the other rooms she had seen in the realm, there were no entry or exits and no windows.

The feeling in the air was diametrically opposed to the rich organic feel she experienced standing with her hands against the interior walls of the first tower.

It was so claustrophobic Faye could feel the top of her head touch the roof and she couldn't stretch her arms out horizontally without touching the sides of the hole in the ground.

The room lacked anything that made it a habitable living space. No bed or running water, much less a bathroom, making it impossible for anyone to live there and Faye truly hoped no one did.

"This is where I lived before being moved into the towers." Faye could almost feel the suffering Cahira experienced.

Faye knew there wasn't anything she could say that could erase the pain, so she took hold of Cahira's hand, gripping on for dear life, hoping to get her empathy for Cahira across when words had failed her.

Faye no longer wanted to stay, and it was clear Cahira didn't either when she felt the ground disappear beneath her feet.

***

"Thank you for showing me." Faye spoke for the first time since arriving back in the forest.

Sitting in the rock circle, Faye expressed her gratitude and then stayed quiet. She didn't want to speculate what Cahira must have felt and continued to feel after living in that mound. She had no point of reference to rely on, so she stayed quiet and hoped to learn.

Admiring the freshly healed forest, Faye couldn't see a blackened scorch mark anywhere. The tree trunks had returned to their previous stature, with vibrant green leaves and thick brown branches, and the grass was back to the luscious green Faye had grown accustomed to. There was no hint of destruction or burnt debris anywhere.

Faye started to practise her control, not wanting to pressure Cahira into sharing any more than she had already. Fuelled by the ever-growing dislike of her great-grandmother, Faye found it easy to keep the orb in her palm for an extended amount of time.

Faye's concentration was broken by Cahira's voice, although not quite catching what she had said.

"You keep channelling your anger, Faye. Try focusing on using a different emotion," Cahira repeated.

"Like what?"

"Positive emotions," Cahira suggested.

"I don't think I have any left." Faye had spent the majority of her time in the Faerie Realm confused, angry or scared, she didn't remember what it felt like to not wake up and feel that way.

"Negative emotions only cause destruction. Positive emotions lead to creation. Try to focus on a moment of joy and happiness and use those feelings to create energy."

Faye closed her eyes, trying to conjure up an image of her mother's face. She was thinking of the fun they have together, indulging in movie marathons and eating copious amounts of junk food. She could only hold onto the feeling of happiness for a fleeting moment before she was reminded that she was alone. The happy feeling was so short; the buzz of energy didn't even start to flicker under her skin before her emotions turned dark, and she focused on the fact she was alone. In that moment Faye felt the energy pool in her palm and create a dark red orb.

"I can't." Faye was disappointed to see the same red colour orb in her hand but was not surprised.

"Try again," was all Cahira said.

Faye did as she was told and thought about her family. All the trouble she got up too with her grandpa, driving her mum and grandma crazy. Always being there for each other, no matter the time or distance. All it did was remind her once again of their separation and her lonely circumstances.

Faye no longer felt happiness or anger, only sadness. She was without her support system, through the most difficult and challenging time of her life. If ever there was a time she needed them, it was now.

"It's not working. Can I try again tomorrow?" Faye asked, needing to process the day's events.

"Lunch is almost here. You will need to change," Cahira replied as she took Faye's hand.

Without a word spoken between them, Cahira teleported her back to her room, where she quickly changed, before being deposited in the dining hall.

# CHAPTER 19

"How did you like the fabric studio? Did you choose something appropriate?"

Faye heard her great-grandmother break the awkward silence. Neither of them had said a word since sitting down for lunch.

"I didn't want to waste fabric for a dress I wouldn't wear." Faye avoided answering the first question, not being able to comment on a place she never actually visited. Even if she had visited and seen the fabrics, she still wouldn't have chosen anything. She detested having to wear the dresses from her walk-in wardrobe, now more than ever.

"Oh well. I would like you to leave with something to remember your time here." Faye watched as her great-grandmother kept up the act so flawlessly, no hint of lying.

Faye wanted to scream that she knew the truth, that she was a lying murderer or just launch herself across the table and do something violent, but she remained in her seat, silent. She tried to maintain her poker face without letting on to the Queen she knew the truth.

"I have plenty of memories thank you," Faye said, not feeling the gratitude she was expressing. She didn't want anything connecting herself to the realm and if she could, she would leave her memories of the Faerie Realm in the realm as well. Once she finally worked out a way to get back home.

"I'm sure we can find you a little trinket to take home."

"That's not necessary."

"I insist."

Faye didn't want anything, no matter how small, tying her to the place or to her great-grandmother. Faye knew it would only bring a whole world of pain and hurt, a constant reminder.

Faye really didn't want to back down, but she knew she had to pick her battles, and this one could wait for another day. So, she chose not to reply and just nodded.

"Cahira can take you to the jewellers. You can pick something out there."

"I'm actually feeling pretty tried. Can I take a rain check on the outing?" Faye feigned tiredness, yawning just for good measure. She may not have been physically tired, but she was mentally exhausted, and desperately needed some alone time.

"Of course. Take the day. Let's see how you feel at dinner time. If needed, food can be bought up to you."

If Faye didn't know any better, she would have thought her great-grandmother was looking out for her. But she knew the truth and imagined her great-grandmother sneering at her behind her back, relishing the thought of destroying the young fool who had stumbled into her realm.

"I've finished; can I be taken to my room please?"

"Of course. I'm needed back in the throne room," the Queen stated crisply.

Faye almost rolled her eyes. She realised, having a sudden epiphany about the woman sitting before her: she had gone to school with people just like her. They always needed to have the last word and to make sure everyone knew they were the most important person in the room. Faye felt an odd level of comfort knowing her great-grandmother was acting like a petty teenager.

"Take Faye back to her room and get her anything she needs," the Queen ordered before disappearing.

Cahira appeared out of the dark corner of the room behind the Queen's chair.

Faye was now alone in the dining hall with Cahira. It was so dark in the vast hall, lit only by candles placed sporadically along the table. For a second Faye wondered what else might be lurking in the corners of the hall.

She gave a look towards Cahira that said, 'Get me the hell out of here' and in an instant they were gone.

\*\*\*

"I don't need anything, and I definitely won't be going to dinner," Faye said once they were back in her room. She was really starting to dislike the feeling of Cahira waiting on her.

Faye grabbed a pillow and blanket off her bed before curling herself into a ball on the floor, in the corner between her bed and the wall. It was almost as if she didn't want to allow herself to be comfortable on the magnificent bed. The more comfortable she was, the more she would let her guard down. Faye lay down, determined to do some thinking followed by a nap. Instead of turning into the wall, Faye faced out, looking at Cahira, her head resting against the pillow.

"Can I ask you a question that's been bugging me and I just haven't been able to work it out?" Faye asked, not really wanting Cahira to leave.

"When I saw you in my dream, was it real? And I know mind manipulation is apparently making me see us all as the same height, but in the tapestries, King Lugh was the same height as me. What does that mean?" Once Faye started asking questions, she just couldn't stop at one.

Cahira took her time to answer.

"As belief in our Goddess Danu lessened, so did her power, which in turn caused the people of this realm to get smaller. It started gradually; each generation smaller than the one before. And yes, your dream was real."

"Thanks for letting me know." Faye smiled, appreciative of Cahira simply answering her questions, rather than speaking to her in cryptic riddles.

Faye closed her eyes, her smile remaining as she tried to fall asleep. She knew she would need all the energy she could muster if she was going to work out how she got to the realm, and how she was going to get out of it.

Faye didn't realise how exhausted and hungry she was until she awoke from a deep sleep and opened her eyes to see a plate of food on the bedside table next to her. She didn't think she had closed her eyes for more than a few minutes but given the change in light in her room she guessed it was now early evening. The whole afternoon had passed.

Faye sat and ate her meal in the welcome silence. She found she could shut her mind down in the peacefully quiet room so she crawled back into her corner on the floor. As she waited for sleep to take her once again, she decided to save all the heavy thinking for tomorrow.

# CHAPTER 20

The next morning Faye was already dressed and waiting when Cahira appeared, fully rested from her day nap and a full night's sleep. No dreams or nightmares had manifested to keep her subconscious awake. Just an endless sea of darkness, giving her mind a much-needed break.

She had been ecstatic when she had woken up to see breakfast placed beside her, meaning she didn't have to suffer through another meal with her great-grandmother until much later in the day.

"You look prepared for the day ahead," Cahira said as she entered the room from behind the closet door.

Faye was sure she detected a hint of surprise in her tone.

"Yep, ready to go."

Faye held out her hand for Cahira to take, eager to get out and into the fresh air. Faye felt Cahira take her hand, before the soft carpet beneath her feet disappeared, replaced in an instant by much sturdier ground.

Faye saw she was standing on cobblestones, quickly realising she was in the village not in the forest where she had hoped they were going. Faye looked up at the moss tower positioned behind the cathedral and her mind flashed to everything she had learnt the day before. She struggled to fathom how anyone could function properly if they lived in the conditions she had seen in the 'burrow' under the hill. But Faye quickly reminded herself that certain fae folk didn't have a choice, their free will had been taken away.

Conflicting emotions were whirling around in Faye which seemed to be her default functioning status in the Faerie Realm. She was saddened and angry at being in such close proximity to the towers, but Faye was also excited to speak with other faeries and hear their stories. She was also aware of the fact that they were there to see the jewellers and have a 'special token' made.

Faye walked after Cahira, going into the tower, and the sight before her nearly brought to her knees. Instead of a jeweller, Faye came face to face with a sweat shop.

Everywhere Faye looked were row after row of wooden wheels spinning away, as faeries sat next to them, twisting raw fibre silk into a useable material. Their legs were busy, moving up and down on a pedal to manually control the speed at which the wheel was turning. On the other side of the room were large steaming barrels, stirred continuously by even more faeries. They were standing on small wooden platforms, leaning over and stirring using long wooden poles. Further back in the room was more equipment to dye and weave the silk together creating fabric. The sweat shop room took up the entire ground floor, every part was utilised by some form of equipment and the faeries responsible for operating it.

Faye noticed that the faeries controlling the wheels wore gloves that were worn through and falling apart around the fingertips. She could only assume it must be the result of friction burns, making her wonder what their hands must look like.

Holding onto the wall for support, Faye was frozen, trying to take in everything she was seeing in the room. The people in front of her were only skin and bone; their cheekbones protruded from their faces giving their eyes an unearthly, sunken look.

Faye didn't want to know what the state of their bodies must look like, hidden away under their flimsy clothing. Faye could practically feel the tiredness and hunger rolling off everyone in the room. They all looked like they would collapse if a breeze went through the place.

Everyone was so focused on their work they hadn't even looked up when Cahira and Faye entered the room.

"This is where all the fabric is made for the royal family and those who attend court," Cahira explained, scaring both Faye and everyone else in the room when she spoke.

Faye watched as the attention of every faerie in the room turned towards Cahira and herself, noticing a horrified expression take over every one of their faces. It took Faye a long moment to realise what they were seeing: her face and that she must be related to the Queen. The person responsible for their suffering and squalid conditions.

Having never experienced a reception filled with such negativity or hostility, Faye felt as if she had taken a physical hit. She took a short step backwards into Cahira, seeking comfort.

"Can you do your teleport thingy and make food appear? These poor people look like they haven't eaten in days, let alone slept." Faye slightly turned her head to whisper to Cahira.

Faye was amazed to watch as plates and bowls appeared in front of everyone in the room. Faye watched the faeries' fear and hesitation retreat from their faces, as sparks of life appeared in their eyes.

"Thank you," Faye said to Cahira, that time in a much louder voice. It started a chorus of 'thank you' echoing from across the room. Grateful to Cahira for creating a sense of joy in a room that had been completely devoid of it only moments ago.

She was overjoyed at the look of happiness and appreciation spread across the faces of everyone in the room. Faye couldn't stop herself from reaching behind her, feeling for Cahira hand, and grabbing a hold. She couldn't take her eyes off the scene that was playing out before her.

Faye remained still, in her position near the entrance, not going any further into the room, not wanting to scare the fae folk any more than she already had.

Faye watched as they enjoyed their meals, wanting nothing more than to help them further, but she had no idea how. There she was, just a seventeen-year-old high school student. She may have learnt about the past atrocious acts done in the Human Realm in history classes, but she was not equipped with the knowledge or skills required to save the beings suffering in front of her.

She settled on taking care of the bare minimum — like finding out how many of the fae folk were suffering in similar conditions and making sure they were fed and clothed appropriately. Faye hoped it would be enough in the interim, while she continued to work things out.

Faye turned around and faced Cahira.

"Can you show me the real jewellers, please?" She asked in a determined voice. Faye was surprised when Cahira simply pivoted around, and still holding Faye's hand, walked out of the tower and into the tower next door.

When they arrived at the jewellers, she was greeted by a similar sight as the silk workshop. The room was a burning inferno of heat. Lined up along one side of the vast room were huge furnaces, surrounded by utensils Faye assumed were used for melting metal. On the ground were graphite crucibles and pair after pair of large, elongated tongs. On the other side were rows and rows of wooden work benches, covered in a variety of tools. Some benches held hammers and mallets of all shapes and sizes, while others had both empty and full moulds. Faye realised these moulds were filled with gold and silver ready to be used for making the type of jewellery she had seen in the cases in her room. At the end of each bench, gold and silver pellets were piled high, awaiting their turn in the smelting furnaces.

Just as before, the room was filled with deathly looking faeries. A realisation suddenly struck Faye as she stared into the jewellery workshop. As far as she could see the workshop only contained male fae folk, and the silk spinning workshop had contained only female fae folk. Great way to maintain the gender balance in the Faerie Realm.

They were only stood in the doorway for a few seconds before beads of sweat began to form along Faye's hairline and her dress started to feel suffocatingly hot. She quickly realised the room lacked any form of ventilation. There were no windows to let a breeze in, carry the heat out, or let light in. The only light source was emanating from the furnaces, casting an eerie orange glow over the room.

Their arrival went unnoticed as Faye and Cahira remained still and quiet in their spot by the entrance, hiding in the darkness the room provided.

"Could you do your food thingy again please?" Faye quietly asked Cahira

Faye watched as the food magically appeared for all the men working in the room. She was happy to remain unseen, so she turned around and walked out of the tower. The thought of the faeries enjoying a surprise meal, without her presence frightening them, brought a smile to her face.

"Thank you for doing this." Faye thanked Cahira again when she stepped outside to join her.

"The Queen will want you to present her with your chosen item this evening."

"I don't want to scare them or have them think I'm like my great-grandmother. Do you think you could find the smallest item, like the teeniest, tiniest thing in the room? Please?"

Faye had barely finished her question before Cahira disappeared once again.

Faye realised she couldn't wait to learn how to control her teleporting. Having full control of moving from place to place, without taking a step, was becoming increasingly appealing to her.

Cahira suddenly reappeared bringing Faye out of her thoughts of teleportation.

"Can we go back to the forest. I really want... no, I really *need* to practise. I have to be able to help." Faye didn't question Cahira about whether or not she had chosen a piece of jewellery. She simply held out her hand for Cahira to take.

She was relieved when Cahira took a hold of her offered hand, and everything disappeared.

# CHAPTER 21

Faye felt at peace when they arrived back in the forest. It was her favourite place in the realm now, for a whole raft of reasons. Not only was it a beautiful and serene forest, but it was also becoming the one place she felt safe in the strange and crazy realm she found herself in. Working on her powers with Cahira was an added bonus.

She resumed her position in the rock circle, sitting cross-legged in the grass. Faye closed her eyes and tried to put all the thoughts of what she had seen that morning out of her mind. She was determined to harness her positive emotions and use them to manifest a physical orb of power.

Putting all thoughts of her family and how much she missed them out of her mind as well, Faye tried to focus instead on her desire to help the fae folk she had seen in the realm. With her eyes squeezed shut, Faye's mind started to flash to images of the women sitting at the spinning wheels and the men working the hot furnaces. All the horrific slave labour for her great-grandmother's benefit.

Immediately, Faye started to feel the buzz of energy within her, being fuelled by her anger. This time, she felt more in control of her emotions and managed to subdue the anger as she channelled her focus on her willingness to protect. She desperately wanted to protect the innocent faeries from being forced into a life of servitude to a malicious Queen and made to live in isolation away from their loved ones.

Faye felt her anger dissipate and a sense of hope start to take its place. The Forsa Beatha started to travel quickly around her body, getting stronger and stronger, looking for a way to escape. Faye concentrated hard to guide the energy to her palms, willing it to form an orb.

Faye slowly opened one eye to take a peek, afraid to see what she would find, afraid that she had failed. She was overjoyed to be greeted by the sight of a large violet orb floating on the palm of her hand. Quickly opening her other eye, Faye couldn't stop the squeal of delight that escaped her, causing the orb to grow ever so slightly by her happiness.

She was enamoured as the orb became a deeper shade of purple, pulsing in her hand at a rate that matched her heartbeat. Faye couldn't take her eyes off it. A quick image of the red orb and all its power flashed in her mind, and Faye was excited to see what the energy of this purple orb could do.

"Place the orb on the grass."

Faye's eyes remained on the orb even as Cahira spoke, worried it would disappear if she took her eyes off it, even for a spilt second. She lowered her palms towards the ground, concentrating on the hope she currently felt. When the back of her hands touched the grass, the orb began to fade, Faye started to look up in Cahira's direction, but couldn't bring herself to make direct eye contact.

"Watch."

Confused by Cahira's simple directive, Faye saw her do a small head tilt towards the ground. Faye quickly turned her attention back to the grass and saw a purple light starting to glow from the grass beneath her hands. In a flash Faye realised the power from the orb was being transferred into the ground. She sat and stared, transfixed by the amazing sight before her. She didn't know what to expect, given the devastation she had recently caused with her powers, and she flicked Cahira a tentative glance. But her guard, now instructor, was staring at the ground just as intently, not having teleported out of harm's way.

Faye was overjoyed when a flower bud suddenly sprouted out of the purple tinted ground in front of her. As quickly as the first one came, another one popped up. Soon, Faye was surrounded by flower buds. She turned her head around and found the whole circle was engulfed by freshly sprouted flower buds, not yet ready to bloom.

Faye looked back up at Cahira, with a beaming grin, only to see Cahira with a small smile as well. The achievement of making Cahira smile, was as rewarding for Faye as what she had just done with the power orb. In that moment Cahira looked every bit as magical as Faye imagined a faerie would. Faye was transfixed by how transformed Cahira appeared to her when she was smiling. There was something so enchanting yet also familiar about her that Faye felt her brain begin to go a little fuzzy. She literally could not think straight.

Faye dragged her eyes away from Cahira and back to the flowers just in time to watch them bloom. Faye let out an involuntary gasp of surprise when the petals opened, and they were the same violet colour as her orb. A sea of purple wildflowers filled every space in the small rock circle around Faye's body. She reached out and touched a flower to find the petals had a velvety texture, similar to the flowers found in the Human Realm.

Faye didn't know what she expected from magically created flowers, but it wasn't the floral arrangement she saw surrounding her now. It didn't detract from the unbelievable act of creation that just happened but there was a small part of her that waited for the flowers to start singing and talking like they did in *Alice in Wonderland*.

Faye stood up from where she was sitting and stepped out of the circle, careful not to damage any flowers. In the now free space where she was once sitting, Faye was amazed to see more flower buds begin to sprout.

Faye was delighted to now have a new memory of creation to counteract her memory of the destruction she had previously caused.

"Thank you, Cahira. I couldn't have done this without you." Faye looked Cahira in the eyes, hoping if her words didn't convince her, then her eyes would convey the message.

"You did this yourself."

"That's not true. I have had no idea about anything while I've been here, but you were the one that has shown and taught me. None of this would have been possible without you." Faye continued to stare directly at Cahira while she spoke. She waited for a reply, a response of any kind, but Cahira offered nothing by way of a reply. She simply stared back at Faye, watching her carefully..

Blinking her eyes, Faye sat back down, just on the outside of the rock circle, wanting to be closer to the flowers but not wanting to squash any of them. She ran her fingers through the petals, assuring herself they were real. She desperately wanted to pick a few, to have as a bunch to take back to her room and back home as proof of the powers she had, but she decided to be satisfied with simply watching them. Just as she had been transfixed earlier by the smile on Cahira's face, staring at these flowers she had just created was having the same effect on her.

Considering her practise space was now taken up by flowers, Faye knew she wouldn't be able to do any more practice until they disappeared. As if reading her thoughts, Cahira issued another clear instruction.

"Stand in the circle and harness your negative emotions; channel that into your hands and turn the flowers to ash."

Faye looked up at Cahira, feeling like she had just been punched in the gut. It was one thing to create an orb using her hate and anger but being able to control it was taking things to a whole other level. Controlling that raw energy enough not to repeat the destruction to the forest she caused last time was one step further than she felt comfortable taking.

"Please don't ask me to do that," Faye pleaded, the joy of the last few minutes completely gone.

"You have mastered making the orb, now you must control the power it holds. You must create an orb from your negative energy, then place your hands while holding the orb on the flowers and envision the flowers turning to ash," Cahira instructed Faye. The cold, matter-of-fact tone had returned to her voice and her face was once again neutral.

Faye was reluctant to do as Cahira told her, but she knew she couldn't stay afraid of herself and what she was capable of forever. Learning to control her powers and trusting herself would become a power of itself. She also knew she trusted Cahira to keep her safe while she was learning.

Stepping into the rock circle and taking a seat, Faye felt uneasy as the flowers she had just created, started to crush under her weight.

Closing her eyes and taking a deep breath, letting the forest fall away, Faye focused her thoughts on her great-grandmother keeping her trapped in the Faerie Realm and away from her family.

Faye concentrated on feeling alone and frightened, and her mind flickered to how upset her mum must be back in the Human Realm. She felt the now familiar buzz of energy just under her skin as it came alive, growing and building up from the pain and fear she felt, begging to be let out and unleashed. Faye forced the energy to channel down her arms and into her palms, determined to control the destructive orb when it materialised.

She concentrated, visualising an invisible cage around the orb, containing it to her will. She felt her palms and fingers heat up with Forsa Beatha, and Faye quickly opened her eyes to see a bright red orb the size of a melon sitting in her palms.

Taking another deep breath, she focused on the orb, shrinking it to the size of a grape, testing herself to see if she had the level of control she wanted, before releasing the power onto the flowers.

She watched the orb flicker and shrink smaller and smaller until it reached the size she wanted. Faye felt a small sense of pride at what she was achieving, pleased she was obtaining a sense of control with her power.

Faye slowly lowered her hands with the small orb sitting still within her palms. Keeping her breath steady Faye rested both hands gently on the top of the ground where she was sitting, willing the orb to flow into the soil, with the intention of destroying only her wildflowers within the circle.

When the orb dissipated from her palms, Faye moved her hands away and watched as the red glow travelled through the soil and up the stems of the flowers. When the glow dimmed out, the flowers slowly lost their colours and blackened, crumbling to the ground, leaving only a pile of ash. Faye quickly looked around at the rest of the circle, only to find it covered in more ash. Where the beautiful flowers had once stood proud, now stood a pile of ash. Faye quickly looked beyond the circle to see if her destructive powers had spread outside the circle, into the wider forest, but she was pleased to find she had managed to completely contain it within the ring of rocks.

She was astonished by what she had just achieved; she was quietly in awe of herself. She had actually managed to control her emotions, direct her power as she wanted and create the type of energy required. Faye picked up a handful of ash, only to realise there was still grass, perfectly green and alive grass, in the circle, left untouched by her orb. The observation only reinforced Faye's sense of achievement, ecstatic at the level of control she had displayed.

"Did you see that? I actually did it." Faye jumped up and out of the circle, rushing to stand next to Cahira.

"I actually did it!" Faye repeated, not quite believing her eyes.

"You most certainly did. You have made great progress today."

Faye couldn't help herself from beaming with pride at Cahira's validation. Faye never cared what anyone thought of her, outside the opinions of her family and close friends, and Cahira had now made her way onto that list.

"The sun will be setting soon, and you have dinner with the Queen to attend. You will also be needing to present this." Cahira held a closed fist out towards Faye. As she finished speaking, she opened her hand to reveal a small silver ring with an amber rock in the centre.

Faye's happiness instantly died, revolted by the fact she had to wear a product made by so much pain and suffering. But she knew she couldn't avoid it, no matter the fuss she made. She was now well aware of the fact her complaining and whingeing about something made no difference at all. So, biting her tongue, she took the ring and tried it on her pinkie finger. It fitted perfectly, of course, and with no worries of it slipping off, she left it there trying not to give it another thought.

She held out her hand, the one that didn't have the ring on it, for Cahira to take and teleport her to dinner. Dreading the sight of her great-grandmother and having to pretend to be ignorant of all the horrible scenes she had witnessed in the towers, Faye tried to clear her mind and put her game face on.

Cahira watched Faye, bemused by the internal struggle she was going through. The young woman was clearly learning to control her powers, but her thoughts were written all over her face.

"Shall we?" Cahira said with a hint of a smile as she took Faye's hand and teleported them both to the dining hall.

# CHAPTER 22

Faye arrived in the dining hall and was greeted with the now familiar set-up. Dark room, candles down the centre of the table producing the only light, two chairs placed at either end of the long table ready with plates, cutlery and glasses. The only difference was that Faye had beaten her great-grandmother to dinner.

Faye had only ever arrived at the hall when her great-grandmother was already seated and waiting for her. Maybe it was one of the Queen's power plays, to remind Faye she was always second best. But that wasn't going to be the case tonight. Faye was buzzing with her newly found power and she couldn't stop herself from wanting to sit in her great-grandmother's seat — even if it was a petty, juvenile move. The fact it would extremely annoy her great-grandmother was all the encouragement she needed.

It seemed Cahira knew exactly what she was thinking and gave a stern shake of her head in Faye's direction and disappeared. Fighting against the immature impulses, Faye sat down on her own chair, bummed her dinner wasn't already there in front of her so she could start eating and avoid any interaction with the Queen.

Faye was just about to start twiddling her thumbs when her great-grandmother appeared in her chair opposite her. On one hand Faye was stunned to see someone teleport while sitting down and on the other she was annoyed at being impressed by anything the older woman did — but she couldn't deny it, teleporting while sitting on your butt was now added to the top of Faye's 'Must Learn How To Do' list.

"You arrived earlier than expected." The Queen was the first to speak.

"I go when and where I'm called, Your Highness," Faye said with faux obedience and a hint of sarcasm. She tried to cover her insubordination with a laugh, but she didn't think she succeeded very well.

Faye watched as her great-grandmother clicked her fingers and two faeries appeared out of the shadows with plates of food. One faerie placed a plate in front of her, while the other did the same to her great-grandmother. The simple act reminded Faye that many of the faeries in the realm were servants and slaves, and suddenly her appetite was gone. She didn't know how to sit back and pretend she hadn't seen all the horrible, barbaric things she had seen — did it make her complicit in the barbarity if she knew about it but didn't act? Faye knew she had to find a way to play along with the Queen — at least until she found a way to help the fae folk.

Faye pushed the rice and vegetables around her plate, trying to make it look like she was eating, lost in her thoughts when the Queen broke the silence.

"Did you find something more suited to your taste at the jewellers?" Faye heard her great-grandmother ask, immediately looking at the ring that sat on her finger.

"I found a ring that fits perfectly," Faye answered in reply.

Not being able to lean across the table because of the length and show her, Faye just held up her hand by the candlelight, hoping she wouldn't be asked to go any closer.

"Why would you pick something so small?"

Faye watched her great-grandmother ask, clearly appalled by her taste in jewellery.

"I can't exactly go back home with a large golden necklace or bracelet. That would raise too many questions." Faye threw out her first comment about going home, subtly trying to test the waters before going all in.

"You're right, we wouldn't want that."

Faye quickly hid her smile by taking a mouthful of food. She could only imagine the pain it must have caused her great-grandmother to agree with her.

Not being automatically shut down about the topic of going home, Faye went in for the kill, trying to act nonchalant about it.

"When can I go home?" Faye watched and waited for any sign, no matter how small, that her great-grandmother was playing her for a fool, but she got nothing. No small twitch of a lip or squint of an eye, absolutely nothing.

"There's no rush. You haven't been gone for more than a few hours in the Human Realm. Take your time and explore."

Faye would have been impressed by her great-grandmother's ability to lie if she wasn't so damn angry at her. Faye wanted to help the folk of the Faerie Realm, and right some of the wrongs that her great-grandmother was responsible for, but she wanted to do it on her own terms. She hated the fact she was trapped in the realm and had no control over where she went and when, and whether she left or stayed.

"It just feels like I've been away for so long."

"You might feel that way, but your family doesn't."

The statement sounded so ominous that Faye couldn't fight the shiver that ran through her body. She thought she was stronger than a few words thrown at her by her great-grandmother, but that sentence scared her to her core.

"What do you mean by that?" Faye asked quietly, as she shoved a few more fork loads of food into her mouth to stop herself from saying anything else.

Her great-grandmother chose to ignore the question and had obviously decided dinner was done.

"I will see you for lunch tomorrow. I have matters to attend to. Breakfast will be brought to you in your room."

With that declaration her great-grandmother disappeared, leaving Faye relieved to be alone again, and happy to be having breakfast in her room. Feeling the tension ease from her body since the Queen had gone, Faye settled in and managed to finish the all food laid out in front of her, taking her time to enjoy the beautiful flavours of every dish.

Faye placed her knife and fork on her now empty plate and stood up, knowing Cahira would be standing in the shadows waiting to take her back.

Just as she thought, Cahira walked towards her and gently took her hand, teleporting out of the dining hall.

\*\*\*

Faye was pleased when they reappeared in her bedroom, glad to be back in what she considered her own space. Despite the upsetting scenes she had witnessed in the towers, and the comment made by the Queen regarding her family, Faye was feeling relaxed and happy with the progress she had made earlier in the forest. She was also pleased that Cahira was still standing in her room and had not simply vanished once she had delivered her from the dining hall.

"I have so many questions after today," Faye stated as she spun to face the faerie commander.

"Do you think you would be able to get more food to all those faeries we saw today and the many more we didn't?" Faye started to pace her room in her agitation.

"Hang on a minute — when do you get to eat?" Faye gasped, horrified that she hadn't even thought to ask before. She realised she had never seen Cahira eat or drink and she is with her all day.

"In the morning and at night," Cahira replied in a matter-of-fact tone.

"I'm sorry."

Faye didn't know whether she was apologising for the fact Cahira only ate twice a day, or for the fact she has eaten lunch in front of Cahira while she now knew Cahira went without, or the fact she had never asked the question before, even while she was asking Cahira to feed everyone else.

"I'm really, really sorry I haven't asked this of you before."

Faye felt like a truly terrible human.

"I will get food to everyone," Cahira simply said and immediately disappeared.

Faye didn't even have an opportunity to object or try to make sure Cahira fed herself first, before taking food to the others. She still had so many questions for her quiet instructor, questions she hoped she would answer now they were getting along so much better.

Faye decided to save her breakfast in the morning for Cahira, in case she had not taken care of herself as Faye suspected she mightn't have done. With that thought in her mind she settled back into her bed and fell asleep almost immediately as her head touched the pillow, exhausted by all she had seen, learnt and done during the day.

# CHAPTER 23

Faye was sitting on her bed, her breakfast untouched, when Cahira arrived. She as dressed and ready for the day, only mildly peckish for the breakfast she had set aside.

"Eat," was Faye's welcoming morning greeting to Cahira, cutting right to the chase, before the faerie could say anything.

"That is not mine. I have already eaten."

Faye wasn't going to take no for an answer. She stood up, picking up the bowl of fruit at the same time and walked over to where Cahira stood by the bathroom door, shoving the bowl in her hands.

"I didn't see you eat. I've never seen you eat. So just give me this one meal. Please." Faye's guilt from the night before returned.

Faye stood defiantly in front of Cahira, trying to show she wasn't joking and was relieved when Cahira hurriedly ate half the bowl's contents. She ate so fast, quicker than Faye could ever shove food in her own mouth, and she had made eating fast an art form. It just proved to Faye how hungry the faerie standing before her actually was.

"Thank you. The rest is yours." Cahira placed the bowl back into Faye's hands, half full.

Faye silently took the bowl back, shocked by Cahira's words. It was the first time Cahira had ever thanked her. She didn't quite know what to do with it, so Faye sat on her bed and finished off the food, grateful to have something in her stomach. Faye placed the bowl back on the bedside table and walked back over to Cahira, holding her hands out.

When Cahira placed her hands in Faye's, there was a moment, just a fraction of a second, when everything was still and quiet in the room, and their eyes met with an intense gaze that shot right through Faye like lightning. Then they were plunged into the darkness of teleportation.

As Faye felt her surroundings materialise around her, she saw she was back in the forest. It seemed to her that Cahira was oblivious to what had passed between them, right before they teleported but Faye couldn't shake the intensity of the look. She had no idea what it meant but it intrigued and terrified her in equal measure.

As a means to distract herself, Faye looked down at the rock circle and was glad to see no evidence of ash anywhere. Taking her position back in the circle, she got comfortable, ready to learn.

"What's on the agenda today?" Faye looked up at Cahira, waiting for instructions.

"Channelling both emotions at once. Separate the positive and negative, guiding each emotion into a different palm."

Faye was puzzled. She knew what was needed to create an individual orb from negative and positive emotions, and that was difficult enough to practice and master. But being able to control all her emotions and make two orbs at once was something Faye didn't think she had the mental strength to do.

Faye was about to voice her concerns when Cahira stated:

"Focus on creating an orb in each palm at the one time, using the one emotion. Then we can work from there."

"So, two orbs, one in each hand, using positive or negative emotions. I can do that."

Faye let out a sigh of relief, now Cahira's instructions sounded more doable. She closed her eyes, letting out deep breaths, calming herself and getting in the zone. Faye relaxed her shoulders, resting an open palm on each leg and took another deep breath, letting the forest fade away.

Faye focused on the anger she was feeling towards herself. Angry at the fact she was trying to take care of the multitudes of faeries before thinking about the well-being of the only one that had taken care of her. It hadn't even occurred to her to ask whether or not Cahira had eaten when she asked her to feed all the working faeries. She was extremely disappointed in herself.

She felt the energy come to life. She tried to imagine halving her energy, sending half to each palm and visualised a barrier down the centre of her body, blocking the energy from crossing over and going anywhere other than where she wanted it to go. Faye slowly felt the buzz in each hand, getting warmer and warmer, stopping just before it became uncomfortable.

Faye slowly opened her eyes, still concentrating on the form of the two orbs, making sure they stayed an even and stable size. She was excited to see that she was holding a red orb in each palm but remained completely still, worried she would lose one or both orbs if she made even the slightest movement.

The thought of the orbs touching the ground and causing unwanted damage, terrified Faye. She did not move a muscle except to breathe. Despite the fear percolating within her, she couldn't help but feel incredibly proud of what she was achieving. As she watched the orbs, completely under her control, she spared a quick thought of just how far she had come from the first savage burst of power. She was confident in the knowledge she could use her fear, harness it somehow, to guide her on her journey.

"Now keep a hold of enough of your anger for one orb and focus on a positive emotion," Cahira said, interrupting her thoughts.

Faye kept her eyes on the orbs but listened very carefully to Cahira's words. While her instructions were always somewhat cryptic, Faye seemed to know exactly what she meant with each directive. Faye closed her eyes and reimagined the barrier separating her body down the centre, continuing into her brain. Keeping a hold of her anger, she pushed it to one side, feeling the red orb in her right hand fizzle and fade out, and turned half her focus on creating a purple orb.

Thinking about the comfort and safeness she felt in the forest around her, and the happiness she had experienced there, Faye remembered the inner peace she found when she saw her flowers grow from the earth. She had never felt so complete until she had witnessed the creation of the flower buds and watching them bloom.

She felt a calmness wash over her and the warmth of energy humming, searching for a place to settle. Guiding the warmth towards her fingertips, she willed the energy to pool in her palm, slowly filling to create an orb.

When she felt a heat in both palms, Faye opened her eyes and saw one red and one violet orb, strong and powerful, no flickers or sparks. Faye had total control. She couldn't tear her eyes away from her hands, scared that if she looked away even for a fraction of a second, she would lose control.

"Slowly bring the energy together. The positive and negative will cancel each other out."

Faye listened to Cahira's direction, slowly and carefully bringing her palms together, meeting at the centre of her body. The two orbs slowly became one and then died out, disappearing, leaving Faye's hands resting together, in a praying motion. Faye slumped forward, taking deep breaths, feeling like she had run a marathon. She was completely exhausted and ready to fall asleep.

Faye crawled out of the circle and lay flat on her back, looking up at the sky. There were no clouds or birds flying above, it was just a vision of clear, brilliant blue. The sound of the wind travelling through the trees was lulling Faye into a slumber she was ready and willing to surrender to.

Just before sleep could claim her, Faye heard Cahira's voice.

"I need to return you to your room."

Confused by the sudden need to be back in her room, Faye couldn't help but notice a touch of urgency in Cahira's voice. But before she could question her, Cahira had knelt beside her and placed a hand on Faye's shoulder, teleporting them out of the forest.

When Faye's body hit the bed in her room, her stomach rolled. She hadn't felt like that since the first couple of times she had teleported and could only guess it was due to the rush and suddenness of Cahira's action and that she hadn't had a moment to relax. She felt so ill she didn't even think about the fact she had just been teleported while lying down or acknowledge surely that trumped her great-grandmother teleporting while sitting in a chair?

Lying with her eyes shut, trying to settle her stomach, Faye took a minute before speaking to Cahira about the day's lesson. As Faye sat up and looked at Cahira's usual standing place by the bathroom door, Faye was disheartened to see she wasn't there nor anywhere else in the room.

"I thought we had moved past this." Faye couldn't help but voice her irritation, even if it was to an empty room.

She stayed sitting on her bed watching the bathroom door and waiting for Cahira to reappear, mulling over the events of the previous night and that morning. Faye didn't know how long had passed before a plate laden with food appeared on her bedside table, indicating it was time for lunch.

Hadn't the Queen said they would be having lunch together? Not that she was complaining, Faye was pleased not to be stuck sitting in the long dining hall alone with her great-grandmother. While she guessed the Queen must be busy with other engagements, she was growing more confused by Cahira's absence.

Faye was fully aware Cahira was her prison guard-cum-babysitter, responsible for keeping an eye on her ever since her arrival in the Faerie Realm. So, where the hell was she now?

It suddenly occurred to Faye that maybe somehow the Queen found out about their visit to the fabric sweatshop and the jewellery manufacturer floor and Cahira was in trouble. She couldn't help the feeling of dread that started to creep into her soul at the thought of Cahira suffering at the hands of her great-grandmother.

Faye tried to eliminate the negative thoughts threatening to consume her brain, knowing they weren't going to help. Giving herself a little pep talk in her mind, she decided there was no use in panicking until she had all the information.

For all she knew, Cahira could have been called away to do her actual job. Faye was quite pleased with herself and the reasonable way she was reacting to the situation — it was most unusual for her. Maybe the realm was having a more positive impact on her than she first realised.

The simplest answer was usually the right one, so Faye sat back and ate her lunch, confident in the knowledge Cahira would reappear when she could. Without her phone or a book to keep her entertained after she had finished lunch, Faye paced around her room a few times before she grew bored of the repetitive activity. At a loss as to what to do, she stood in the exact spot Cahira usually appeared when she teleported into her room and closed her eyes, trying to figure out how the whole teleportation process worked.

She tried to visualise the forest and transmit out into the universe her deep desire to be there. She even tried to image her body breaking down to the molecular level and shooting across time and space in an effort to leave the room. For an instant she felt a weird sensation, almost like the beginnings of the vertigo that encapsulated her the first few times she teleported with Cahira. Terrified at the thought she may actually pull it off, Faye opened her eyes and the feeling passed, leaving her standing alone in her bedroom.

Faye felt a wave of exhaustion overtake her and realised she had expended a great deal of energy in her attempt at teleporting, combined with her efforts in the forest earlier that morning, Faye was wholeheartedly exhausted. She decided to rest while she waited for Cahira to reappear and made her way back to what she was referring to as her snuggle corner. Within minutes of her lying down with her pillow and blanket she was sound asleep, snoring ever so quietly.

# CHAPTER 24

Faye was staggered to find the next time she awoke it was morning. Even though she didn't have a clock or natural sunlight to track time, she could measure it by the meals that were present on her bedside table. And there, as she sat up in her snuggle corner on the floor, was breakfast. But still no Cahira.

Faye could not remember a time in her life when she had ever slept so soundly, and for so long. She wondered for a moment if she had been put under some sort of spell to contain her. She instantly shoved the thought out of her head, not wanting to know the answer. So instead, she let herself get distracted by her hunger, as she was absolutely starving, having missed dinner. So she distractedly ate the food on the tray while she tried to work out what may have happened to Cahira.

Faye was so consumed with her thoughts and the process of eating, she did not realise someone had appeared in the room — until she heard a throat being cleared. A male throat.

Faye turned her head to the opposite side of room and was literally floored by what she saw.

"Dad?" Faye couldn't help the small whimper that escaped her.

Standing on the other side of the room was her father. Or as things go in the realm: his doppelganger. The faerie standing before her had blonde hair instead of her father's brown hair, but her father's face with the same brown eyes. Faye realised he was the first faerie she had seen that didn't have blue or green eyes.

She was stunned into complete silence. Her brain did not know how to process what her eyes were seeing.

"Eamon," Faye heard her father's doppelganger say, in a voice that sounded exactly the same as her father's.

She knew he wasn't her father; the being in front of her was definitely a faerie. Even with everything she had seen and learnt over the last couple of days, she could not work out how it fitted into the grand scheme of things.

For her own mental well-being, she chalked it up to the mind manipulation that was constantly being used in the realm and blamed her great-grandmother for being so cruel. She didn't know how the Queen knew what her father looked like, but she kept reminding herself that the faerie Queen was more powerful than she could comprehend bundled up in a whole lot of evil.

Faye just couldn't work out why the Queen was going to these lengths to torture and upset her. As the shock of seeing her father's face — worn by a faerie, wore off, she was glad it was his face the Queen was using to taunt her and not her mother's. That would have been the straw that broke Faye's resolve to survive the Faerie Realm and make it home. All the thoughts flashed though Faye's mind in a blink of an eye as she tried to steady herself after the shock.

Trying to put her game face back on and lock all thoughts of her family in a box firmly tucked away at the back of her mind, Faye focused on Eamon's presence and what that meant.

"Where's Cahira?" Faye asked, concentrating on the differences instead of the similarities between Eamon and her father, reminding herself it was just a trick to screw with her.

Faye didn't get a reply. Instead, Eamon stepped forward, grabbing a hold of her upper arm in a vice like grip and teleported them out of the room.

Her stomach violently jerked, threatening to expel her breakfast out into the ether. As Faye felt her feet hit solid ground, she ripped her arm from Eamon's hands, despite the fact his grip was the only thing holding her upright.

Falling to her knees, Faye rested her forehead against the cold tiles and tried to concentrate on the coolness instead of the need to vomit.

"Never touch me again," Faye growled out, in between taking deep breaths, forcing the food in her stomach to remain where it was.

"Good morning, Faye."

Faye ignored her great-grandmother's greeting, keeping her head down while the need to puke lingered. She knew if she looked up at her great-grandmother, the sight alone would be enough to purge her stomach.

As the sick feeling started to subside, Faye got up off the floor only to realise she was back in the dining hall. Taking her seat and careful to keep her gaze away from her great-grandmother's direction, Faye was desperately trying to re-establish her poker face. As she took a large gulp of water, testing out whether she would be able to keep anything down, Faye couldn't help but notice Cahira's absence from the room. Faye may not have been able to see Cahira during her previous meals, but she could always sense her presence in the room — and the feeling was missing from the hall right now.

Faye took a deep breath before looking up and across the table at her great-grandmother, determined to find out where Cahira was.

"Where is Cahira?" Faye stated flatly, as she maintained eye contact with the Queen, not backing down or looking away until she got an answer. She would sit there all day if she had to.

"Cahira has been called away to deal with a matter of the realm."

"What matter? When will she be back?" Faye demanded.

"When the matter is resolved," was the simple answer she received.

Faye hated the vagueness of her great-grandmother's response, but she resigned herself to being patient and wait. Something Faye was terrible at doing.

Faye knew there was no use in questioning her great-grandmother any further, so she turned her attention to the food in front of her. Faye tried to keep her focus and thoughts solely on the food, trying not to worry about Cahira or the desperate desire to go home that was again threatening to take control of her.

"Eamon will take you to the fabric shop to choose some appropriate material to be made into a dress for you. You will wear it to your last dinner here before leaving," the Queen stated as a matter of fact.

Faye didn't know what her great-grandmother was playing at, but her sense of fear and panic was prickling again — and she didn't like it. She knew the woman sitting across from her had no intention of allowing her to leave and go home, so what was she really intending to do with her?

"I'm done," Faye stated flatly, as she dropped her knife and fork on her plate.

Cahira's absence was reinforced when the Queen clicked her fingers and Eamon walked out of the shadows and stalked towards her.

Faye took a few deep breaths and reminded herself that she knew exactly what was happening and where Eamon was taking her. She relaxed her body and stepped toward Eamon as he reached for her arm and teleported.

Faye was relieved when her stomach didn't roll and churn during their travel away from the dining hall. When the darkness faded, she found herself standing in front of a moss tower, wondering what she was about to walk into. The one thing she was sure of: she was going to be shown an actual fabric store, not the sweat shop Cahira had taken her to.

Eamon motioned to Faye to enter the tower in front of him as he followed closely behind. The room they walked into was like any fabric store in the Human Realm, with rows and rows of benches filled with rolls of fabric. There was a central table topped with multiple pairs of scissors, pin cushions, and measuring tapes. The rest of the room was lined with benches in rows, piled high with rolls of fabric. Each bench seemed to represent a different colour, and was covered with ornate lace and silks, transparent material and a myriad of shiny and matte fabrics. The resulting effect was a spectacular rainbow across the tables in the room.

"Select your fabric and someone will be in to take measurements."

Faye looked towards Eamon as he spoke, standing in the doorway of the room, watching her every move.

Faye had no desire to choose materials and have a dress made for her, but she would play along to get it over and done with as quickly as possible. The only colours in her wardrobe in the Faerie Realm were pale blues and silvers, and that couldn't be further from Faye's taste in colours if she tried. Walking around the room she gravitated towards the tables holding the fabrics in her usual colour scheme: black and red. If she really had to have a dress made, she would create the coolest gothic style ballgown the Faerie Realm had even seen.

Choosing a red lace to sit on top of a matte black material, Faye picked up the fabric and carried them to the centre table. Thinking of what her great-grandmother's reaction will be when first seeing the dress, Faye was not able to suppress the smile that begun to flicker at the corners of her mouth. She was actually starting to enjoy it.

When Faye placed the fabric on the table, a female faerie suddenly appeared and picked up a tape measure. She tapped Faye's arm and gestured for her to lift her arms above her head. Faye did as she was instructed, and the faerie slid the tape measure around her waist then bust, travelling down to measure the length of her legs before finishing.

Once the faerie was done, Faye watched as she picked up her selected materials and promptly disappeared, leaving her alone with Eamon. *Okay,* Faye thought, *so you can teleport while holding material objects — good to know.*

"The Queen would like you to see the tailors," Eamon said.

Faye almost couldn't stop her eyes rolling back in their sockets. For goodness' sake, she hated being a part of the ridiculous façade her great-grandmother was running. Hated being treated like a fool. She followed Eamon as he walked out of the moss tower and into the tower next door. Faye stood at the doorway of a room filled with more benches. On each bench sat an ancient-looking wooden sewing machine. The sewing machines were hand operated with a wooden knob to control the needle. They reminded Faye of photos she had seen of sewing machines in the Human Realm that were used in the early nineteen hundreds.

The benches were covered in dresses in different stages of completion. The faeries working behind the benches and sewing machines looked healthy and as if they were treated well, the complete opposite of the faeries working in the silk and jewellery sweatshops Cahira had taken her to.

Faye was struggling to see the reasons behind why the Queen was orchestrating it all, ordering her to this fabric shop and having the dress made. Why did she have to see all the well-fed faeries, happily going about their business? The complexity of the charade was sending chills down her spine.

Ever since the tapestry had shown Faye the evil her great-grandmother was capable of, she had been able to identify the methodical and cunning manipulation, and the tangled web of lies she used to create the picture-perfect faerie-tale realm. But she had seen the truth. She knew it was all a lie. What she couldn't work out was why. What was her motive for all of the deceit?

Faye saw the same female faerie who had taken her measurements lay the black material on the bench and get to work. There were no patterns to trace, the faerie only had a plastic tape measure and a pair of scissors to create a ballgown silhouette to sew. Faye watched in fascination as the faerie laid the tape against the fabric and made small cuts to mark a length, before moving it around a few more times. The process was repeated several times before she gathered up all the materials and set to cutting. She cut in some places and tore in others to create a basic outline of a dress.

Faye had never seen a piece of clothing being made before, and quite possibly never would again, but she couldn't imagine anyone in the Human Realm creating something that fast. It was truly mesmerising. She didn't know if the faerie was using magic of some type to create the outfit, but Faye loved the idea of wearing clothes that had been made of magic.

Faye continued to watch the faerie seamstress as she moved onto cutting pieces out of the red lace, then turned to a sewing machine to begin combining the pieces of fabric, excited to see how it would all come together.

She had no sense of how long she had stood there watching until Eamon moved into her line of sight, grabbing her arm before she had a chance to move out of his reach. Before she knew it the room disappeared, leaving her in a sea of darkness.

The darkness lasted longer than Faye had grown accustomed to and she was on the brink of panic when the blackness faded, and she was welcomed by the sight of her room. She felt both relieved and bummed out to be back. Faye wanted to watch the creation of her ballgown through to its completion and possibly speak with the faerie who was making it. But of course, she had no control over where she went and when.

"The Queen has been called away to tend to some royal matters. She will not be attending lunch or dinner. Both meals will be provided to you in your room."

Honestly why did they even bother telling her that stuff? It made no difference to the fact she was being left trapped in her room, no matter what the bloody Queen was supposedly doing.

"Royal matters. Yeah right, whatever," Faye replied like a petulant child.

Faye was relieved not to be having lunch and dinner with her great-grandmother for a second day in a row, but she was worried about Cahira. She was frightened that Cahira was involved in her great-grandmother's latest scheme and Faye desperately hoped Cahira would finally reappear tomorrow morning to escort her to breakfast.

Faye snapped out of her thoughts when she realised Eamon had disappeared, and a bowl materialised on her bedside table. She hadn't realised just how much time had passed in the fabric and sewing rooms until her stomach growled at the smell of the food.

Looking at the bowl, Faye saw an orange-coloured soup and even though she wasn't a big fan of food in a liquid form, she was ready and willing to give it try. So, braving a spoon full, Faye was pleasantly surprised by the earthy taste and continued to guzzle the soup quickly.

With a full belly and nothing to focus on, Faye could feel the buzz and hum of energy inside her body, ready for a release. She had got into a routine with Cahira of practising her magic each day and she missed doing it that morning.

Faye tried to relax and keep calm at the thought of having no access to the rock circle for the day. She wondered what would happen to all the energy within her. Now that it had been acknowledged and released a few times, would it need a regular outlet? Did she need a rock circle to channel the power and use her magic? She had so many questions and no one to answer them.

Faye wasn't comfortable running the risk of practising outside of the circle without Cahira there to help if things got out of control. So, she sat back, tried to get comfortable and started doing a few breathing techniques that had helped to settle her so many times before.

Faye retreated to her snuggle corner and tried to concentrate on the rise and fall of her chest instead of feeding and growing her energy into an orb. Within minutes she had achieved her mediative state and unintentionally fell asleep.

# CHAPTER 25

Faye awoke from her post-lunch nap with a start, sitting bolt upright, so sure Cahira was in her room. But no. It was just a dream. She lay still for a moment longer, settling herself before she stood and thought of what to do next. She was guessing it was mid-afternoon, and given what Eamon had said earlier, she was confined to her room until the next morning.

Once again Faye kicked herself for not asking Cahira to teach her to teleport. Faye assumed her room was made of bricks and mortar — the Queen herself had said she resided in a room beneath the cathedral and the other faeries live in the towers. She walked along the perimeter of the room, running her hands along the walls, pushing into the corners, but she could not find any places where timber or brick or mortar were visible.

"Arghh! This is so bloody annoying," Faye roared as she slapped her hand against the door leading to the bathroom.

"Let me out of here!"

Of course, no one answered her.

Faye seriously thought she would go crazy in the room and contemplated throwing things against the walls, but that would be a more strenuous activity than she was willing to do. Considering someone could just materialise and click their fingers to fix it all. It was just not worth the trouble.

Faye paced a few more times around the room, then flopped herself onto the bed. She lay still, calmed herself and tuned into the energy coursing through her veins. She decided to concentrate on how the energy felt under her skin as she thought of different things. Faye focused on her mother's face, trying to bring it clearly into the focal point of her mind.

She almost let out a gasp of joy at the clear image of her mum that appeared before her eyes. Faye felt a surge of happiness as the Forsa Beatha quickened through her veins. The feeling encouraged Faye to visualise an orb in her hand and grow the orb into a physical form of her mother, willing her to appear in the room with her. Although it was happening in her mind, Faye was confident she could make it happen for real — if only Cahira was with her.

The thought of Cahira caused an immediate change to the flow of the energy within Faye, and she wasn't one hundred percent sure what it meant. The image she held fast in her mind was of Cahira giving the small smile while they were in the forest. There was no denying the faerie commander was attractive in a breathtaking kind of way. She had no real idea what to do with the power coursing through her, so she took a few deep breaths, quietening her energy, and decided to head to the bathroom for a long hot shower as a means of distraction.

***

The rest of the night passed without Eamon or any other random faerie minion appearing in her room, sent by her great-grandmother. Faye awoke the next morning feeling unrested and fidgety. Her anxiety around not knowing the whereabouts of Cahira was driving her crazy. Maybe the Queen was telling her the truth and she was just off on some secret Queen mission. But every fibre in her being was telling her that was not the case. And the thought of Cahira going off and leaving her without a word certainly disappointed her.

Faye had turned so many possible scenarios around in her head she was getting dizzy. Finally deciding on a course of action, she marched into the bathroom and looked at her reflection, ready to launch into the biggest pep talk of all time.

"Pull your big girl pants on, Faye. Buckle up and get ready to take the crazy old bag on."

She stood with her hands on her hips and almost cringed at the forced tough girl smirk she had plastered on her face. She was ready to play the Queen's game more seriously than ever.

Faye was prepared when Eamon appeared in her room and grabbed at her shoulders to teleport her to breakfast in the dining hall. She stumbled to her seat opposite her great-grandmother, feeling a little lightheaded and began to eat, not sparing a glance or a single word. Faye had decided to eat as much as her stomach could take at breakfast because she didn't know how the day would unfold. And she would definitely handle it all better fully fed.

When Faye had finished, she looked directly at her great-grandmother for the first time since arriving in the dining hall.

"Can I spend the day in my room?" Faye didn't have the spare brain capacity to try to orchestrate a lie that sounded believable enough to warrant a day to herself. It had taken the whole of breakfast to psych herself up to speak. She was ready for an argument, but all she got was a simple reply.

"Of course. Eamon will take you back."

Out of the corner of her eye, Faye saw Eamon move into the light and readied herself for the uncomfortable teleport that happened every time she travelled with him. She had just got accustomed to teleporting with Cahira and enjoyed the feeling of disappearing and reappearing. But now, she was back at square one with Eamon's abrupt and rough approach to teleporting.

Travelling with Eamon always knocked the wind out of her and when the blackness didn't fade quick enough, Faye was left lightheaded, hunched over with her hands on her knees.

"Cahira's better," Faye mumbled under her breath while her eyes were closed and she tried to fight off the dizziness, not caring if Eamon was around to hear.

Slowly opening her eyes, Faye quickly looked around her room, making sure she was completely alone. Even going as far as to check her bathroom and closet.

Satisfied that she was alone, Faye stationed herself at the end of the bed, staring into the bathroom.

The first stage of Faye's new plan was to teach herself to teleport. The quiet time she took yesterday afternoon and last night concentrating on the power within her, and all the things Cahira has said to her over the last few days, had instilled a new confidence in her. She wasn't afraid of her power any more and she was ready to embrace it.

She knew she had no real idea of how teleporting worked but she figured the best plan of attack would be to concentrate on the spot she wanted to be. Faye concentrated on her breathing first, taking a few deep breaths to centre herself and the Forsa Beatha began to radiate within her.

Staring at the door that separated her bedroom from the bathroom, Faye willed herself, with all her might, to be standing on the other side of it. A strong wave of vertigo overtook her, causing her to stumble forward. Black spots clouded her vision and she stretched her arms out in front of her, ready to break her fall. To her surprise and absolute glee Faye's palms made contact with smooth cold tiles.

Blinking rapidly to clear her vision, Faye was delighted to find herself resting against the wall inside her bathroom, unceremoniously crouched between the toilet and the shower. She rested for a good five minutes, waiting for the dizziness and nausea to pass before she stood. Faye was so encouraged by her success in teleporting from her bedroom to the bathroom she decided to tweak her technique.

She stood straight, with her back flush against the cool bathroom wall and shut her eyes. In her mind she pictured the interior of her closet, a dark space filled with racks of ballgowns hanging above glass cases of expensive jewellery. She felt her energy heat up and in an instant Faye was hit with another wave of dizziness, losing all balance and falling to the floor.

Taking a minute with her eyes still closed tightly shut, Faye waited for the vertigo to pass. She steadied herself and opened her eyes to find herself nestled between the racks of ballgowns and drawers of jewellery.

Faye was momentarily unable to process what had just actually happened. She spun around in place, letting out a high-pitched squeal so loud that it wouldn't be a surprised if her great-grandmother could hear her from her throne.

She couldn't believe she had teleported. Twice on her own. Without anyone's help. Without Cahira.

She was on a roll now and so confident in her ability. Faye stood in the centre of the closet, away from the walls, ready to try teleporting without leaning on anything for support. She had to get use to not falling on her ass each time she did it. Faye closed her eyes and concentrated on where she wanted to be: back in her bedroom.

Within seconds Faye felt her energy respond and the air was knocked out of her. She opened her eyes and saw she was back in her room. It helped to solidify her belief in herself: that her first two attempts at teleporting had not been flukes. Once she caught her breath, Faye was relieved the vertigo passed quicker. But she didn't kid herself into believing that she had mastered teleporting — she was well aware there was a vast difference between teleporting a few metres in a familiar room and teleporting across the realm to an unknown location.

Now she needed a plan of action. Faye had no clue where Cahira could be, and the Queen and Eamon hadn't given her a straight answer when she had asked. So, she was on her own, something she grew more familiar with.

Faye didn't know if she could teleport to a location she didn't know, based only on a thought of a person she wished to visit, but she was going to give it a try. Walking out of the bathroom, Faye sat cross-legged on the floor of the bedroom. This was how she felt most relaxed and comfortable, and she needed to clear her head and focus first.

Closing her eyes, Faye focused on her breathing, letting everything else fall away. As her pulse became a steady thump and her breathing evened out, she thought of Cahira. How Cahira had gone out of her way to show Faye the truth and about all the hours spent teaching her not to be afraid of herself and to embrace the wonders of her powers. Faye thought back to where they had met and how far they had come. She couldn't deny that Cahira had become her family whilst being in the realm and was someone Faye would cherish for the rest of her life. She knew she wouldn't even think herself capable of doing something so incredible as teleporting if it weren't for her.

Faye was so engrossed by her thoughts of Cahira that she didn't really notice as her energy started to react, and her skin warmed up. She only snapped back to the present when she felt the ground disappear and she was unable to breathe. On instinct, Faye's eyes snapped open, only to see complete darkness. Her panic took hold as she gasped for air, trying to take a breath. She was flailing about, starting to feel faint.

Just before Faye reached the point of losing consciousness due to the lake of oxygen, she felt solid ground beneath her, and air fill her lungs. It took her a few moments before she realised that she was still sitting cross-legged on the floor — more specifically she was sitting on the floor in a puddle of water. Confused, Faye looked out into the darkness, only to find she was back in the place she would have been happy avoiding for the rest of her life: the cave dungeon. Faye's sense of claustrophobia quickly levelled up to high intensity when she saw that was where she had teleported herself.

"Faye?"

Faye was suddenly brought out of her terror when she heard Cahira's voice. Looking up in the direction it had come from, Faye saw a cell in the far corner of the cave, and behind the bars sat Cahira. She launched herself up from the floor and staggered towards the faerie. Cahira was still in the clothes she was wearing the last time Faye had seen her, but she was filthy, head to toe.

Faye's eyes watered at the atrocious smell that radiated throughout the dungeon. It was a mixture of the damp mouldiness, body odour and the unspeakable mess of the buckets in the corner of each cell. She could practically taste it.

"What are you doing here?" Faye and Cahira asked in unison.

"Are you okay?" Faye quickly followed up. She knew it was a stupid question, but she couldn't stop herself. She stood with her hands wrapped around the bars of the cell that separated her from Cahira, quietly waiting for an explanation.

"The Queen. She found out we never went to the silk room and jeweller — well not the one she wanted me to take you to. She is busy now, trying to find out what we have been doing."

Faye absorbed everything she was just told. The actions of her great-grandmother didn't surprise her, but she was stunned by the fact that Cahira was actually speaking freely with her, providing a clear answer to the question she had asked, with no avoidance. Cahira was speaking without the indifferent tone or politician mumbo jumbo that always frustrated her.

Cahira sensed Faye's surprise and quickly continued.

"The Queen's magic doesn't reach inside the cells; no magic does. Out there, I am prevented from speaking the truth regarding the Queen's actions and plans. Don't you know I did all that I could to work around these spells to give you as much information as I could? But in here I can tell you everything."

"How do I get you out of here?" Faye asked, ignoring this new information to focus on getting Cahira out. She would have plenty of time to process all that later.

"She has no intention of keeping you alive."

Cahira ignored Faye's question and voiced what Faye had suspected since the day in the tapestry hall. So, the little nugget of knowledge was pushed to the back of her brain with the rest of the truth dump she had just received.

*Later,* she kept telling herself. *I will deal with that later.*

Faye stuck to the simple questions.

"How do I open the cell?"

"Faye, how did you get here? Who teleported you here? Does someone else know where you are?" Cahira was deadly serious when she asked those three questions.

"We don't have time for this Cahira. I need to get you out of here. No one brought me here. I taught myself to teleport around my room, firstly to go back and forth between my room, the bathroom, and the closet. Then I just concentrated on you, and I materialised here — in my favourite place in the whole world." Faye tried to jest at the end of her rambling, in a vain attempt to defuse the tension.

"You taught yourself to teleport," Cahira said in a whisper. "Of course you did. You really are extraordinary."

Faye was beaming now, but she calmly repeated her question: "How do I open the cell?"

"Yes of course. Your magic will work down here because you teleported into the observation isle, which protects you from the power cancelling magic cased over the cells. Unfortunately, mine does not. Settle yourself, Faye; call your energy forward into your palm. Just before it manifests into an orb, place your hand on the bar."

Faye listened carefully to each and every word that Cahira said. She found it easier to feel her energy now having worked on the teleporting. She guided the buzz and hum towards her hand, focusing on the thoughts of freeing Cahira. When her fingers warmed up, Faye raised her hand and placed it against the bars. Feeling the warmth leave her hand, Faye watched as the metal bars glowed then disappeared, dematerialising before her eyes.

Before she knew what she was doing, Faye ran forward, falling to her knees and hugged Cahira. She didn't care that Cahira was dirty or smelled, she was just relieved she was in front of her and looked unharmed.

"Are you okay? Are you hurt? What did she do to you?" Faye couldn't stop herself from talking a mile a minute. Desperately hoping Cahira was both physically and mentally okay.

"We need to leave."

Faye noticed how Cahira ignored her questions but knew it wasn't the right time to grill her for answers. She didn't have a plan. She had only thought as far as finding

Cahira, not where they would go or what they would do after Faye found her.

Cahira rose from where she was still sitting on the ground and took a few unsteady steps forward, through the space where the bars had been.

"Those bars inhibited my powers Faye, but now you have freed me."

Cahira held out her hand to Faye and she took it gladly, trusting that Cahira would keep them safe.

# CHAPTER 26

The teleport with Cahira lacked all the uncomfortable and sickening feelings she had felt the last few times. Faye was able to breathe, and she wasn't left feeling dizzy or sick when they arrived at their destination.

Faye didn't have to open her eyes to know where they were. It was the smell of dirt that gave it away instantly. Cahira's original home. It was still the small and bare hole in the ground that she had visited a few days prior. Faye hoped they didn't have to stay there too long because it was barely big enough for one person, let alone the two of them.

"Won't we be found here?" Faye was worried — surely it would be the first place they would look once Cahira's escape was discovered.

"The Queen does not know of my original home."

Faye couldn't even look Cahira in the eye because they were still standing as they had been during the teleportation: side by side, holding hands. There wasn't much room to move around so Faye shimmied her body until she was facing Cahira and waited for her to copy. Getting the hint, Cahira followed Faye's actions until she faced her, and looked down at their entwined fingers.

Cahira dropped Faye's hand like it had stung her.

Faye ignored the pang of hurt her action caused and ask her next question.

"Will she have people out looking for us?"

"The Queen would have to tell the fae folk who she was looking for and why. So no, I do not think she will initiate a search party for us. At least not out in the open. She does have spies everywhere, so we need to be extremely careful. I want to keep you safe and out of her hands so you can reach your true potential."

Faye thought about what Cahira was saying and had to agree it made sense. How could the Queen of the Faerie Realm announce to her people some random human had managed to enter their world undetected, the world she protected, and now that human needed to be hunted down. And how could she explain why she had imprisoned her most trusted commander? Most importantly, how could she hide the fact that the missing human was in fact the next rightful Queen of the Tuatha De Danann?

Faye shivered as she imagined her great-grandmother working on some elaborate plan that would end up with her death and Cahira's imprisonment.

"Okay. Right. What do we do now?" Faye asked, feeling terrible for putting the responsibility to create a plan on Cahira.

"We rest."

It wasn't the answer Faye was looking for but decided against voicing her opposition to it when she watched Cahira take a small step backwards and lay down. With her back right up against the wall, she couldn't even stretch out because the room wasn't long enough.

Faye copied Cahira's actions and curled herself up against the opposite wall. She kept her eyes on Cahira. Faye watched as Cahira's eyes closed and her breathing evened out. She was glad Cahira could get some rest; she couldn't imagine what Cahira was subjected to over the last few days in the dungeon.

Faye wasn't tired, she was still buzzing from the successful teleportation from her room to the dungeon and using her magic to help Cahira escape. She knew she could have teleported the two of them out of there as well but was happy to let Cahira take the lead.

Contradicting her positive, empowering thoughts were her familiar friend negativity. Faye didn't like being left alone with only her thoughts. Every thought of how skilled she at controlling her power was countered with a thought of how her great-grandmother, her own flesh and blood, wanted to kill her. Her thoughts of how amazing it was that she taught herself to teleport were being suppressed by the louder voice in her mind telling her it was all just a dream, none of it was real, and she was having a mental breakdown.

That voice was breaking her down, piece by piece. The possibility of a reality where she never met Cahira, never discovered who she really was and the power she was capable of wielding, terrified Faye more than any death threat the Queen could throw at her.

Faye desperately tried to quell the thoughts and get a head start on formulating a plan. She knew for a fact no one would ever be safe in the realm while her great-grandmother remained on the throne, but Faye had no intentions of becoming Queen. She didn't think it was fair that an outsider, someone who had never lived in the Faerie Realm, let alone knew of its actual existence, was able to waltz in and be given power over all the faeries' lives. And all this just because of who they were related to, and a legacy put in place hundreds of years ago.

So, the crux of her plan was to help get her great-grandmother off the throne, then the faeries could choose who they wanted to rule, and she could go home. That was the light at the end of the tunnel, getting home, but she still had a whole tunnel to travel through first.

Faye was counting on Cahira to have enough connections and influence with the faeries to get the support they would need if they were going to succeed. She also had to work on uniting the whole realm and breaching the gaps the Queen created when she divided the faeries by their skills and power levels.

Faye didn't know how she fit into it all. She wondered if faeries had short memories, and if they would think she was just like her great-grandmother, especially given the fact that she looked exactly like her. She trusted that Cahira would help solve that dilemma if it arose.

Faye tried not to think about the all too real possibility that the faeries would demand justice in the form of taking the Queen's life. And then wondered if they may turn on her too. If she was honest with herself, Faye was conflicted about it. She knew her great-grandmother was a monster who seemed to be capable of terrible acts. She treated the faeries in a heinous way and knew she must be made to pay for those things. But who was she to say what the punishment should be? One thing she knew for sure, she did not want the responsibly of making that decision.

When Faye saw Cahira open her eyes and sit up, she couldn't help but wonder how long she had been stuck in her thoughts for. Was it a few minutes or a few hours?

"Did you sleep okay?" Faye attempted to start up a conversation, unnerved by Cahira's stare and silence, but only got a nod in return. She didn't know what to do besides sit up as well, and stare back.

Faye remained in the same position until Cahira stood up and held out her hand. Due to the size of the room, when Cahira stood up, her crotch was right at eye level for Faye, so she scrambled to stand up and take Cahira's offered hand.

\*\*\*

Faye found herself in a forest. It wasn't the usual place Cahira brought her to, it was missing the rock circle and dense tree foliage. She could see clearly through the trees to an open field lined with rows of earth mounds. Faye was quickly reminded just how sad and dire the situation was for the majority of the faeries.

"What are we doing here?" Faye turned her attention towards Cahira.

"You will grow our food."

Faye gave Cahira a sceptical look. Growing flower buds in the safety of the stone circle was one thing but growing crops out in the open was taking things to a whole other level. Cahira sensed Faye's hesitancy and placed a reassuring hand on her arm.

"You can do this, Faye. Create your orb from positive energy, and before you place it to the ground, imagine what you want to grow."

Faye really wanted a cheeseburger but unfortunately knew she couldn't make one grow from the earth. At least Faye didn't think she could grow a burger from the dirt. Instead, Faye thought of a fruit salad. Taking a seat in the grass, she closed her eyes and basked in the encouragement and faith Cahira had given her. She was no longer alone, and Cahira was safe, standing right next to her. Faye felt her energy react in an instant and without guidance, began to travel to her hand. When her palm started to heat up, Faye opened her eyes to see a vibrant purple orb, resting in her hand. It was the same palm that held the purple orb when she had practised handling the two orbs created from positive and negative energy, so it seemed her mental block remained in place.

Faye's confidence was increasing but she still didn't know what to expect. Maybe fruits were just going to pop up from the dirt, whole and ripe, or trees would grow, or something entirely different. She had no idea but was ready to find out. Thinking about the fruits in a fruit salad, Faye slowly lowered her hands to the grass and felt the heat in her palm disappear. Taking her hands away, Faye watched as a dim glow spread out across the grass around her, going far beyond, then fading out.

She waited for something to happen and wasn't disappointed when a shoot sprouted at the base of a tree and ever so slowly wound up around the trunk of the tree. Faye jumped up to her feet, ready to run over and check out the vine but was stopped in her tracks when more plant shoots started to appear. Slowly the shoots grew to chest height before stopping, then they started to sprout fruits. Faye and Cahira were suddenly surrounded by a mini orchard. There were apples, perfectly ripened bananas, grapes growing on vines entwined around the trees and even a pineapple.

Faye couldn't believe her eyes. It was beyond her wildest expectations. In the Human Realm she couldn't even grow something from seeds she had planted and watered attentively. But in the Faerie Realm, she had used her power to create and grow actual edible fruits.

She was ecstatic and almost felt bad for walking over to the mini apple tree and plucking one, but when Faye took a bite, she was reminded how hungry she was, and any thought of guilt was gone in a flash.

Faye quickly devoured the apple before moving onto the little banana tree, but she stopped her actions when she saw Cahira was still standing in the place where they first arrived, and her hands were empty. Faye picked another apple instead and walked back to Cahira, handing it to her. She was pleased when Cahira took it and ate it just as fast as she had eaten hers. That encouraged Faye, so she took a few quick steps around the apple tree to get to the bananas. She tore a bunch of bananas off the little tree before moving back over to Cahira. She handed one banana to Cahira, then started to eat one as well. She stopped herself from scoffing them all and decided to save a few to take back for later.

Faye gathered the bottom of her dress to make a basket for carrying the fruit she was picking. Placing the bananas there, she walked over to the tree where the grape vine had grown and began to pick clusters of grapes, dropping them in with the bananas. She left the pineapple as she had no clue how they could eat it without a knife. Surely someone else would find and enjoy it.

Faye looked around at what she had created — a garden of food capable of feeding the faerie clans that lived here. What else was she capable of doing?

Walking back over to Cahira with her improvised basket, Faye was ready to go back to Cahira's home and start brainstorming the next part of their plan.

"There is a section of woods further in, which you can use to relieve yourself. Did you need me to show you?"

"What do you…" Faye's question trailed off, as it dawned on her just what Cahira meant. Embarrassed, she shook her head, unable to voice a reply. She didn't like the idea or feel comfortable going to the bathroom in the middle of a forest. She had never even been camping before. Now she had something else to worry about. Faye really didn't know how she was going to go if and when the time came.

Faye tried to shake her mortification away when Cahira held out her hand, indicating she was ready to go. Taking her hand, Faye left her embarrassment in the forest, letting it disappear just as quickly as she did.

# CHAPTER 27

Faye and Cahira sat against opposite dirt walls, with the fruit in the middle. Neither of them had said a word since arriving back, both lost in their own thoughts. Faye was still trying to push the thought of peeing behind a bush out of her head and focus on the problem at hand, their lack of a plan.

"What happens now?" Faye broke the silence.

"Now? Now you must learn how to teleport objects and mind manipulation."

Faye's blood turned to ice at the mention of mind manipulation. As someone who struggled with her own mind, the thought of using someone's mind against them was disgusting to Faye. It was one power she did not want to learn.

"What is our plan, Cahira? What is the end goal?" Faye needed to know Cahira had a plan to stay out of the Queen's dungeon, and ultimately to overthrow her.

"You stay here and work on your powers. I will contact certain faeries I know who will help us in our cause. This will take a few days as I will need to travel to all corners of the realm. When the time is right, we will all come together and attack. You are the key Faye. No one can match the Queen's power but another Queen. It is your destiny."

Those last four words hung thick in the air. Destiny.

Faye had a million things running through her head. The air in the tiny underground burrow was so thick Faye could hardly stand it. She could feel the familiar creep of a panic attack. As if sensing Faye's distress Cahira took Faye's hands in hers and said in a voice that was almost a whisper:

"Remember what was said in the dungeon. This is your birth right, to become the next Queen and ruler of this Faerie Realm."

Faye was starting to feel a little lost under the intense gaze of Cahira, and when she dropped her eyes to their hands, the faerie relaxed her grip.

"I don't know how I'm supposed to do what you need me to."

"Practise. You taught yourself to teleport Faye. You have not even begun to tap into your potential."

If Faye was honest with herself, she didn't want to know what her full potential was. What if she turned into someone like her great-grandmother? She wanted to know how Cahira felt about her, other than the fact she was a future Queen. She wanted to know who Cahira was leaving her to meet with and plan to overthrow the Queen. She wanted everyone to know she didn't want to be Queen — it seemed no matter how many times she shouted it out, no one seemed to listen.

Why would the faeries want a seventeen-year-old human, with no knowledge of how to lead a kingdom, take the throne, especially after all the oppression they had suffered at the hands of her great-grandmother. Why did Cahira have so much faith in her?

Faye returned her gaze to Cahira's face, trying to convey all her conflicting thoughts and emotions with her eyes. She thought she saw a moment of hesitation in Cahira's eyes but then the faerie commander's mask was set back in place, and she was all business. Reinforcing her commander persona, Cahira untangled her fingers with Faye's and snatched her hands back, putting distance between the two of them.

"Practice," Cahira repeated.

"You can leave this burrow but only go to the forest and field above us. Practise moving yourself, and objects, between these two locations. Practise growing more food. I will check in on you as often as I can."

Faye could tell by Cahira's tone that was the end of their conversation. Not knowing what else to do, Faye dropped her hands, rested her head against the wall and closed her eyes. It triggered an onslaught of tiredness from the excitement of the day — successfully teaching herself to teleport, to finding Cahira, and creating the fruit trees. The extensive use of her powers came crashing down on her and she was completely exhausted. Faye knew she was about to fall asleep, and nothing could stop it. She was barely aware of Cahira standing over her before she teleported out of the burrow and Faye fell into a restless sleep.

\*\*\*

Faye wasn't really sure how much time had passed when Cahira reappeared in the burrow. She had slept for a long time, eaten some fruit and tried to teleport a banana from one side of the burrow to the other. It had worked but it wasn't really much of an achievement given how tiny the space was. She wasn't brave enough to teleport out of the burrow by herself just yet. She was worried she would end up back in the dungeon.

Cahira returned to find Faye sitting in the burrow talking to the banana. "Oh, look our leader has returned," Faye said looking up at Cahira.

Cahira simply stared.

"Where did you go?" Faye quickly threw the question out and watched for any changes in Cahira's schooled expression, but she was a master at keeping her face neutral. Faye wondered if it was another skill she had learnt from working so closely by her great-grandmother, or maybe Cahira just didn't show much emotion. Faye couldn't decide which one sounded more likely.

"Word has spread that the Queen is keeping a fae prisoner in the dungeons and they are not happy," Cahira offered as an answer regarding her whereabouts.

"That's perfect! The faeries need to be united and what better reason than unjust imprisonment of an innocent." Faye was starting to feel the faint flicker of hope start to crawl into her being. If what Cahira was saying was true and the general faerie population were starting to realise their Queen was not the benevolent monarch she pretended to be, maybe they could do it.

The faerie clans had been kept separate for so long — maybe their current situation was the one spark to reunite them?

"You need to learn the last two abilities."

Cahira's voice, and general presence, seemed so loud and large in the tiny burrow, and it brought Faye out of her small celebration with a thud.

"Okay. Where do we start? I did manage to teleport this banana from here to there." Faye pointed to the other side of their enclosure, less than two feet away.

Cahira did manage a smile in acknowledge of Faye's achievement.

"While that is a great start to teleporting objects, I need you to call on your energy, bringing it forward. Concentrate on an object that you know is inside the Faerie Realm. Instead of teleporting yourself to the object, push your energy towards it, then pull it back to you."

Faye couldn't think of any personal items she had there with her in the Faerie Realm, and she was struggling to think of an object she would want to teleport to the burrow. Then she had an epiphany, like a light bulb suddenly went off in her head, and she thought of the perfect thing. She didn't know whether they had been kept or destroyed but she had to give it a go.

Picturing her nicely folded clothes she wore into the Faerie Realm, Faye felt her energy surge. She focused on her power, wrapping itself around every surface of her clothing, and like a fish on a hook, she pulled her energy back towards her body. She opened her eyes and sitting in front of her was a pile of her clothing. Reaching out and tentatively touching them, Faye had to make sure they were real, afraid they were merely a hallucination. When she was satisfied they were in fact real, Faye couldn't help but bring the fabric to her nose and breathe in, relishing in the smell of home. It was just the boost she needed, making her more determined than ever to get home.

Taking a moment, Faye kept her face in the clothes, surrounded by the smell of home and letting that fuel her for the task ahead. Slowly Faye lowered the item of clothing, trying not to look at Cahira in case she saw a look of distaste at Faye's display of weirdness. Cahira only looked on with a look that was a mixture of slight interest in Faye's behaviour towards her clothes, and satisfaction with Faye's ability to teleport such an object across the realm.

"What's next?" Faye asked, still clutching her clothes and avoiding eye contact with Cahira.

"I am very impressed by this first — no sorry, second, attempt at teleporting an object, Faye. I mean it. I have never seen a novice learn such control of their powers so quickly," Cahira said feelingly, causing Faye finally looked up at her.

"Next is mind manipulation. There are multiple different abilities associated with this power. The first is telepathy. In the first instance this is simply thinking of a word and pushing it into someone else's mind using your energy. You won't hear a reply unless the faerie shares the same ability. Now, try it on me."

When Faye thought of mind manipulation, she automatically thought of the twisted control her great-grandmother had used on her mind, not the cool things she could do herself. Taking a deep breath, Faye made solid eye contact with Cahira, the first time since the clothes sniffing incident. Concentrating on a single word, Faye pushed it with her energy to Cahira's mind, repeating it until Cahira gave any indication it had worked.

It took a few minutes before Cahira finally gave her the sign she was waiting on.

"What is an elephant?"

Faye stopped pushing out her energy and laughed. Happy that it worked and delighted she would be able to teach Cahira something after all the teaching Cahira had done.

"It's an animal that lives in Africa." Faye then realised Cahira probably didn't know what or where Africa was.

"Try projecting an image of this animal."

Faye was relieved that she didn't have to explain what an elephant looked like to Cahira, guessing it was unlike anything Cahira had ever seen. Faye realised then she had yet to see any living animals in the Faerie Realm, so she didn't know if the realm had any reference other than chickens she had eaten.

Faye tried to conjure up an image of an elephant, from all the documentaries she had seen. She was concentrating on the sheer size and weight of the animal, with its wrinkled tough grey skin and large tusks protruding from both sides of the mouth, encasing the trunk. Pictures of Dumbo and his big floppy ears kept popping into her mind, threatening to create a hybrid image of a real elephant and a carton elephant. Faye squeezed her eyes shut tight in concentration to clear her mind of everything except the image of a magnificent elephant and pushed it out towards Cahira.

Unlike with telepathy, Faye couldn't just keep repeating a word until Cahira heard it; instead, she had to hold a constant image in her head and a constant stream of energy beaming towards Cahira, draining her a lot quicker than anything she had done before.

Faye sagged in relief when Cahira made a noise of surprise. She blinked a few times, clearing the haziness from her eyes before refocusing on Cahira. Cahira didn't have her usual stoic expression; she had an ever so slight smile that she wasn't quick enough to cover up.

It made all the dizziness and tiredness worth it.

"So that is an elephant," Cahira simply said in quiet amazement.

Resting her head against the wall, Faye tried to stop the world from spinning. The coolness from the dirt helped ground her and it wasn't long before the dizzy spell passed, but the tiredness remained. She barely had enough energy to take the banana that Cahira offered.

Once Faye had finished eating, she could only just lift her head off the wall without fear of passing out, but she knew she was in need of a long sleep to restore her strength.

"That was impressive, Faye. We will work on blocking and improving your endurance another time. For now... rest."

Faye couldn't argue. She was completely exhausted. Grabbing her clothes from home out of her lap, she placed the folded stack on the ground and swung her body around, so her head rested against her clothes like a pillow. Closing her eyes, the last thing she remembered before she fell asleep was Cahira standing over her before she once again disappeared.

# CHAPTER 28

"Where do you get all the fruit from?" Faye asked, using her new skill of telepathy, while sitting across from Cahira in their little burrow and eating.

"Your garden," Cahira replied out loud.

It had been the same routine for the past couple of days. Faye would wake to find a newly replenished pile of fruit, before eating as much as she could and starting her practise.

It was a simple routine, wake, eat, practise, eat, practise, eat, sleep, repeat. Faye found the mind manipulation skills the most draining of all her abilities she had learnt. It was taking a substantial amount of time for Faye to build up a tolerance to the significant energy drain each practice was taking on her — each episode left her feeling like she would pass out. She needed to build her stamina and quickly.

The telepathy aspect didn't take long for Faye to master but it was frustrating because Cahira did not hold the same ability. While she could hear a voice projected into her mind, she could not respond in kind — she had to speak her side of the conversation out loud. It left the whole telepathy experience anticlimactic for Faye, it was easy, but one-sided mind conversations were a bit boring.

Instead, she spent more time practising image projection as it took a greater toll on her. She figured she would get 'fitter' the more she worked on it — just like cardio and spin classes, or so she guessed. Faye was successful in projecting other images of safari animals and the African landscape to Cahira with a mixed bag of an energy toll.

After two days of practice, she could now project without strong bouts of dizziness or feeling completely fatigued, but she had yet to practise standing up.

Faye hadn't left the burrow except to do the unspeakable, and that's only when she couldn't hold on any longer, so she didn't know what had happened to the mini orchard she made. She had hoped it was where the fruit was coming from, but without Cahira's confirmation, she was unsure. She was elated it was still growing fruit and hopefully supplying the faeries in the area with food too. Faye's happiness was tainted by the fact Cahira was leaving the burrow without her and she had no idea what she was doing.

Every time Faye brought up the subject of where Cahira went or what was she doing, the faerie commander remained tight lipped, refusing to discuss it. Her feelings of frustration increased each day and she felt like she was back in square one with Cahira, only getting one or two worded responses, which usually revolved around instructions about practicing more.

The frustration was compounded by the fact Faye was literally going stir crazy. She hadn't left the burrow for an extended period in at least four days. Faye didn't really know how many days had passed because there were no windows to see the sun or stars. She certainly wasn't counting the quick visits to the woods for a bathroom break because they were over and done with in a flash.

"Can we go there please? I would love to see it again," Faye almost pleaded

When Cahira gave Faye a nod in agreeance, Faye didn't know if it was the desperation in her voice or the picture of herself banging her head against the wall, she projected into Cahira's mind that persuaded her to agree. But Faye didn't give it much of a thought before grabbing Cahira's hand and teleporting them out of there.

"Wow, that's a lot harder than you make it look." Faye stated, arriving in the forest. She had to lean up against a tree trying to steady herself as she caught her breath. Faye hadn't teleported another being before, and it certainly took a heavy toll on her. She felt they had spent longer in the darkness, without the ability to breathe, then she usually did when teleporting alone. Teleporting with Cahira had been a real test, showing her that she still had a way to go with her training.

Faye had a newfound respect for Cahira after her attempt at teleporting them both; she didn't know how Cahira did it so smoothly and frequently.

Faye rested her back against a tree and started to lower herself to the grass, pulling her dress up, bunching around her waist as she slid down. She didn't care how she looked to Cahira; all she thought about was the fresh air filling her lungs, the grass tickling her legs and the breeze that caught her hair.

The sunlight shone through the trees, heating her skin, a feeling that seemed so foreign after being in the cold, dark burrow for so long. She followed the beams of light to the sun and saw it was high overhead, and Faye guessed it must be around midday. She was happy to work out that she had been at least sleeping in a regular cycle — given she had woken from her 'long sleep' as she liked to call them, only a few hours ago. At least Cahira's deserting her in the burrow hadn't turned her nocturnal.

Faye was content just to sit and basked in the open air and sunlight, but her plans were interrupted by Cahira getting straight back to business, in her usual cryptic way.

"Walk through the forest while projecting the scene. Anchor your energy to me then push your surroundings through."

Faye didn't know what Cahira meant by 'projecting the scene' and 'anchoring' - Maybe it meant she could live stream projections of things into Cahira's head. Whatever it was, she was determined to give it a go — just like everything else. Not once had Cahira's methods failed her, so she stood up, leaving her small piece of heaven on the ground, and started to walk in a random direction.

Calling on all her energy and trusting her instincts, Faye imagined a golden glowing tether connecting her mind to Cahira's. When she turned her attention to the forest around her, Faye hadn't even realised she had continued to walk while she was anchoring her mind to Cahira's. Looking around she realised she could no longer see any signs of the garden and fruit trees, instead she was surrounded by enormous trees. The leaves on the tops of the trees created a canopy so dense only tiny factures of light could break through, creating an eerie, surreal atmosphere. Faye took her time taking all the scenery into her mind then pushed the imagery down the tether to Cahira. Instantly she was overcome by a paralysing dizzy spell.

Before she was aware of what was happening, she was laying on the grass with Cahira standing over her, watching with that intense stare of hers. Faye had no memory of falling to the ground and realised she had no injuries apart from a mind splitting headache — so she guessed Cahira had appeared just in time to catch her.

"Did it work?" Faye was eager to find out, hoping she hadn't fainted for nothing.

Once again Faye only received a simple nod. If she didn't feel so drained, she would have tried to get more out of Cahira, and challenge her about the nonverbal responses, but Faye just didn't have the energy. Instead, she took the time to lay out in the fresh, forest air and bask in her success at completing another task. The particular exercise really took it out of her, and she would need to practise more so she could transmit images of what she was looking at or where she was without passing out. She knew it would be a very useful skill to master for any further plans.

Faye was feeling sick to her stomach every time she moved a muscle so she was desperately hoping her exhaustion would turn into a nap. Cahira must have sensed her discomfort and Faye was more than happy when Cahira lay a hand on her shoulder, and everything disappeared.

\*\*\*

Faye woke up sometime later, alone again in the burrow. She was disappointed to see Cahira was gone but pushed the thought of not being included in the faerie's activities aboveground aside and concentrated on sitting up. Faye positioned her hands on the ground by her hips and pushed all her weight through her arms, causing them to tremble and shake in her efforts to push her torso up. She was alarmed at how drained and weak she still felt, but Faye was grateful that the dizziness had passed. Shuffling her body around until her back rested against the wall, she took the pressure off her arms and waited for the trembling to ease.

As the shaking finally subsided, Faye lent forward to pick up a bunch of grapes and an apple to test if her stomach was still queasy. After swallowing the first few grapes without triggering her gag reflex and throwing up, she quickly shoved the rest of the grapes in her mouth before polishing off the apple. Feeling pleased with how she had recovered, Faye decided to practise teleporting the remaining pieces of fruit above ground, back to the garden, then back to the burrow. She knew she was successful at it when she could feel the warmth of the sun on the skin of the apple in her hand.

Faye continued at the task until she felt she could do it without really thinking about it.

She desperately wanted to teleport herself to the garden, but she knew Cahira would be furious with her if she returned to an empty burrow. Faye leant back against the cold wall and let her mind run over the skills she had been learning and the toll each one was taking on her. She was confident in controlling and using her powers now without fainting, except for projecting her surroundings into someone else's mind. That one still needed some work. And she did not know what other skills Cahira had yet to teach her, or what role she would play in their attempt to overthrow the Queen. As these thoughts consumed her mind Faye fell back into a restless sleep.

# CHAPTER 29

Faye woke up and for the first time, Cahira was lying on the opposite side of the burrow, sound asleep. Faye stayed still, not making a move to sit up, too afraid her movements would wake Cahira. She stayed curled up in a ball on her side facing Cahira and just watched the small rise and fall of the cloak hiding the amour Cahira always wore. Faye had no idea how it was comfortable to wear metal plates sewn into clothing, let alone sleep in it.

Faye knew it was Cahira's role to guard, but guard what against? That's what she didn't understand. They were in a realm shut off from everyone that wasn't a faerie. Why did Cahira look like she was always ready for war? It was just another thing Faye put on her list of ever-growing questions she had for Cahira.

The movement of Cahira's cloak snapped Faye out of her thoughts, and she refocused her eyes back on the faerie. Cahira had sat up and begun eating a banana before Faye had even made a move to sit up. She was impressed by Cahira's swift and flawless actions. She wondered if it was a perk that came with the ability to teleport, or if Cahira just moved quickly. Another question to add to her list.

Copying Cahira, Faye sat up and took a banana. Eating it, then an apple, Faye wanted to consume as much nutrients as she could get for the unknown day ahead.

"What's todays plan?"

"Blocking. You need to develop the ability to stop any outside force tampering with your mind. For a start, concentrate on blocking the influence that stops you from seeing me in my true form."

There was so much in that last sentence for Faye to unpack, so she waited for Cahira to explain further, but in her typical fashion Cahira remained silent.

"How do I block someone else's magic? How do they even get control over my senses? For that matter, how do I even know if someone is controlling my mind?"

The questions just kept rolling out of Faye, she needed some clear detailed direction on how to accomplish her new task.

"There is no set way to block. It works differently for everyone and depends on what controls have been placed on you."

"Great, just what I wanted to hear." Faye mumbled under her breath but the close quarters made it impossible for the comment to go unheard by Cahira.

Faye had no other option but to work out how to block whatever magic her great-grandmother was using to control her experience in the Faerie Realm. She honestly had no idea the extent of the control her great-grandmother had over her — was it only limited to controlling how she saw faeries and keeping her trapped there, presumably until she could kill her?

Closing her eyes, she concentrated on the energy running through her veins, and instead of guiding it into her palms, Faye directed the energy to settle on every surface of her skin. She could feel her body temperature start to rise - not in a negative way as if she had a fever, but like the warmth of the sun was glowing within her. Faye pictured every fibre of her energy interlocking to form a barrier over her skin, creating a glowing shield.

When Faye opened her eyes, she was startled to see Cahira was no longer the same height as her, but now the size she was when she first met her — an adult the size of a human toddler. She didn't know where to look, she didn't want to stare at Cahira, so she cast a quick look around the burrow.

It dawned on her that the little room under the mound was not quite so small if she looked at it from the perspective of Cahira's true size. It was still an atrocious place to make anyone live, but the ceiling was height appropriate to a faerie. Lost in her thoughts, Faye didn't realise she was in fact staring down at Cahira, until she subtly cleared her throat.

"I'm sorry Cahira, I don't mean to stare. I haven't seen you in your true form for so long I forgot."

"Does my size bother you, Faye?"

Faye blushed at the question and started to stammer. "No, no, of course not."

She realised Cahira had reverted back to the same height as Faye. "Hey, what, okay." Faye continued to stammer.

"So bright side: I managed to block whatever was manipulating my mind to stop me from seeing you in your true form. Not so bright side, it didn't really last very long, did it?"

She thought once she put the barrier in place that was it, it would stay in place and continue to work. But so much for that theory. While she had managed to block her great-grandmother's power, it was only for a very short time.

"It will take constant work and energy to resist an outside influence for any substantial amount of time." Cahira reassured Faye.

"You are still learning these new skills. Practise. Then practise more."

"Aye, aye, Captain," Faye said as she gave Cahira a fake salute. Faye honestly could never read Cahira's expressions but for a split second, she thought she may have cracked her, as her faerie guard slash instructor gave her a look of amusement mixed with tinge of something Faye couldn't quite identify.

She knew Cahira would never ask for clarification or an explanation if anything confused her, so Faye decided to leave her to try to work it out for herself.

Faye was so pleased with her progress and the new skills she had learnt, she refused to be disheartened in any way. She settled back and closed her eyes. Imaging the glowing shield back around her body, she commanded the barrier to sink into her skin and infuse with her skin cells to form a permanent barrier. The feeling was remarkable, almost like getting an instantaneous sunburn from the inside out, then it faded away to a warm glow. When she opened her eyes, she saw the exposed skin of her arm glowing faintly — a pale red gleam, and then it was gone.

The effort quickly took its toll and Faye felt weak, her head fell against her chest, her neck no longer strong enough to hold it up. She rolled her head to the side and glanced at Cahira — who was again back to her original faerie height.

"It actually worked." She murmured before she slumped to the ground, completely exhausted.

Her last thought before sleep claimed her was, she would never underestimate her own abilities again.

\*\*\*

Faye woke up ready and raring to go. But there was no denying she felt like she had been hit by a bus — a bus that then ran over her, stopped, backed up over her again, then ran over her body one last time before continuing on its merry way. Her body was exhausted, but her mind and spirit were determined.

Once she had determined her shield was still in place, by the fact Cahira was still at her faerie height, she sat up and waited for Cahira to wake up. She was quite happy to sit and watch Cahira sleep, she was always so still, but the stillness was different when she was asleep. The hard edges were softened a little and her face looked serene.

Faye was startled when the faerie snapped her eyes open, almost as if she knew Faye was staring at her. Maybe she did know, maybe Cahira could be aware of what was going on around her while she slept. Or maybe she wasn't asleep at all?

"Shut up Faye." Faye muttered to herself as she broke eye contact with Cahira.

"Good morning, Faye. Did you sleep well?" Cahira offered as a reply.

"Um yes I did thank you," Faye responded formally.

After a moment's silence Faye decided to get straight into it.

"So, I have managed to create a shield, well I call it a shield, it's more like a blanket I have all around me, so you still appear to me now in your regular form. Now I am wondering if my shield is effective against all forms of power and influence." Faye paused for a breath.

"I was thinking back to when I first arrived in this realm, in the forest, you were able to control me, essentially binding my hands and making me move against my will. I was wondering if you could try doing something like that to me now, so I know if my shield gives me complete protection?"

Cahira was watching Faye intently, listening to what she was saying.

Faye was more than a little perplexed by the shadow that crossed Cahira's face.

*Oh God did what I just say about binding my hands sound weird?* Faye asked herself.

"You truly are more powerful than anyone could have imagined," Cahira said in a hushed tone before collecting herself and continuing more loudly.

"This is great progress Faye, and a good idea. But it was another faerie in my patrol unit that holds that ability. I will try to scout another with this ability for you to practise. I unfortunately cannot make any guarantees."

Faye beamed at the compliments. She felt a weight lift from her body when her shield settled into place permanently. She could feel the energy under her skin without needing to concentrate on it. The energy wasn't trying to push out and escape, it just hummed and buzzed below the surface, as if it was letting her know it was there when needed.

Whole and complete. Those were the two words Faye would use to describe herself in that moment. Learning about her powers and new abilities was like finding all the missing pieces of a puzzle and finally putting it all together. She could feel the last sliver of her soul settling and aligning with the rest. She was no longer scared of the power she held, instead she consciously submitted to it and embraced it.

She was ready to take on the Queen.

There was one thing that was always floating in the back of her mind, the unanswered question: would she still have her power when she returned to the Human Realm? She was more confident than ever that she would make it home, but the unknown around if she would have powers and how they may manifest, was unsettling.

"Faye. Faye!" Cahira repeated her name twice, trying to make her snap out of her ruminations.

"What? Sorry."

"Here, eat some grapes," Cahira instructed as she handed a bunch to the younger woman.

"I would like you to practise blocking for someone who is unable to."

Faye waited for more from Cahira, but it seemed the faerie had spoken her share for the time being and had reverted to her usual practise of sitting quietly and staring. Trying to read between the lines, Faye gathered Cahira wanted her to create a barrier To block out the Queens influence, mimicking the dungeon.

Nodding in understanding, Faye closed her eyes and took a few long, deep breaths. She was ready to try it now and didn't want to wait until they were above ground. She opened her eyes and fixed Cahira with an intense stare. Imagining a golden glow around Cahira's body, strong enough to withstand any outside interference, Faye pushed her awaiting energy towards Cahira. She felt a tremendous whoosh, as if she was winded by the surge of power leaving her body and heading into Cahira.

They both let out a simultaneous gasp as the energy transferred from one body to another, and Faye saw Cahira's shoulders sag. In an instant the faerie looked like a large weight had been lifted from her, and her body relaxed. For the first time since she had known her, Faye noticed Cahira wasn't frigid with tension. She decided to try a tester question to see if it worked. May as well start with the big ones.

"What does my great-grandmother plan to do to me?"

"Kill you." Cahira didn't even hesitate in her answer. And there it was. Out in the open.

No matter how horrifying it was for Faye to hear that someone wanted her dead, a someone that also happened to be a family member, she couldn't help but smile at Cahira's answer.

Cahira mirrored Faye's smile and breathed out a quiet "Thank you."

Faye wasn't sure how long her energy could hold both shields in place, but she was pleasantly surprised by the fact creating another barrier to protect Cahira did not affect her as severely as creating her own.

"I don't know how long this will last so fill me in on everything you know but haven't been able to tell me," Faye blurted out.

Cahira faced Faye and began.

"Do you remember the tapestry hall I took you to? That part of the cathedral is enchanted, its main purpose being to capture every important event that occurs throughout the history of the realm. This is a way for the rulers to know of things that have happened or are happening that they cannot personally see. I would accompany the Queen to the hall once a week to review the tapestries, to see if any new event or action had been added. This is where I learnt of our previous Queen's death. I don't know if she had hidden the tapestry from me in the past and didn't mean for me to see it, or if she meant for me to see it and was happy for me to know she was a murderer.

"When the Queen knew I had seen it, she quickly set the first of many mental blocks that have stopped me voicing what she has done. No one else in the realm knows what she did. We all thought our previous Queen, who was much loved by all, had returned to the Human Realm, as she was supposed to. I am the only one, besides you, who knows your great-grandmother killed her."

Cahira paused and looked down at her hands. Faye didn't want to interrupt the verbal diarrhoea coming out of Cahira's mouth, but she couldn't help herself. Everything Cahira had just said confirmed the little Faye assumed to be the case after she was tossed out of the tapestry.

"How long have you known?" Faye asked quietly.

"Ten years now. That is how long I have been waiting for you, Faye."

# CHAPTER 30

The next thing Faye knew, she was back in the open forest with Cahira standing at least five metres away from her. But Cahira was also back to being the same size as her. How did that happen?

There was no way she could deny there was something going on between them. She had sensed a shift in Cahira's but Faye wasn't sure what it all meant.

Cahira of course was the first to regain her steely, shut-off manner.

"I apologise Faye. I should not have said that."

"No need to apologise," Faye replied "I..."

"We have a place to start now, Faye. We need to stay focused on our main goal."

"And what is our main goal exactly Cahira?"

Cahira fixed Faye with her gaze and opened her mouth "We need..."

She stopped speaking, blinked a few times, and actually stamped her foot. It was the most adorable thing Faye had ever seen.

"I can't finish my sentence. It is in my head, but I cannot speak it. The shield you created must have fallen. Can you try to create it again?"

"I will. But first can I offer my ideas on what our plan should be?"

Cahira simply nodded in assent, gesturing to Faye to continue.

"What is our end goal? To get my great-grandmother off the throne, right?" Faye looked at Cahira for confirmation, but she got nothing but a stare.

"Okay the answer to that is yes. What do we do if, or should I say *when*, we manage to kick the current Queen off her shiny throne?" Faye was pacing around in a circle now, animated by the one-way conversation she was having with herself.

"I don't want to replace her as Queen. I really want to get home to the Human Realm." She shot a quick sideways glance to Cahira when she said that, looking for any kind of reaction, but got none.

"Maybe you can start a democratic election — let the fae folk choose who they want to lead them?"

That question got Faye the smile she was hoping for. She stopped quickly in front of Cahira and grabbed her hands. Before Cahira could react, Faye shot a blast of pure energy into the faerie, determined to create a permanent shield.

Cahira staggered back as the power enveloped her and her skin started to glow red.

"So how do we bring down the Queen?" Faye asked, wanting to see if her gamble had paid off.

"We need to make the Queen confess her crimes publicly. Once every faerie knows what she has done they will unite, and her regime will come falling down."

The words rushed out of Cahira in flood, as if the dam had finally broken.

"Goddess be praised. Faye, you have done it again."

"I think this time it may be more permanent, but we will see," Faye replied slightly out of breath from the exertion of creating the shield.

"Now, back to the subject at hand… it's not like she will just stand up and shout to the realm, 'Hey everyone! Guess what — I killed your old Queen so I could take over forever and rule you all like a maniac'."

"This is the human sense of humour, isn't it? I do not understand it at all," Cahira stated with mock seriousness.

"Come on, Cahira. How are we going to get this crazy old woman-cum-faerie Queen to confess?"

"This is where your powers of projecting come into the plan. That and your ability to be very human and annoying."

"Hey, wait, you think I'm annoying?"

"No Faye, I do not think you are annoying, but I know you and I know the Queen. If we can create the right situation, you will be able to exploit her hubris, and goad the Queen into admitting what she has done, while projecting it to all the fae folk to see."

Faye stared at Cahira like she had truly gone mad.

"Cahira, do you recall two days ago when I couldn't even project the forest scenery without passing out. And I was only projecting it to you. How am I supposed to aggravate my great-grandmother, an extremely powerful faerie I might add, into confessing a murder, protect myself from her magic, and project the whole shebang to a whole race of faeries?"

Faye didn't realise her face echoed the doubt she had just voiced until Cahira spoke again.

"We will practise. Then practise some more. I want you to project a message from me to all the fae folk across the realm — all the fae except the Queen and Eamon, he is completely loyal to the Queen. You must think of a way to stop the message travelling telepathically to them."

"Right. Okay. So that made things just a little more complicated Cahira. Come on. This is a lot."

"I believe in you, Faye. And you should believe in yourself. We will practise now, and I know you will do it."

Those three crisp, clear sentences sparked a new wave of determination in Faye.

She nodded and closed her eyes, imaging the same golden glowing tether that connected her to Cahira, connecting her to all the faeries everywhere. Like a glowing spider web, her tethers spread out across the entire realm, finding anchors then stretching back to her. In the midst of the tethers stretching out from her mind, she brought an image of the Queen and Eamon into sharp focus. She then pictured a red stop sign and hoped the simple cliché would work to stop the message reaching the two fae she despised.

When she felt a sense of completion, Faye opened her eyes and nodded at Cahira, signalling she was ready to go.

"My name is Cahira. Most of you know me as the Queen's head guard. My job has been to accompany the Queen wherever she goes. During this time, I witnessed the truly horrific murder of our previous Queen. We were led to believe she returned to the Human Realm, just as it is decreed in Tuatha De Danann Legacy. All other Queens in the past have honoured this code, but that was not the case this time. Queen Faye the thirty fifth stabbed her ancestor to death. You do not have to believe my words. The time will soon come when you will hear the Queen's confession from her own mouth. When that time comes, all I ask is you stand together against the injustice."

Faye let out a sign of relief when Cahira finished talking. She didn't think she would have been able to carry on for even a second longer. She felt faint and her head was spinning from the effort, but she was relieved that she actually felt okay. Exhausted but okay. And she really needed to sit.

As she sat down Faye asked, "Do you think it worked?"

"I will go out and see," Cahira replied, looking ready to teleport out of the forest.

"Wait. Before you go, can you teleport me back into our hide away?"

Cahira touched Faye and teleported them back to the burrow. As Faye felt the damp dirt floor materialise beneath her, an almighty jolt smashed into her skull, as the weight of thousands of faerie voices crashed into her mind.

Faye jerked back, tearing herself away from Cahira. Faye cowered, cocooning her head in her arms, trying to block out the noise radiating throughout her mind.

"Faye are you okay?" Cahira asked, alarmed and concerned.

"No, no, it's not you.," Faye said.

"It's not you," she repeated. "I'm ok, I think …it's just…" Faye staggered and took a gasping breath. "I think your message was received loud and clear."

# CHAPTER 31

"I can confirm it worked."

Faye was startled awake by Cahira's loud return. It took her a few moments to clear the fog of sleep from her brain before she realised what Cahira meant. After their quick return to the burrow, Faye succumbed to the pressure of all the voices in her head and she was left alone to rest. "Oh my Goddess! That's amazing. Did it reach everyone? It sounded like I had a million different voices in my head. All clamouring for answers." Faye could not contain her excitement.

Cahira let out a small laugh. "I was not able to speak with the whole realm, Faye. But the fae folk that I did speak to, all said they saw and heard me. Remember not all fae have the ability to reply to messages back telepathically, but the ones who can, caused the overload on your mind."

"Did they believe you?" Faye asked in a more subdued manner.

"Some did."

"Right. But some didn't. I get it."

Disappointment shouldn't have been the first emotion Faye felt after their success, but she couldn't help it.

If Cahira had straight up told her that her great-grandmother had murdered someone, she would not have just believed her, without any proof. So, how could she expect thousands of fae to just accept the fact that their Queen was a crazy murdering psycho only off someone's word? But if she factored in how they were mistreated and how their families had been split apart, she couldn't possibly fathom how scared they all must be.

"Do you know if I was successful in stopping the Queen and Eamon from hearing your message? How do we know that the plan will work? Everything hinges on all the faeries coming together."

Faye's doubts started to creep in again and she couldn't stop from voicing them out loud. She also desperately wanted to ask what Cahira intended for her great-grandmother — once all of it was over. She was pretty sure she already knew the answer but if it was confirmed, Faye didn't know how she would deal with that piece of news, so she kept that question unvoiced.

"I will answer your questions one at a time, Faye." Cahira said patiently.

"Firstly, I am confident the Queen and Eamon did not hear the message — I asked a member of my guard platoon whom I trust implicitly, if the Queen had issued any orders for my arrest and she said no; the Queen has not changed her behaviour at all."

Cahira took Faye's hands in hers.

"Secondly, I know the plan will work because I know. It is that simply. We are ready. You are ready."

Faye wanted to believe in Cahira's confidence but the fact that the entire plan rested on her shoulders was more than a little overwhelming.

"What happens now? When do I confront my great-grandmother?" Faye couldn't help the questions spewing out of her mouth. Now that Cahira was actually answering them, she just wanted to keep asking them. And not just about the plan to deal with the Queen. She desperately wanted to ask Cahira questions about what was going to happen when it was all over.

"It is very late, Faye. Now you must rest. Tomorrow morning, I will teleport you to the throne room — early before anyone else arrives. There you will confront the Queen and broadcast it throughout the realm."

"Tomorrow." Faye let the word hang in the air.

Faye's heart started to violently thump in her chest and her breath quickened. She knew they had to maintain the momentum they had built, but tomorrow? She was glad she didn't know the timeframe Cahira was working on before, otherwise she would have had an intense panic attack. Now she had less than twelve hours to overthink every possible scenario — most of which ended with the Queen overpowering her and the whole plan failing.

"Eat then rest. I will wake you when we need to go." Cahira said softly, knowing Faye was struggling with what was to come.

Cahira manoeuvred herself to sit beside Faye, as best she could in the cramped little burrow. They ate a small amount of fruit silently, then Faye rested her head on Cahira's shoulder.

"We can do this right?" Faye asked in a whisper. Cahira took Faye's hand and answered.

"We can do this."

Faye took one last look at their hands entwined, resting on Cahira's thigh, then shut her eyes and drifted off to sleep.

***

"Faye... Faye... Faye!" Cahira tried to jostle Faye awake.

"Okay, I'm awake. I'm awake," Faye whimpered.

"Please don't hand me any more fruit. I can't face another banana." Cahira smiled.

"How about an apple? You need some sustenance before we tackle today."

Somewhere in her dreamscape, Faye had decided to wear the clothes she had on when she first arrived in the Faerie Realm. She knew her jeans, T-shirt and converse would help her feel comfortable, and piss off her great-grandmother at the same time.

They ate quickly as Cahira went through the plan one last time.

"I will teleport you to the throne room to wait for the Queen, while I gather as many fae to the cathedral steps as possible. If at any time you feel in danger, teleport straight back here to the burrow."

"Got it. Throne room, deal with the Queen, lots of fae, back to the burrow at the first sign of danger. Did I miss anything?" Faye joked.

Cahira was used to Faye's sense of humour by this stage. So, Cahira smiled and nodded her head.

"You did not miss anything."

Faye stretched, stood up and extended her hand out to Cahira. "I'm ready Cahira. Let's do this."

Cahira took Faye's hand and rose to stand in front of her.

"Shall we?" Faye asked as she held out her hand.

\*\*\*

The throne room was dark, lit only by a few burning candles along the far wall. The sun hadn't started to rise yet leaving the stained glass windows to present a darkened version in the place of their splendid colourful façade.

Faye and Cahira stood in the deep shadows, looking out into the gloom to make sure no one else was there. When Cahira was satisfied they were alone, she turned to Faye.

"The first sign of trouble you must leave. I do not want you to risk being injured or worse."

"I will be okay Cahira. Relax. You have trained me well. I need you to stay safe and hold up your side of the plan."

"Who are you and what have you done with Faye?" Cahira asked with mock seriousness.

"Really! Really? Now is the time you drop in a clanger of a human joke?! I could ask you the same question."

"You are unusually calm and at peace this morning. Not like your normal fidgety Faye human self. You are becoming more like a fae as each day passes."

Faye decided to take it as a compliment.

"Umm thank you. Okay, go and do your thing. I will see you on the other side." Faye pulled Cahira in for one last hug, catching her by surprise.

"Sorry. You should probably get out of here before she shows up," Faye said, letting go of Cahira and stepping back.

Even if it was a while before her great-grandmother made an appearance, Faye didn't want Cahira anywhere near the throne room.

"First sign of a threat, get back to the burrow," Cahira instructed before disappearing.

Once she was alone, nothing was going to stop Faye from sitting on the throne. She had no desire to be Queen, but she knew her great-grandmother would be royally pissed off if she saw Faye, sitting in her place of honour. And she just couldn't pass up on the opportunity.

Taking a seat on the throne she didn't feel powerful, she just felt lonely. She sat on a raised platform overlooking a vastly empty room, and the feeling of disconnection between monarch and subjects was tangible. The Queen sat up there on her mighty throne, surrounded by her sycophant flunkies, while all the peasant faeries milled about below looking for handouts. It certainly created a clear image that whoever sat there was so much better than everyone else.

The emotions Faye processed while she sat on the throne helped to solidify her decision of wanting no part of it — even if she would be a different kind of Queen, one with compassion and empathy for the fae folk. She wanted to give them the opportunity to make decisions for themselves and set up some form of democratic system. She had no idea how that would happen, but she trusted that Cahira knew what she was doing. Once the Queen was dealt with, she just wanted to get home. What came after that…who knew.

Faye sat quietly on the throne and closed her eyes. She focused on the glowing spider's web of connections between the faeries and herself, strengthening the tether, getting ready for her great-grandmother to make an appearance.

Faye felt her great-grandmother's presence before she heard or saw her. She snapped her eyes open and there she was, standing on the ground level looking up at her. Faye couldn't help but notice the look of surprise on the older woman's face.

"Faye what are you doing here? And where have you been? I've been going out of my mind with worry."

Faye started to push her energy through the tethers, capturing and projecting everything her great-grandmother was saying.

Faye had to give her great-grandmother some credit: she was very good at playing the concerned Queen slash great-grandmother. She was not giving away any hint that the concern was fake. Faye had never seen a person lie so flawlessly and it sent a small tinge of fear through her. She couldn't let her doubts take a hold of her mind. "WWJLD?" she said quietly to herself.

With her great-grandmother expressing an emotion besides her usual stoic look, Faye smiled and got to work.

"You don't have to act any more. You have played the intrigued and concerned grandmother role long enough don't you think?"

"I don't know what you are talking about, Faye. Why don't we go and have some breakfast? We can talk over a meal together." The Queen held out her hand for Faye to take.

"I am actually quite comfortable here." Faye began to run her hands up and down the armrests of the throne.

"I think I might just stay here." She said the last sentence staring straight down at the Queen.

The Queen regained her composure and retorted,

"You have played enough, Faye. You should not be sitting there."

"Neither should you," Faye fired back as she stood.

"I am the rightful Queen of this realm, by the blood of my ancestors. Your time will come soon enough."

The anger was clear in her voice now; Faye was encouraged as the mask of deceit was slowly fading away.

"That's a lie and we both know it." Faye paused momentarily before continuing and firing the first shot. She was tired of the cat-and-mouse game they were playing, ready for it to finally come to an end.

"You have gotten away with treating the beings of this realm like they are shit on your shoe for long enough. You tried to put a good act on when I first got here, but thanks to how I was raised I know what real family is. And that family includes the son you abandoned, who grew to become a wonderful loving grandfather — no thanks to you."

The blow landed on the Queen hard; Faye could tell by the fractured look that flashed across her face. She was on an unstoppable roll now, ready to land the killer blow. Faye walked down the stairs until she was standing directly in front of her.

"I know you will kill to get what you want. No one will get in your way, will they? Not the previous Queen. And certainly not me. I'm not the meek and mild little Faye from the Human Realm any more. I know a few tricks."

The Queen continued to play the bewildered old lady.

"Faye, I don't know what you are talking about. I have not killed anyone, and I certainly do not want to kill you—"

*"Enough!"* Faye screamed as she reached out and grabbed her great-grandmother by the arm and teleported them to the tapestry hall.

As they hit the floor, the Queen staggered back away from Faye, a look of shock across her face.

"Enough with the lies." Faye continued.

"I know what you have done — *look!*" she said as she pointed to the tapestry on the wall. They were standing in front of the tapestry depicting her great-grandmother murdering the previous Queen with her sword. There was no denying what they were looking at — and Faye was broadcasting it to the whole fae population. She could feel the sense of shock and anguish flooding back down the tethers towards her mind. It was so loud she thought she might go insane.

"I…" the Queen began.

"Enough," Faye repeated, in a more subdued tone.

She reached out and took the Queen's arm again, amazed she put up no resistance. This time she teleported them to the steps outside the cathedral, where she hoped Cahira would be waiting with an audience of faeries.

When Faye felt the solid steps beneath her feet, she took a few steps back away from the Queen. She was relieved to see Cahira making her way up the stairs towards her and a sea of fae folk in the forecourt of the cathedral. She was struggling now, the stress of maintaining a projection for so long, coupled with teleporting, was taking its toll. But she needed to land one last jab on the Queen, in front of everyone. But the Queen beat her to it.

"I do not know what you have orchestrated here, Faye but I demand answers," the Queen stated as she saw the multitude of faeries below her. Then she noticed Cahira, and her gaze hardened.

"How did I know you would have something to do with this. So, was it you, Faye, who helped Cahira escape from the dungeons, with your newfound abilities. It all makes sense to me now. Very clever, Cahira. Guards, seize her!"

Nobody moved. Cahira stopped where she was, a few steps down from Faye.

The ripples of murmurs throughout the faerie crowd got louder and louder, some were even starting to ascend the stairs. It was all the encouragement Cahira needed to speak out against the Queen.

"You are the one that betrayed us by dishonouring your vows as Queen. You were supposed to protect us but all you did was divide and destroy. Forcing fae folk to work endlessly in poor conditions, underfed and sleepless, only to feed your greed and never-ending need for power."

Cahira's rage was palpable, the distress of all the fae evident in every word, and now they were all murmuring in agreement. The voices in Faye's head were so loud that she decided to break the tethers that bonded them to her. The relief was instantaneous.

"I am your Queen, and you will treat me as such. Guards, restrain Cahira and take her to the dungeons." The Queen tried to re-establish her authority, but no one moved.

"You are no Queen and never should have been!" Cahira threw back with intense venom.

Faye was just a witness now to what was unfolding, unsure of what exactly was happening.

The Queen looked from Cahira to Faye, then scanned across the faces of her subjects. When she saw only disgust and hostility, she knew she had only one last option.

The Queen materialised a golden dagger that looked like a smaller version of the sword from the tapestry, and with the speed of light the dagger was in its way through the air towards Cahira. How Faye anticipated the action she will never know but she was ready for it. Just as quickly as her great-grandmother shot out the dagger, Faye sent a burst of power towards Cahira that reinforced the shield she had already created around her, and the weapon simply recoiled against the invisible barrier and fell to the ground.

The blatant act of violence carried out by the Queen towards her most loyal subject was the final spark needed to ignite the tinderbox on the cathedral stairs.

The faeries, one by one, produce their own energy orbs, aiming and projecting them at the Queen, in fear she would try to hurt anyone else. It created a dazzling chain reaction that successfully immobilized her. Faye stood in awe, watching the unified fae folk standing up for themselves against the tyranny they had been living under for so long.

Different coloured orbs of energy were combining around her great-grandmother, creating a glowing, magical cloud that shot bolts of energy into her body. Faye could tell the exchange of energies was working up to a catastrophic climax. As more faeries joined in with their energy, Faye saw a glow appear beneath her great-grandmother's skin and it quickly became brighter and brighter. Within seconds it was too much to look at and Faye turned her head away.

In that moment, there was an explosion of light and energy so intense it knocked everyone off their feet.

# CHAPTER 32

Once the brightness died down, Faye saw everyone splayed out across the cathedral forecourt. Some were lying down, staring unblinking up at the sky, others were slowing pulling themselves up to a sitting position. The quiet was unnatural and unnerving.

Faye looked to the space where her great-grandmother had been standing, only to find it empty. She was gone. Nothing was left in her place. Faye was both relieved and frightened in equal measure. Relieved the woman was gone but unsettled that there wasn't a body. She did not want to deal with the gruesome reality of a dead body but without the tangible piece of evidence, Faye was not one hundred percent sure their plan had worked.

As if reading Faye's thoughts Cahira stood beside her and took her hand. They stood together, in silence as they watched the fae struggle to their feet, helping each other stand and dusting themselves off.

"Believe me when I tell you Faye, the Queen did not survive that massive blast of pure energy." Cahira raised her voice and shouted out to the crowd, raising their entwined hands as she said, "She is gone. It is finally over, and we are finally free."

The cheers that erupted across the crowd were deafening, and in that moment, Faye knew everything was going to be all right.

\*\*\*

"What happens here now?" Faye asked Cahira as they sat together on the steps, in the shadow of the great cathedral. They had organised food to be distributed amongst the faeries as they got reacquainted with family members they had not seen in a very long time. The air was filled with laughter and squeals of joy. It was definitely how she wished to remember her time in the Faerie Realm. "Will someone else be made queen or king?" Faye asked, desperate to know things would be okay once she left. She needed some relief from the guilt she felt for refusing to take the place of her great-grandmother and thus halting a tradition that had been carried for thousands of years. Faye knew Cahira understood her refusal to take the throne, but she did not know if the rest of the fae folk accepted her decision. She was just glad they did not hold her responsible for the Queen's past actions against them.

"Everything will work itself out, Faye. As you said yourself, we will set up a system whereby the fae folk can decide for themselves who they want to rule, be it one person or several representatives. You have helped us pave the way for a new order in our realm and we will be eternally grateful," Cahira stated with as much passion as Faye had ever heard her express.

Faye sat staring at Cahira almost reluctant to say what needed to be said.

"I have to get home," she said quietly.

"I know. The block the Queen had placed on the bridge between the Human Realm and Faerie Realm would have been broken with her death. It will be safe for you to return via the stone circle," Cahira offered by way of reply.

It was a bittersweet feeling when Cahira held her hand out for Faye to take. Faye knew it would be the last time they teleported together, but she also knew it was one step closer to getting home. She took one last look up at the cathedral, the surrounding moss towers and the faeries celebrating with each other. Faye closed her eyes and for the first time in her life, she prayed. She prayed to the Goddess Danu, wishing for the faeries to be kept safe and happy now that the legacy of her bloodline ruling the realm was broken.

Placing her hand in Cahira's, she watched as the faeries disappeared from her view and the deep, dense forest materialised. She loved this place, and was so in tune with it and the energy that dwelled there that she could hardly reconcile how she felt now compared with the scared, anxiety ridden teenager that first arrived. She knew the Faerie Realm was in safe hands with Cahira and that her part in the realm was done. And she also knew her place was in the Human Realm with her family. But... there was also a part of her that did not want to leave any more.

"Thank you for everything you've done. I wouldn't be here if it weren't for you." Faye couldn't look Cahira in the eye, as she choked out her words of gratitude.

"I should be saying that to you, Faye. You saved us all. You will never be forgotten."

Faye let out a mangled laugh, her throat too heavy with the need to cry. She wrapped her arms around Cahira and hid her face in the faerie's neck.

"You should be happy. This is what you wanted. You are finally going home."

Slowly detaching herself from Cahira, Faye gave herself enough time to wipe the tears off her face before raising her head to meet Cahira's eyes.

"I am. I am glad to be going home to see my family but I…" she left the rest unspoken as she tried to fake a smile that came out more like a grimace.

"Thank you again," was all she could eventually manage as she stepped away from Cahira.

"You are welcome, Faye." Cahira was reverting to her stiff-backed, single-sentence self, expressing very minimal emotion.

Faye walked into the stone circle and turned to face Cahira.

"Hey if you're ever in the Human Realm come find me," she said with a wink. The possibility of seeing Cahira again, sometime in the future, made Faye's face light up with a genuine smile.

Faye closed her eyes with image of Cahira's face burned into her mind. She turned her minds focus to the graveyard and headstone of her great-grandmother Faye Burke, with the fading, eroded text, covered in moss and vines.

"Goodbye," she whispered as she felt the energy start to build, pulling her back to the Human Realm.

"Thank you for your help, Faye. I didn't expect things to go the way they did and bond with you. I am truly sorry for what you are about to face."

Faye's eyes snapped open when she heard Cahira's voice, rattling clearly in her mind, booming louder than she had ever thought possible. But it was too late to react.

She felt the grass beneath her feet disappear and she was suspended in the dark void that must exist between the two realms. The inability to breathe was back and she was virtually unconscious when she landed back on solid ground.

Faye gasped in deep gulps of fresh air, in-between bouts of heaving and retching. She rolled over onto her back and looked up at the sky, a clear blue, cloudless sky. A sky that looked particularly familiar. She gingerly turned her head to either side and was relieved to see headstones all around her.

She was back. She had actually made it back! She closed her eyes again and tried to piece together what had just happened as she started to teleport.

She heard Cahira say something but what did she mean by it and why was it so loud?

"What the actual hell!" Faye exclaimed. "She was in my head! She is telepathic!"

Faye sat up, struggling to comprehend the meaning of what she just realised. How did Cahira speak to her in her mind? Why would she be sorry? It didn't make any sense. Did Cahira's ability to speak to her telepathically start only after the death of the Queen, or could she do it all along?

"What the hell?" Faye repeated. She decided to park those thoughts until after she got back to her mum. She stood up and started to zigzag through the headstones, picking up the pace as she made her way to the cemetery gates.

She skidded to a halt when she saw Orla sitting on the footpath just outside the entrance, looking quite serene.

"Hey girl. What are you doing here?" Faye stopped in the front of the enormous dog and gave her a scratch behind the ears.

Faye looked around, scanning the car park for any sight of her grandpa.

"Shit. How long have I been gone pooch? Where is Pa?" Faye was feeling more than a little worried now.

"Woof!" was the only response she received.

"Right, okay, lets head back to Niamh's, she must be wondering where we both are," Faye said as she looked over the dog's head, in the direction she thought the BnB was.

Faye did a double take, looking down at the dog; she could have sworn Orla shook her head.

It quickly occurred to her she didn't know the way back to her accommodation. She hadn't paid any attention to where they were going when her grandpa had driven them into town. So, she didn't know how to get back to her family.

Orla stood up and gently took Faye's hand in her mouth. In that moment Faye knew exactly what she had to do.

She closed her eyes and pictured the beautiful Faerie House BnB. Before she had time to think about whether teleporting would work in the Human Realm or not, she was standing in the gardens on the edge of the driveway. And sitting all together on the veranda, swinging in the comfy porch chairs, was her family.

Faye released a sob and summoned the last ounce of her stamina to cross the remaining twenty metres that stood between her and her mum. She hadn't even realised she had managed to teleport Orla with her as well, or that the dog was standing back in the shadows of the garden.

"Oh my Goddess, Mum! I can't believe I made it back. You will never believe where I have been," Faye gushed out as she climbed the stairs, ready to hurl herself at Elaine.

Niamh rose and walked to meet Faye at the top of the stairs.

"Can I help you dear?"

"Very funny Niamh. Mum, Grandparentals. Come on. Sorry I was gone for a while, but I have all the answers now." Faye was getting a little frantic now, looking back and forth from her mum to her pa, from Niamh to her grandma. She couldn't deny they were all looking bewildered.

"This is private accommodation young lady; you must have these people confused with someone else. I'm sorry but I will have to insist you leave."

And just when she thought her world was finally coming back together, it completely shattered into a million tiny pieces. Just like her heart.

THE END